Chiaroscuro
a novel

LAURENCE BRADY

ISBN: 978-1-7393440-0-9

Cover design & typesetting by Raspberry Creative Type

For Clare

CONTENTS

CAST OF CHARACTERS

Francisco Zurbaran, artist.

Leonor Tordera de Zurbaran, Francisco's wife.

Don Diego Lozando Villasandino, investigator and representative of the Order of Santiago.

Don Fernando de Salcedo, investigator and representative of the Order of Santiago.

Michelangelo Merisi da Caravaggio, artist.

Fermo Merisi da Caravaggio, father of Michelangelo.

Ranuccio Tomassoni, head of a Roman prostitution ring.

Fra' Alof de Wignacourt, Grand Master of the Sovereign Military Hospitaller Order of Saint John of Rhodes and Malta.

Vincenzo dell'Antella, the 'Commendatore', personal valet to Grand Master Wignacourt.

Alonso Cano, artist and sculptor.

Fra Giacomo Marchese, a Sicilian Knight of the Order of Saint John.

Aaron and Gomu, Maltese farmers.

Sor Maria, Abbess of Agreda.

Padre Inquisitor Antonio del Moral, a Trinitarian and representative of The Inquisition.

Juan Feixo de Naboa, a lieutenant in the Spanish Infantry.

Diego de Vegas Hoyos, a captain of the Spanish army.

AUTHOR'S NOTE

Michelangelo Merisi da Caravaggio and his two later Spanish disciples, Francisco Zurbaran and Diego Velazquez, were by no means the only artists to make the light-and-darkness technique of *chiaroscuro* an art in itself, but they were unquestionably among the most gifted. Caravaggio's influence over Zurbaran and Velazquez, who were not yet teenagers when he died in 1610, would last a lifetime.

Of the three, arguably Zurbaran is the least well known today, though this was not always so. The churches and monasteries in Spain that contained most of his work were comprehensively looted by Napoleon's armies in the Peninsular Wars of 1808 to 1814. In the decades that followed, when Francisco Zurbaran was displayed in Paris alongside the art of contemporaries including Velazquez, Alonso, Ribera and Murillo, it was he who was considered to be the greatest of the masters of Spain's Golden Age. In 1838, for the opening of the Spanish Gallery at the Louvre, 180 of the 400 paintings on display were attributed to Zurbaran (though not all of these were his work). The Spanish art historian, Juan Gallego, once wrote, '*It has been said that if just fifty paintings had to be saved out of all the cultures of mankind, at least one would be a Zurbaran.*'

From Milan to Rome to Malta to Seville to Madrid, the painting facts and life events of these three exemplars of *chiaroscuro* are well documented. Yet virtually nothing is known about what they said and thought, how they arrived at the choices they made, what childhood, marital and family influences, what friendships and broken relationships, made them who they were. They are unknowable. One thing we do know for sure is that they lived in an age and culture of unshakeable belief in God and the certainty of eternal life.

We know, too, that in the last decade of his life Diego Velazquez makes the claim that he is descended from nobility. He petitions the Holy Order of Santiago to be accepted as a Knight. King Philip IV alone cannot sanction it. Due process must be observed, an investigation undertaken. With the sanctity of the venerable Order of Santiago wrapped around his knighted shoulders, eternal reward for Diego Velazquez would not be in doubt. If only he could prove his nobility.

Foolish and misguided though such beliefs may seem to many in the twenty-first century, in seventeenth century Spain they were core to the meaning and purpose of life. Velazquez knew that, so did the investigators, and so did the witnesses, one of the last of whom is Francisco Zurbaran. The king and his spiritual mentor, Abbess Maria of Agreda, knew it too.

Out of these events, my story of Chiaroscuro is born. I have taken the liberty of creating imagined thoughts, actions and motivations of historical figures, Caravaggio, Zurbaran himself, his wife, Leonor, and the two investigators, the most notable among them. It is for the principal purpose of telling a story, making them knowable, their lives real and, not least, bringing them to the moment in December 1658 when all is revealed.

They knew only their past and present but not their future – and definitely not how history would regard them.

In taking this liberty, I am acutely aware of the centuries of scholarship and thousands of articles, dissertations, lectures, documentaries and books on Caravaggio, Velazquez, Zurbaran and the Golden Age of Spanish painting. I am neither art historian nor art critic, nor an academic for that matter, and have relied upon the deep knowledge and recent books by acknowledged experts such as Laura Cumming, Sir Simon Schama, Andrew Graham-Dixon and the late Michael Jacobs.

Further back, the writings of the French art historian Jeannine Baticle, Martin Soria, Juan Gallego whom I have already mentioned, Jonathan Brown, and the *doyenne* of Velazquez scholars, Enriquetta Harris Frankfort, have also contributed hugely to my understanding of the artists and the period. Works by Eamon Duffy, Diarmaid MacCulloch, Desmond Seward and the late, renowned Spanish historian, Hugh Thomas, have provided invaluable political and religious insights of the time. I am also indebted to the American academic, Marilyn H Fedewa, for her biography of the 'Mystical Lady In Blue', the remarkable Maria, Abbess of Agreda.

Miguel de Cervantes has been another indispensable guide: to the Spain of the early seventeenth century; to the workings of the human mind; to the complexity and unpredictability of every person. As Dostoevsky once said of Don Quixote, 'a more profound and powerful work than this one is not to be found.'

Chiaroscuro is fiction, but a story that I would like to think may lead you to search for more opportunities to see the astonishing achievements in art of Caravaggio, Velazquez and Zurbaran and imagine for yourself what life was like for them. I hope you will be content for now with the thoughts of Francisco Zurbaran where this story begins, one night in Madrid in December 1658.

Laurence Brady
Selkirk, 10 March 2022

PART 1

Chapter 1

THE QUEST

Can you remember the twelve sons of Jacob? Their names, their faces, their look? You should. You painted every one of them after all. And their father, bent over a stick, his long grey beard hanging down. Leonor says she likes Joseph best in all his finery at the court of the pharaoh. What a surprise! Your wife, the goldsmith's daughter, picks out the golden threads on his coat, the gems in the brooch around his neck. She even delights in the bows of silk on his sandals. Of course she does, but do you not think it's Joseph's story she loves even more? Thrown down a well by his jealous brothers, left for dead, rejected, redeemed, restored, resurrected, lifted from the darkness of the well to a new and unimaginable light.

Leonor flatters you with her vision of the thirteen portraits of Jacob and his sons. Among the finest works of the great Francisco de Zurbaran, she likes to tell you, adding that you are the most accomplished of Seville's artists, past or present. 'Francisco,' she says, 'your gift is eternal.' What she really means is that she sees your doubts. You are not as sharp, not half as confident as you once were, but twice as bitter. Believe in yourself, Francisco.

Don't allow your achievements to remain in the past. She even quotes Saint Benedict at you, 'Run while you have the light of life.' Run, Francisco. Run through the twelve sons, know their names, use them, your memory of how you created them, to remember that you are one of the great artists of our age. The city of Seville owes you so much.

Leonor, sweet Leonor, as good and gentle a wife as a man could wish for. What are you saying? She cuts down to size any man who treats her like a weaker vessel when it comes to buying and selling her precious gold. She wields Jacob and his twelve sons like a club over your head. Don't you sit at the bottom of the well in the darkness. It's not where you belong. Look on your works and do not despair.

You are not, you know, whatever she believes. You are not the painter you once were. You are not the beloved son of Seville, not any more. If that were true your commissions would still be flowing. It would be your *reals*, not Leonor's, paying for this house, feeding the children. For that matter, you would not be in Madrid, not dreading the moment you must address Velazquez.

It's that thought, that Diego Rodriguez de Silva Velazquez is alive and here in Madrid. Obviously. No-one can doubt his presence this Advent in the year of Our Lord, One Thousand Six Hundred And Fifty-Eight. He lives and paints, year after year, in the court of the king at the pleasure of the king. It's who he is, what he has always been. Gifted. Privileged. Speaking through his art. Never saying too much, careful not to offend. Discreet, always mindful of the need to satisfy the king. At least that is how it seems. It must be thirty years now, thirty-five maybe, years of building Philip's trust. Slowly becoming the only fixed point when wars, wives, children, advisers, nobles, ha! even Olivares, come and go. Diego didn't even have to be painting all of that time. It's not as if the king demanded great years of service.

'Yes, Velazquez. You go to Rome and Venice now and procure more art for my Hall of Mirrors.'

'Ah Velazquez, you have returned, but only after three years. Not so much buying or painting on this trip? Too much time perhaps, meeting Bernini. Or Cortona? Poussin? Domenichino? No matter. Welcome back, Velazquez. These antique sculptures and paintings by the Venetian masters are magnificent. Excellent purchases, my roving Court Painter. Well done.'

Yes, well done, Diego. Philip thought you had brought him such treasures. Your own works too. I cannot deny that your portrait of Pope Innocent is masterful. Did King Philip compliment you on the technical brilliance of the painting? Those layers of red, that hard expression revealing both a sharpness of mind and an untrusting nature. So political. So temporal. As far from the fishermen in Galilee as it's possible to be. And in his left hand, well what could that be? Your signature on paper, proof of Innocent's assent? The pope who promotes Spanish cardinals. The pope who must outwit Cardinal Mazarin and the French. The pope who refuses to recognise the independence of Portugal. The pope who agrees to sit for a Spanish artist from the court of the king of his ally. The pope who will give the papal seal of approval to your quest for nobility, sacred membership of the Order of Santiago. Of course he will. He is holding you by the hand, after all. So subtle, Diego. So subtle. The perfect way for you to start the conversation with the king.

A life of painting. Travelling. Purchasing. Advising. Curating. Counting the accolades. Collecting payment. Hearing the applause, always led by the king. The way you have survived in the politics of the Escorial. Only to reach this late stage in life and be obsessed with a noble and holy order that is not rightfully yours. Is it not enough? And now this. Why are you so obsessed?

Once. Once it was only your art that mattered. To us. To the three of us. You Diego, Alonso and me, Francisco Zurbaran. Remember me? Sometimes called the Spanish Caravaggio. Or is that you? Teenage boys in Seville hanging on every word of our mentor and master, the great Pacheco. Is that true? Well, partly. One minute marvelling at his knowledge, his explanations and illustrations. The next, joking about his mediocrity as a painter; too clever, too arrogant for his own good. Except you wouldn't let on in front of the old man, would you. Funny to remember that's how we thought of him then. Only later, when Alonso challenged you about your charm all being an act, I realised.

Diego, Diego. I could never tell what you were thinking. Even when you were forced to admit to *amor*, you gave no sign of emotion, no passion. No Don Quixote speeches for your fair Dulcinea. When I think about it now, you played the game so well with the old man. How naïve Alonso and I were, thinking the great Francisco de Pacheco was always in control. There was Diego, doing his bidding, following his instructions like the hungry apprentice he was. It makes me sick now. I can see you as clearly as if you were standing in front of me, nodding your acceptance every time Pacheco re-stated his belief that we should imitate the techniques of those Flemish painters of Antwerp, Bruegel, *El Bosco* and all the rest.

Quite a performance for five years. To be so calm, attentive and flawless in following Pacheco's instruction. Never intending for a moment to copy the Flemish or anyone else for that matter. I wonder at what point did you realise that you had fallen in love with, or at least wanted to marry, Juana Pacheco? I could never tell with you. Not one to confide, not in me anyway. You and Alonso were always closer. Maybe you knew about Alonso long before I did. Diego Velazquez and Alonso Cano, separated only by two years. I can't believe that you looked up to him, Diego. Even then, do you remember, Alonso would lose his temper with the slightest teasing or provocation. So many opportunities with Alonso's bluster, for you to blend into the background, quietly going about your business, your art, your plan for self-promotion. I always knew where I stood with Alonso. I could see his mood or confession ahead like a storm coming over the horizon. I loved him for it.

Why am I thinking about those days, anyway? Such ancient history. All because of this final quest of yours. And we, Alonso and I, we must, it seems, remain in the shadows, though now we three are in Madrid. In Madrid, but not together. Not equals. The bright light that went to the king's court thirty-whatever years ago has shone brightly ever since. I should have known. I should have known. You recognised your exceptional talent as a teenager, didn't you. And, I mustn't forget, at the same time you discovered your power to influence people most likely to advance your prospects. What I can't work out is whether the acceptance as royal painter on his second attempt before you had reached twenty-five years old was unexpected good fortune, or an arrogant assumption.

First Pacheco, the greatest teacher and mentor in Seville and possibly all of Spain. Second, King Philip IV, the undisputed patron of patrons, the single most certain route to wealth, reputation, stability and influence. And others on this gilded life journey? Alonso, for example. Foils? Deflectors? Protectors? Like the characters who complete your paintings but who do not, must not, cast a shadow over the bright light that is the artist of artists.

This arrogance, Diego Velazquez. It must be that. Your conceit. That we are all in your shadow, is unbearable to contemplate. Who do you think you are? What gives you the right to eternal life? Pacheco, the king, the queen, Alonso, princesses, the Church, the army of advisers – we are all somehow means to your end. Now this. I once shared your youthful energy, lived day by day in your friendship, cheered your talent and good fortune. I had assumed your reserve was humility, your success a distraction from the purity of your art. Now I can see what your obsessions have done to you. For over thirty years you have assumed control of the king no matter what anyone else thought of your paintings, your marriage or even your parentage.

Ah yes, Diego, your parentage; even the king can't do anything about that; and this obsession you have, this vain quest to become a member of the most holy and venerable Order of Santiago, how noble is that? An aristocrat of pure, noble blood whose ancestors, the defenders of our faith, fought for the Holy Lands in the Crusades or on Rhodes or in the Great Siege of Malta? You think that because you are the king's *confidant,* because you make this great gift of a family portrait with the maids of honour to him, that somehow you are entitled.

No, you must have pure and noble blood, Diego, my friend. Your father was a church notary of Portuguese stock. He came from merchants. Possibly some Jewish heritage too. At least that's what I remember you telling Alonso and me in confidence. More convenient, was it not, for your parents to follow Andalusian custom and take your mother's family name of Velazquez, not your father's name of de Silva.

This is not like Charles V simply deciding to award Titian the title of Count Palatine. Philip cannot just anoint you, even if he wanted to. Calatrava, Alcantara and Santiago, those are the three great military orders of Spain, Diego, or have you forgotten? It was they who fought the holy war of *Reconquista* to drive out the Muslim invaders. White habits for the knights of the Order of Santiago, black for the canons, emblazoned with a red cross. *Rubet ensis sanguine Arabum*, Diego. Their motto, their history, our history of *Reconquista*, an Order of nobles confirmed in its defence of the faith by more than twenty popes, twenty Successors of Peter, starting with Alexander III. When the knights were not colouring their swords red, they painted a picture of compassionate Christianity. Caring for the sick, they risked their lives exposing themselves to diseases as deadly as any Berber sword. The knights of the Order of Santiago are the *hospitaliers*, the men who nursed lepers. Their rewards, Diego? In this life, gifts of land, money and castles. Castles everywhere: France, the Holy Lands, Hungary, Carinthia, as far as England, even Portugal. In the next life their reward is eternal, of that there can be no doubt.

So, my friend, the Order's Council will decide whether you are to be admitted to this sacred brotherhood. You. Even I, the newcomer to Madrid, have heard of the king's desire to see you achieve this crowning glory. It says something about the sanctity of the Order of Santiago, doesn't it Diego, that the king cannot demand for you to be accepted. What would he say anyway?

'Please, please let my dear Velazquez in. He cares little for the Faith or the glory of God and he prefers to paint what he can see and touch in this life with little concern for the life eternal yet to come. Don't worry about the noble birth issue. A bit old-fashioned, and anyway, I'll vouch for him. I am the king after all. So please let him enter your most sacred and holy Order of Santiago.'

We all thought that was that. The Council would approve. The king's wishes known, his now holy painter anointed. A knight of Santiago, a guarantee of the last rites of the church being a passage to eternal life. The red cross emblazoned on the shoulder of a burial habit. Accept me, Lord. Here I am. See. I am your most faithful servant.

That was not what happened though, was it? I know the date, the Fifteenth of July in the year of Our Lord, One Thousand Six Hundred And Fifty-Eight, when the Council of Santiago assembled to hear the testimony of the king's court artist. The applicant, the moment of truth, the crowning of your career, Diego. All you had to do was read out a list of your ancestors. Lo and behold, it would be a noble line, an evangelic revelation, a record of the genealogy of Diego Silva de Velazquez, the son of, the son of, the son of.

Speak up, members shouted. How upsetting it all must have been for you. You, a man whose life gains were realised by remaining in the shadows, the artist in the background. They wanted names, Diego, evidence of lineage. Good enough reasons to see a brother of noble heritage in their midst, one whose face had been in plain view but hidden all these years. The real Diego Velazquez would break bread with them and be recognised for who he really was for the first time.

But how could they, Diego, without ridiculing themselves and everything the Order stood for? How could they not, without delivering a public insult to the king? For men faced with such a dilemma I am inclined to think the Council's solution was a clever one. Your candidacy is of such great importance to the Order that it 'merits further investigation.' Note: merits. Very clever, and smart, too, in appointing two opposites as their investigators. One, a young lawyer whose sharp questioning in the courts of Madrid had won him a reputation for dispensing with distractions and digressions offered by witnesses. Sharp, but not cold, not heartless, giving way to flights of fancy at times. A romantic, they say. The other, well, a pedant. Sorry if that seems harsh. Overweight, overbearing, over the age of contributing anything useful to society as far I can see. Yet, admired in the Council. A devout man undoubtedly, a good man even, one obsessed by facts and without compare as a living historian of the Order.

So, the Council appointed these two who had never, as far as I know, so much as exchanged a word. Can you imagine? Of course you can. That the carefully crafted life and reputation of my friend, Diego Velazquez, should rest in the hands of these two and however many witnesses their investigation requires. Not the king, not any Council member, could countenance a rejection of their findings. The Council would give them less than six months to carry out their work, free, unimpeded, unlimited resources. Their first task, to get the measure of each other.

* * *

'The king actually said that?'

'Those were his very words. I heard them from his own lips.'

'Say them again.'

'Why do you need me to repeat what I have already told you?'

'Was that all he said?'

'No. I've told you.'

'You didn't say very much.'

'What more is there to say? I've given you the facts.

Those are what matter. The facts.'

'Yes, but the facts don't tell you everything.'

'In this case they do.'

'Facts are as bald as you are. They need dressing up a little.'

'There is no dressing up the fact that I am bald.'

'My point is that that there is more to you than your baldness. There must be. Though I confess I am struggling to see anything else right now.'

'I am bald. You are not funny. These are the facts.'

'No. The fact is we are getting away from the point. What happened when our most noble Order of Santiago convened in the divine presence of his imperial majesty to discuss the candidacy of the anointed regal adviser, much-travelled curator and peerless court painter, Señor Velazquez?'

'I fear for the future of our legal profession if you are held up as one of its most able representatives. It is clear to me you are not content with facts but thrive on insinuation and gossip. Your question betrays prejudice even before we have started our work.'

'So, before you will answer my question I must defend my profession. I see. Suffice to say that for the law to serve its purpose, information must be obtained. An understanding of the circumstances, a clarity surrounding motivation will – how can I put this to you politely – illuminate the facts.'

'You, Don Diego Lozando Villasandino, and I, Don Fernando de Salcedo, as Council members of the holy Order of Santiago, have been appointed by the same, to investigate the claim of one Diego Rodriguez de Silva Velazquez – born and baptised in Seville on the Sixth day of June in the year of Our Lord One Thousand Five Hundred and Ninety-Nine – to be of noble birth. Our investigations are to begin immediately. They are to comprise of as many interviews as necessary to establish the facts of the legitimacy of Señor Velazquez's claim. On the conclusion of our work we are to submit our report to the Council. Both the Council and the king have made it clear that they want to see this matter resolved at the earliest opportunity and before the end of this calendar year. At this point, Don Diego, I need to know when you are likely to have made a full recovery so that we can make our preparations to travel.'

'One thing at a time, Don Fernando. You still haven't told me what happened in the Council's meeting with the king, what arguments were made, and what was the reaction to Velazquez's evidence to the Council. Secondly, I want to know how this grand decision of appointing the two of us as investigators was reached.'

'At last. I knew you would ask a reasonable question eventually. We have not worked together on Council matters before and few, if any, would call us kindred spirits. And thirdly, I need to be clear on what you mean by travel. Velazquez stated in his testimony before the Council that his paternal grandparents, Diego Rodriguez de Silva and Maria Rodriguez came from Porto in northern Portugal. As you will recall, he also declared that the family of his mother, Doña Jeronima, hailed from Andalusia. Velazquez followed the Andalusian custom of taking his mother's family name. It is perhaps a convenient explanation to draw attention away from his father's heritage.'

'More conjecture, Don Diego.'

'If we are to travel, as you tell me we must, Don Fernando, it is surely our job as investigators to establish the truth. Our interviewees, whoever and wherever they may be, are not going to give us the facts as you would wish. They are not going to show us a ledger of actions and transactions. No. They will choose how they want to interpret the facts and then give us a selective and subjective version. And, as we are travelling they will, as it were, see us coming. The Council will be less concerned with Andalusian stock, but they will expect a thorough investigation of more questionable Portuguese ancestry. Add to that the small matter of Spain's war with Portugal for nearly twenty years. If we are to travel to Portugal to interview Velazquez's Portuguese descendants, how will we do that?'

'More skirmishes than battles, but we remain in a state of conflict, I would say, with Portugal, it is true. This point was raised in Council with the king. Many, myself included, were concerned that we could not establish Velazquez's true identity were we not able to enter Portugal. Velazquez, if I may remind you, Don Diego, has made extraordinary claims.'

'I know. I was there. Remember? I haven't always been this ill.'

'He presented as fact that the De Silva family, from which his father sprang, was descended from none other than Silvius.'

'I know. The mythical founder of Portugal and son of Trojan Aeneas. It was the one moment when our court painter got too carried away and betrayed his desperation to become a Knight of the Order of Santiago. If the king had not been in the chamber that day I'm sure the room would have erupted in laughter. Strange, for, by all I've heard about the man, he is not given to emotion, says little and carries an air of cold detachment. Do you know anyone like that?'

'Perhaps you will be surprised to hear, Don Diego, that I recognise your attempt at humour at my expense. You can be assured that you will not have to endure any

irrational or factually incorrect outbursts from me. We are
to work together as the two representatives of the Council
of our Order.'

'I understand that. The key question is whether you
are ever going to tell me what was actually said in the
Council meeting with the king. If we cannot go to Portugal
what are we going to do?'

'The answer is Tuy.'

'Where?'

'It is a small town in the province of Pontevedra in
Galicia close to the Portuguese border. We are to travel
there and use that as a base for interviewing whoever has
an association with the family of Velazquez.'

'And they will willingly come to meet us? How many?'

'I believe once the word spreads we will have literally
dozens of interviewees. We will send messengers into
Portugal in advance to guarantee their safe passage, no
further action as a consequence of their testimony, and a
holy blessing from the sacred Order of Santiago.'

'And that will be enough?'

'You forget, Don Diego, what acceptance into the Order
will mean for them. You are a member by virtue of your
unambiguous noble heritage. Your family regard it as a
right.'

Don Fernando pauses. For all his attention to fact and
logic, he is not so in love with the sound of his own voice
that he remains insensitive to the impact of this reminder
on his new partner. He has unwittingly silenced Don Diego,
who looks intently at him now with reddening eyes. Don
Fernando might as well have broken the news of a death
in the family such is the emotion so obviously welling up
in his new colleague. Surprised by his own restraint, Don
Fernando resists the temptation to continue with a
reminder of the origins of the Order, starting with the

discovery of the body of Saint James in Galicia, a fact he does not doubt. It is one of many articles of faith that he takes to be absolute truth. His is not a questioning nature. He follows every holy observance to the letter and accepts the Church's magisterium. A personal experience of God eludes him. As with other facts of life, he acknowledges that not everyone of faith can be chosen, as God had chosen Francis of Assisi or Teresa of Avila. It never occurs to him that God exists somewhere other than in the sacraments, in the institutions and sacred orders of the Church, all of which can be traced back to the handing on of faith by the apostles. God's presence lives in the authority of his church, built on the rock of Saint Peter and his successors.

The fact was - as Don Fernando happily reminded anyone who dared to question the divine source or even the authenticity of the Order of Santiago – that not one or two, but no fewer than twenty men sitting in the Chair of Saint Peter had confirmed Pope Alexander III Bull of 1175 recognising the Order as religious. Only the year before this recognition, a Spanish king, Alfonso VIII of Castile, gave the Order the town of Uclès where their monastery was then established. And that, Don Fernando always wanted to emphasise to any victim of his monologue, was still only fourteen years after the Order had been founded in the first place. Though, in the unlikely event of a naïve soul ever pressing Don Fernando to tell more of the Order's history, he would admit that Santiago was just one of three *hermangildas* that evolved in the holy war of *Reconquista,* the other two brotherhoods being Calatrava and Alcántara. Up until the eleven hundreds these brotherhoods were no more than disparate groups of local armed militia defending their land and their farms.

Don Diego, head bowed, responds.

'My father certainly did. And his father. And no doubt every *paterfamilias* since the brotherhood was bestowed on the Villasandinos. It did not matter what kind of men they were, strong or weak, filled with the gifts of the Holy Spirit or gripped by greed or envy or lust, they were assured of a better than fair Judgement. I am following them as will my son. Our merits, our gifts are as nothing compared to the heritage of our birth. It is a burden I find hard to live with.'

As strange to the outpouring of emotion as he is familiar with the release of facts, Don Fernando judges that his fellow investigator would be comforted with a little historical insight. 'Perhaps it is worth remembering, Don Diego, that the Order has five Grand Priors. For Léon, Castile, Aragon and Gascony, as you might expect; but also for Portugal. Guided by the mighty Santiago *Matamoros,* the knights drove off the invaders and, like the Knights of St John of Malta, they built hospitals. They cared for lepers. What set us apart from Alcántara and Calatrava was the allowance of married knights. These were not just *confrères,* but full members whose possessions and families also became part of the Order. They made sacrifices with all they had. They gave their very lives to protect the Christendom of Spain and Portugal and to care for the most diseased of outcasts.'

Don Diego makes no effort to interrupt the flow of his new partner's history lesson. For his part, Don Fernando interprets the silence, the staring at the floor, as an invitation to continue, the lack of requirement of Don Diego itself bestowing a healing power on him.

'No small wonder, then, that gratitude would be expressed by the granting of properties as far away as England.' Don Diego raises his head.

'Yes, England, Don Diego, can you believe that? In France too. Milan. Venice. Florence. Palestine. Even

Hungary, and yes, in Portugal as well, including the town of Palmella as I recall. So, war or no war, do not be surprised by the willingness of people to come to Tuy to be interviewed by the men who can influence the decision to make one of their sons – as they will see him – to become a knight.'

Don Diego smiles at his companion, acknowledging the kindness intended in the history lesson. What could he say now? That Don Fernando had succeeded only in deepening his melancholy? Had reminded him of his father's frequent invocations of the Order of Santiago as his family's guaranteed path to eternal life? The absolute certainty in his voice in the retelling of these same facts. The monasteries, the hospitals, the lepers, not recounted as atonement for the slaughter of other human beings who happened to be Muslims, but as other Christian duties to be fulfilled. Duties that assumed lesser mortals didn't have the stomach for.

Someone had to take care of the lepers so that the rest of the population didn't become infected. Someone had to cleanse Spain and Portugal or they would overrun Christianity. The end justified the means. *Rubet ensis sanguine Arabum.* 'Santiago and close Spain.' That was it, the cry of the knights in battle. That was what they yelled. The louder the cry the more they believed it.

At least it had not been a violent death for his father. The time for defending, for killing Muslims and ministering to lepers had long since past. Only the symbolism remains. The symbolism and the hubris. Don Diego could see his face now. Serene, almost smiling. His dead body purified by the white habit of the Order, the red cross on the shoulder, its bottom arm swishing like a sword blade. Resurrection and life everlasting confirmed by Saint James's and Saint Peter's successors, his sins forgiven. Confessor or no confessor, the divine nature of the Order conferred it upon him. In his first waking thought and in his last breath he knew it. His life had a purpose. He would see the face of Almighty God. As his noble heritage gained him entry into the Order of Santiago, so his membership allowed him at the very least to approach the gates of heaven and humbly ask his God to let him in. That was his belief. That was his hope of eternal salvation. Lost in these thoughts, Don Diego is oblivious to Don Fernando staring at him, eventually giving up and supplying his own.

'We will, of course, also interview known associates of Señor Velazquez here in Madrid and in Seville. You will have heard of some of them, I'm sure. The artist, Francisco Zurbaran? The sculptor, Alonso Cano?'

'I don't understand. Why them?' Don Diego asks.

'They were all apprentices at the same time in Seville, in the academy of Francisco Pacheco. Zurbaran was apprenticed to Pedro Diaz de Villanueva. Before you ask me, we are, as investigators of the Order and acting explicitly on the Council's command, guaranteed truthful evidence from these contemporaries of Velazquez. Whatever they might think of him now, however loyal they might want to be, they must answer truthfully. If Velazquez joked with them about his ancestry or made serious reference to his noble Portuguese origins, we will find out.'

'You mean their word against the word of Velazquez, if they say that he admitted to coming from a family of merchants, or peasants even.'

'Don Diego, our job is only to gather the evidence. It is for the Council to decide based on the facts we present to them. We cannot presume to know what any of our interviewees will say. You are frowning. What have I said that troubles you?'

'Cano.'

'I beg your pardon?'

'Cano. A moment ago you mentioned Cano. There was a case against him some years ago. Accused of murder. Killed someone in a duel. Something about his wife too. I'll look it up. Perhaps we should have some protection when we go to see him.'

Don Fernando betrays nothing of the smile in his thoughts. All of his personal encounters with knights and members of the Order had till this point been framed in politically, no, religiously, correct language. Propriety observed. Appropriate. Based on fact. Without conjecture. Gossip strictly avoided. Verbal exchanges, for they were not conversations, guided by *magisterium*. Nothing prepares him for this candid disarmament by a man seemingly without guile. He can sense no attempt to deceive him, no desire other than to speak the truth. In spite of the warmth of friendship rising in him, in spite of the inexplicable relief that Don Diego's melancholy appears to be lifting, Don Fernando arches his eyebrows in concern, maintaining his own stern appearance.

'This is no laughing matter', he says. 'We must not be prejudiced in any way.'

'Of course, of course', Don Diego leans forward, further compressing the scarlet velvet cushions on the black sofa where he has been reclining, more animated now. 'I'm sure you will look after the integrity of our investigation, Don Fernando, and defend me if necessary. So what's this other man like, Zurbaran?'

'Not for me to gossip if that's what you are looking for.'

'Facts, Don Fernando. Facts. That's all I am interested in.'

'You are mocking me again. Be that as it may, I am surprised that you don't know.'

'Know? Know what? Surely we must both be aware

of – what shall I call it – circumstantial evidence in this investigation. We need to be able to judge how reliable the testimony of any witness – is that what we're going to call them? – shall be. Though this Cano sounds dubious, and what weight we can give to the declarations of people born and bred in Velazquez's father's family, I am even less sure.'

'The fact is, my learned colleague, that Francisco Zurbaran has been talked about in Seville and Madrid for years – '

'Talked about? Talked about, Don Fernando? Is this gossip coming from your lips so early in our working partnership. I may have to report you.'

Ignoring Don Diego's levity, he continues.

'The facts are –.'

'Oh, facts.'

'The facts are that Council members, especially those close to the Jeronomite and Carthusian orders, believe that Zurbaran would have had a worthy claim to be a member of the Order of Santiago. You might say that – '

'Is this conjecture?'

'You might say that, unlike Velazquez, his preoccupation throughout his life has been the eternal reward of the saints, the monks, those who have sacrificed their lives for faith in the resurrection. Zurbaran has shown us what actually happens to a person when God becomes present to them. His paintings, in their simplicity, in their contrast of light and dark, are themselves instruments of faith. I am surprised you do not know of his work, Don Diego. I recommend you visit the Jeronomites at Guadalupe to see his sequence of paintings that grace the walls of the monastery. If there is time during our investigations, we can go together to the Dominican monastery of San Pablo El Real in Seville. Ambrose. Gregory. Dominic. Jerome.

Our Blessed Lady and Virgin Mother. All brought to life for us with an intensity and sharpness of light that make you feel the divine presence. You could even argue that a visit would be pertinent to our investigation.'

Don Fernando pauses in his eulogy. His partner, whose resurrection from the sick bed had taken place only days before, is struggling to sustain their dialogue. This exchange had come several days too early for him and no doctor would have prescribed Don Fernando for recuperation. He dispensed facts with all the certainty of a physician. Opinions, too, were weighted with knowledge and clarity. Don Fernando could only be telling the truth. An ideal witness for the Defence in any court, his would be an authoritative testimony. Few, if any, would detect his evasion, his skill in not answering the specific question put to him, in saying everything but nothing.

Don Diego lacks the will and the strength to continue this first discussion. He has gleaned enough. He has the measure of the man, he thinks. The core fact remains. The Council of the Order has appointed the two of them to investigate the candidacy of the king's court painter, Diego Velazquez. He has no choice, whatever his first impression of the bald inquisitor sitting across from him. Is he being tested? Judged even? Does it matter that he has not come across this supposedly divinely inspired artist, Francisco Zurbaran? The wave of weakness matters more at this moment. He would find out more about Zurbaran and Alonso later. He simply needs to end this meeting as soon as possible. Only one question remains unanswered for the time being.

'Don Fernando, you will forgive me if we leave further questions of Zurbaran, Alonso and others to another time. I confess that my recovery is not yet complete and I am tiring, though there is so much of interest to me in all that you say. If we can resume tomorrow I would be grateful. I only want to put my mind as well as my body at rest by understanding the king's view. You still haven't told me what comments he made about Velazquez in the Council meeting. 'We are – '

'No. No. It is you who should forgive me', Don Fernando stretches out to grip Don Diego's arm. 'The Spanish Caravaggio can wait.'

'What did the king – ? No. Wait. Why do you call Zurbaran the Spanish Caravaggio?'

'We can discuss this another time. I see that you are tired.'

'No, you've got my interest now.'

'I see. I didn't have it before, then.' Don Fernando returns.

'You know what I meant. I have listened carefully to every word you have said and found it all fascinating. It's when you forget your factual principles and stray into opinion or hearsay that I really start to understand. It gives me a more rounded picture. Calling Zurbaran the Spanish Caravaggio would be like calling you the Charismatic Investigator. It goes beyond fact, a value statement if you like, not objective.'

'Are these jibes a symptom of your illness, I wonder? They are the uncontrollable utterances of a semi-delirious invalid. Gradually they disappear as you make a full recovery and you are restored to your essence, that of an honourable lawyer with integrity, charm, conscience and an unswerving desire to serve the Order. Or is this only a mild beginning of something much worse to come? Our interviewees are to be subjected to insinuation and insult, goaded by an intemperate man in a constant fever.'

'I thought you were going to be the grand inquisitor.' Don Diego smiles broadly. 'So tell me some more about him, Don Fernando, if you don't mind me reclining on these cushions and closing my eyes while I listen to your strictly factual account of him.'

'If you insist. Only the facts, mind you, as they are pertinent to our investigation.'

'Of course. I would expect nothing less and nothing more. Please begin, Don Fernando, and pay no attention to my quips.'

'Quips?' the newly elected grand inquisitor asks.

'Think of them as signs that I am looking forward to investigating and interviewing with you; signs that I already believe the bond is strong enough not to hurt your feelings.'

'I don't need signs, thank you', Don Fernando rejoins. 'It is a faithless generation that asks for a sign.'

'Yes, I know that. Your knowledge of the Gospel does you great credit, and my knowledge of the facts about this Spanish Caravaggio as you call him, would help our investigation. Please continue before I expire.'

'Well, then, these are the facts. Francisco Zurbaran is the son of a shopkeeper. Though his family is descended from Basques and is not of noble blood, he was born and baptised sixty years ago in Fuente de Cantos.'

'I've never heard of it,' Don Diego interrupts.

'It's a small village and the only thing to say is that it's about fifty miles from the ancient Roman city of Mérida,' confirms Don Fernando. 'which is not much to say. Now that I think about it, apart from the *Puente Romano* in Mérida I don't have much to say about Extremadura either.'

'Ah, thus speaks the Madrileño. You disappoint me, Don Fernando. A lawyer could argue in court that our glorious empire was built on the labours of sons of Extremadura. Need I remind you that we wouldn't even have found the Americas, never mind conquered them, without the brilliant navigation of Vasco Nuñez de Balboa, himself of noble blood of Extremadura if I recall.'

'Your capacity to rally when criticism is called for is a new source of amazement to me.'

'Really, my friend, even in my weakened state, I can out-factual-ise you.'

Don Fernando's face brightens. 'There's no such word', he smiles.

'And then there's Balboa's friend, Francisco Pizarro. Have you heard of him? Maybe not. He only conquered, civilised and converted the Incas to Christianity as well as founding Lima. Oh, and we musn't forget his half-brother, Gonzalo, who explored the Andes and discovered one of the Americas', if not the world's, great rivers.'

'Is this what you are going to do to our witnesses, Don Diego? Humiliate them?'

Ignoring his partner, the lawyer continues with his prosecution of the facts about the extraordinary sons of Extremadura. Hernán Cortés. Francisco de Orellana. Hernando de Soto. Sebastián Vizcaino. Don Fernando nods vigorously waving his hand for the catalogue of Extremaduran heroes to stop.

'Yes, yes. Great men every one. Conquistadors. Explorers. Soldiers. Missionaries above all. Men whose journeys began no doubt with a pilgrimage to Our Blessed Lady of Guadalupe as Christopher Columbus had done before them. I fear, though, that your exposition of my failing to recall the giants of Extremadura has further drained your energy, so let me proceed with my telling of this other son of Extremadura, before you are too tired to hear.'

Don Diego lies back in the cushions once more closing his eyes and waving his arm as if instructing a witness in court to speak. 'You may proceed', he says.

'Francisco de Zurbaran left Fuente de Cantos as a

teenager seeking an apprenticeship in art. By either luck or design, I'm not sure which, he ended up at various times in the studio of Francisco Pacheco in Seville during or after his apprenticeship with Villanueva. It was there that he came into contact with others like him who would go on to become gifted and renowned artists as painters or sculptors. Think of Francisco Herrera and our friend, Alonso Cano. Diego Velazquez was the first apprentice of Pacheco's.'

'Why Pacheco?' Don Diego asks. 'What was so special about his art school?'

'For one thing he was an established artist himself. Then there's the fact that he was especially well-connected with the Church and at El Escorial. Pacheco painted and taught a strict religious code which is not surprising when you consider that he was also the censor for the Inquisition in Seville.'

'So that was where Zurbaran met Velazquez?'

'Yes, they became friends as far as we know. After his apprenticeship Zurbaran remained in Seville. He married Maria Paez and they had three children together, only she died while the children were still young. In the 1620s Zurbaran secured a number of notable commissions that consolidated his reputation.'

'Like what?'

'Like the Dominican monastery of San Pablo El Real in Seville. Zurbaran produced a series of paintings for them. Saint Dominic. Saint Jerome. Saint Ambrose. But it was his Crucifixion still hanging in the sacristy there which secured his secured his fame and, Don Diego, gave him this title of the Spanish Caravaggio. I have seen it and I have asked why Zurbaran stands out when there were so many other imitators of Caravaggio's stark style of light and darkness after he died in 1610, and not least among them, Jusepe de Ribera, who died only a few years ago.'

'The relative merits of one man's art over another's do not concern me, Don Fernando.'

'By the time of the Dominican commission Zurbaran had re-married, a widow named Beatriz de Morales.'

'More children?'

'No. The fact is, though, that she lived with him through the most successful period of his career. They moved from Llerena to Seville where the elders invited him to be its official painter in residence. He and Señora Morales spent ten years together there, living with his three children, another relative of his, Isabel de Zurbaran, and as many as eight servants.'

'Expensive,' Don Diego observes. 'How do you happen to be so well informed about Zurbaran's life, anyway? This sounds like gossip to me.'

Don Fernando throws his hands up in the air in exasperation. 'I cannot understand you at all. These are facts that are widely known, facts about a man whose art has brought heaven to earth. Zurbaran is, many on the Council and at El Escorial would argue, the greatest painter of our age.'

Don Diego remains passive, expressionless, not rising to the emotion, a detached interviewer, a lawyer extracting the truth from a witness. 'Why is that?' he asks.

'I am no expert on art. I can't explain the technical detail', Don Fernando says.

'I am not asking you to. Never mind what anyone else thinks. Just tell me what you see.'

'I have seen his cycle of eight paintings for the Jeronomites on the walls of the monastery in Guadalupe. Each one is a scene of a monk's vision of God. So simple. So intense. Every monk appears to be physically held by the light of God himself. Outside of that light there is only darkness. It is as though Zurbaran is saying that if you choose to live in the light you need not be afraid of the darkness that surrounds you. You have a simple choice. Remain in the light and do not worry about your life. Do not be concerned with other details or possessions that are lost in the darkness.'

'That may be so, but we both know how influential and wealthy the Jeronomites are in Spain. Did they commission these paintings depicting their own monks like saints with a visionary experience of God to remind themselves of their true calling to spiritual and not temporal matters? Or are these paintings a more cynical political tactic to deflect attention away from any excesses of the monks?'

Don Fernando shakes his head. 'I don't know about the circumstances of the monks twenty years ago. The fact, though, is that the Jeronomites of Guadalupe see those paintings every day of their monastic life.'

'And you are saying that the way Zurbaran painted the monks is in the style of Caravaggio?'

'Pardon. You are almost whispering, Don Diego. I can tell you more about Zurbaran before we meet him. First, we have a lot of planning to do for our trip to Tuy. If you are asking about Caravaggio, I would say that many have tried to imitate him, but only Zurbaran has achieved that intensity of light in his paintings, light in the darkness. The irony is that the contrast between light and dark can be said of the characters of Caravaggio and Zurbaran as well.'

'Thank you. I understand now why he is a key witness. Your facts have given me the context I was lacking,' Don Diego whispers, appearing to travel away from consciousness.

'Now you must rest properly. We can talk again tomorrow.' Don Fernando stands ready to leave. To Don

Fernando's surprise, his partner promptly sits up, extending his arms, opening his outstretched hands. The gestures do not bid farewell or seek a fraternal embrace even less. They ask once more the question he has avoided answering since the beginning of their conversation. He cannot now leave his fellow investigator at the end of this first bonding meeting without telling him. Don Diego's fixed gaze tells him. 'If we are going to work together and trust each other to obtain the truth, we must begin as we mean to continue.'

Don Fernando hesitates, looks at his feet, speaks in a soft, embarrassed voice like a child confronted by the naked evidence of a misdemeanour.

'The king said only this of Velazquez. 'Write down that I am certain of his nobility'.'

Chapter 2

THE DARKNESS

Michelangelo Merisi da Caravaggio is dead: to begin with. There is no doubt about that. Washed up on the shore of a new day, July 23rd, in the year of Our Lord One Thousand Six Hundred And Ten, the fugitive painter could not cling to the wreckage of his life any longer. Not one living soul can say exactly when he gave up his spirit. No account survives of a Good Samaritan who cradles the dying man in his arms or memorises a list of requests for forgiveness. There is no anointing, no final absolution. Only Caravaggio's death is absolute: that is certain.

Whilst the circumstances of his premature demise remain a mystery, its inevitability is not. From an early age, in the darkness of his sleeping mind on turbulent seas, most nights he climbs to the top of the mast to curse the wind, to taunt the raging waters.

'Do your worst. I do not fear you. I will take my chances. I am not praying for calm. I am not asking to be rescued. Is it prayer that will save me from drowning? Really? Do you not know what I have already seen? I was only five years old when the plague became my childhood. I could not understand at first why the children I played with disappeared so often from our games. I was too young to work out why the streets emptied day after day. Four days, five days at most. Do you hear me? Five days! Five at most for those who were strong before the grotesque puss-filled domes on the neck, or under the armpits, or on the genitals, turned each body purple before a foaming death. They all prayed for salvation. Did it come? Did their God save them? He didn't save my grandfather, my uncle, my father, my beloved father. Fermo da Caravaggio. Taken from me before I am even six years old. Do you hear?

And who was left to me as my teacher, my guide in life? The man to whom all Milanese looked for salvation. That's right, the divine Cardinal Borromeo could do nothing. Nothing. Nothing. Is it prayer that will save me now? No. I am a survivor. It does not matter what I believe. I will not play this game of faith. I am an outcast. I will not bow down before the altar of decorum. I cannot, I will not, defer every action, every moment of my life, to a God who allowed my father, my uncle, my grandfather, my grandmother, my countrymen in their thousands to die the most vile death. I see no angels, no redemption. Do you hear me? I will not drown. The only rules in this life are my own, whatever that makes me to other men.' This is how it was for Michelangelo of Caravaggio. The storm of his plagued childhood never abates. Deep in the darkest corner of his mind a memory plays over and over again.

A wide-eyed boy is stumbling over the cobbled streets. Motionless, half-naked purple bodies swollen by plague, are face-down, broken, waiting to be taken, or staring in a trance at the sky in one silent final plea for salvation. They ought to be behind closed doors, out of sight, but here they are, these vessels, full of plague, empty of whatever love and hope once made them human. The boy breathes in the putrid air that infests them. Women, forbidden by quarantine laws to enter any church, are wailing. Some murmur, some gabble the rosary, fingering wooden beads. Some shout, calling on Saint Ambrose to intercede. Others call for the Cardinal, kneeling in in front of candles mounted on makeshift altars at street corners.

The faint creak and clatter of spokes and hooves penetrates the wailing and incantations. The distant rolling sound stops, resumes, each time the rhythm slower, heavier, closer. The wooden body carts are so close in the next street now that the boy hears the thud and squeak of another body thrown on the heap. The skeletal nags pull the overloaded cart into view at last. The purple flesh of a veined arm flops through the wooden slats as if waving a greeting to the five-year old in its path: 'Here we are. You have been waiting for us again, haven't you? Who did we collect yesterday? Your uncle, was it, or your grandmother? Anyway, we're back again. Must be the turn of your father today. Don't worry. We won't forget to pick him up. There's plenty of room on top of me.'

The sheet that bears the dead weight of Fermo Merisi da Caravaggio is knotted at either end. The purple domes on his neck and armpits are no longer visible, only imagined. The boy, Michelangelo, clings to his brother. He too is murmuring. It is a prayer for forgiveness. For mercy. The *monatti*, the gravediggers, take a knot each at either end of the stained sheet and swing his father. One, two, release. For an instant the full sheeted length of Fermo is suspended in the air above the cart. But now he is rolling down and off the slope of heaped cadavers. One of the knots is loosened by the throw, the body bent double exposed above the shoulders. Michelangelo catches a glimpse through his brother's fingers of the contorted face of his father. Beneath an open eye staring in accusation, the hard skin betrays a crack where the puss now escapes running down his chin like a living organism in search of a new host. Death is dribbling onto the street, trickling between the Milanese cobbles.

One other detail plays out in this recurring dream of the five-year-old Michelangelo. The taller of the two monatti, his hooked nose protruding from his cowl of rough grey cloth, steps forward to the side of the cart where Fermo's broken face lies exposed. Careful not to dirty his bare hands with the stained sheet, slowly he pulls a square white cloth from the rope girdle around his waist. He opens out its four corners and lets it drop to cover Fermo's face. Michelangelo hears him whisper 'Thy will be done' before he turns and nods to the boys.

In this moment Caravaggio sees the compassion in the face of the gravedigger. But there is more. Authority. Certainty. He has seen this face before. It is one and the same – it cannot be – of the divine figure most loved and revered in all of Milan, the man his father had called the second Saint Ambrose, saviour of the city. It's him, he whose blessing he had prayed for, gripping his father's hand, holding up his dripping candle with the other, in the procession for the feast of St Ambrose. This is the man sent by God to protect Milan from the plague. His father had seemed breathless, barely able to get the words out in that dusk of candlelit incense and cries for help. *Saint Ambrose, have mercy on us. Holy Archbishop, Blessed Cardinal, pray for us.*

'You are too young to understand now', his father had tried to explain to him waiting for the statue of St Ambrose. 'Cardinal Borromeo is the only man who can save us from this deathly plague. He will intercede for us as a successor to St Ambrose. The Cardinal has saved us before, protecting us from the Inquisition, taking back control of Milan from the Spaniards. He has given our faith meaning again, son. They used to joke outside church that he wanted to turn all year every year into the season of Lent, but no-one says that now. He is the light that God has sent us to face this devilish disease. Quick, Michelangelo. Cardinal Borromeo is passing us now. Hold up your candle and bow your head for his blessing.'

In that instant, Fermo followed his own instruction, so did not notice the disobedience of his son, gazing across the shoulders and the flickering lights of the penitent crowd. His look met a stern, yellowing face exaggerated by the blood-red robes framing it. What a deep sadness the Cardinal's look betrayed. Or was it helplessness in the half-light that he saw? The mitred head turned slowly in its arc of synchronised benediction. Inquisition, Michelangelo had wondered. What does that mean? And how can a red man walking in bloodied bare feet with a rope around his neck save the children from the plague? How can he be the light in this darkness?

Michelangelo stares at the *monatto,* expecting him to turn towards him again and make the sign of the cross in blessing. Maybe the Cardinal *monatto* will stretch out his hand and place it on his brother's shoulder. 'Peace be with you', he will say. 'Your father's sins will be forgiven. He will have his reward in heaven. As for you, Almighty God knows of your suffering. He has heard your weeping and he will put an end to this plague for you, your brother and all the souls of Milan, its towns and villages as well. Now, take care of your brother and your family. Protect them from this pestilence which, I assure you, did not come from God. He is not punishing you. Soon these streets will be clean. Tears will dry and the joy of the Risen Lord will return.'

Only, the *monatto* does not say that. Instead, seemingly unaware of the circle of family and neighbours around him, he berates his colleague,

'Could you not see that was going to happen?'

'I just thought – '

'You should only think when I tell you to think. Our job here is to clear the streets of bodies, pile them high and deliver the cart before sunset.'

'I'm sorry, I – '

'Idiot. Do you know what they say about our kind?'

'That we – '

'They think we spread the plague; that we go into homes for more than cadavers; that we are looters; that we steal and abuse; that we are incompetent.'

'Surely they won't say that about the two of us.'

'And what are these people gathered here watching us supposed to think when you cannot even load one more victim onto a cart?'

'I, I didn't mean – '

'Stop bumbling and get on with it. Fool. Straighten up. Why are you always hunched over like that, your head hanging down. Hurry up. Help me get this one back on the cart.'

Without so much as a nod or a glance behind to the grieving souls kneeling and wailing on the rough stained cobbles, the gravediggers seal, lift and swing the knotted sheets holding the body of Fermo da Caravaggio, on to the sagging cart. Taking the horses' tethers they resume their creaking, clopping, clattering collection.

Michelangelo is too frightened to run after the scolding *monatto* to ask if he really is the Cardinal, truly present in their suffering. He clings to Bernardino. Holding him in a tight embrace, his brother says nothing. The *monatti* fade into the Milanese gloom and with them their father,

Fermo Merisi da Caravaggio. Gone forever.

The memory stops there. It rewinds and plays again and again. Sometimes Caravaggio watches it in his mind's eye. At other times he is oblivious and the sight of the *monatti,* the cart, the twisted white shapes on the cart, the face, the face, play subconsciously.

* * *

Before an age in life when any work is expected of them, boys and girls can dream. Poverty, hardship, means nothing, safely wrapped as they are in a cocoon of play and loving families. Blessed are the children whose dreams of chivalrous knights, of adventures won and cheered, of prizes claimed, flow without interruption. To daybreak. Blessed are the children whose only worries on waking are the hours parents, brothers, sisters, friends, give to their whims and fantasies. If not a worry, then a concern for the child secure in love and circumstance, is the companionship for creating, exploring new worlds.

The imagined, the imaginary, the imagination, all can find a daily expression in play, in learning, in the wisdom of parents and playmates. And blessed, too, are those children of a more solitary nature, who draw more deeply from the well of their own thoughts. Discoveries are made, stimulated more by independent curiosity. Blessed one and all in this tender age, whose eyes close each night having lived through another day of the new, whose dreams filter life's bounty, whose energy is restored for another adventure at dawn. The brightness of dreams herald another day, predictable for its undiscovered treasure of good things.

Michelangelo Merisi da Carvaggio is not so blessed. Before he is ten years old his mind is barely candlelit. The light within does not dispel the darkness. It flickers. It

40

shrinks and retreats, made small by the intensity of the blackness that encircles it. Still, the black does not quench the flickering light. It cannot. At least not yet. It is ineluctable, burning at times with such strength that its yellow beams reach every corner of the boy's consciousness.

In these moments, when the gloom is penetrated, the boy from Caravaggio sees the detail of his world and imagination more clearly. While the light illuminates, he observes. He sees images with a clear focus in his mind's eye and stores them. Subconsciously, the boy knows that, before long, the light will dim again. The bright optimism of his senses will fade and the candle will flicker perilously close to extinction once more.

The boy, soon to be known simply as Caravaggio – as if to embody a whole village of souls as well as his own lost family – is still too young to know that he must endure long periods without the candle burning. For the most part it is the half-light that prevails, a descending darkness from which he cannot escape. Try as he might as adolescent, as young man, and God knows he tries, it is the pervading gloom that dictates his moods, determines his responses, dominates for days of drink and debauchery. On these days, the flame in his candlelit mind cowers in its quick. On these days, frequent, consecutive, unrelenting, pity the whores and young men, bought with charm and tenderness. They realise too late rough hands forcing submission. Or the waiter, whose bruised face bears witness to his audacity in serving artichokes with the wrong dressing. Think kindly of the landlady whose good reputation is undone by each coarse verse acted out as entertainment for the passers-by, for the shopkeepers, for the innocent children playing, for all to hear beneath her windows.

On some days the candle has all but gone out; days like the day when Caravaggio mercilessly taunts Ranuccio

Tomassoni. 'Lavinia's not like other women. No interest at all in any of my brushstrokes. I'll say that for her. There's only one thing she wants from me. She doesn't appear to be concerned with reputation at all. Does she, Ranuccio? But I do think about reputation. I do. Honestly I do. In fact, I have spoken to at least two other esteemed tradesmen of this eternal city at the inn over several weeks. Their tongues, loosened by wine it must be said, wagged all night long about Lavinia. Wagging tongues, Ranuccio. Sweet Lavinia. She never asked them about their work either, apparently. But for the sake of their reputation, I don't think I should say who they are. That wouldn't be right, would it, Ranuccio?'

Never in a quiet place, never discreetly, always in the company of those stalwart friends, associates whose opinion of him the vain Ranuccio cherished. Never so explicit as to leave Ranuccio with no option but to lunge at him, making Caravaggio the injured party. Goaded Ranuccio chooses the only other option. Satisfaction.

Humiliated to the very core of his being, Ranuccio Tomassoni chooses his own time and place with the painter, the philanderer, the parasite. It is not for Lavinia's sake that he lays down the challenge. Not for that whore, no different now from the long line of Roman prostitutes whose lives he controls. Not for the first time he dwells on the truth that he is a make-believe man, dressed up as a soldier but one who could only ever walk ten paces behind the mighty, the valiant Giovan Francesco, his heroic brother in arms. Always Giovan Francesco who would make the wealthy Farnese proud of their patronage of the Tomasssonis. Not Ranuccio. The less said about him the better. He was only good for profiling the weaknesses of Rome's honourable men. Never that difficult for Ranuccio to look the part of a cardinal protector, to brandish the sword and carry enough persuasion to expose the real desires of these paragons of Rome. The Farneses know it. The Tomassonis know it. Ranuccio knows it. He can undo the reputation of any man whatever mask or medals he wears, however much incense he burns. He is helpless in Ranuccio's hands because he delivers his deepest carnal desires, and for that he will pay anything.

Lavinia changes that, or so Ranuccio believes. Through Lavinia's fall he would earn respect and a new engagement. She would be the catalyst for him to forge a new reputation in Rome. He had connections, after all. He had influence with Cardinal Aldobrandini. He, Ranuccio Tomassoni, could eat his own pride and ask his brother's advice on starting a new life. And if Giovan Franceso believed in him, so would the Farnese. It would all change. It had to change. He would not allow the daughter he and Lavinia had brought into this world, beautiful Felicità, to grow up with a pimp as a father. He would choose Felicità.

Ranuccio's day of freedom and redemption is to be May 28th, 1606 on the Campo Marzio. Giovan Francesco, who cannot turn down a request to be his second, will see that his brother, Ranuccio, has honour, too; will defend his family; can fight and win in a swordfight just as Giovan Francesco had done in the battlefield. The selected witnesses are arriving, wearing faces as dark as their doublets. They are dressed for a December funeral when the sky is spectre-grey, nodding to each other as mourners do, sombre and silent.

The pretext of this supposedly spontaneous swordfight – a dispute over a tennis match – hardly seems a plausible way of convincing the Roman authorities that this is not an illegal duel, but it is what Ranuccio's brother has agreed with his brothers-in-law, Ignazio and Federigo Giugoli and Onorio Lunghi, and Caravaggio's second, Petronio Toppa.

It is why Ranuccio faces the lengthening shadow of Michelangelo Merisi da Caravaggio as if he has been playing tennis. No helmet. No body armour. Caravaggio's cruelty does not matter now. What difference that they talk of him as a divinely inspired painter. Ranuccio shivers. He plants his right foot firmly into the soft grass to stop it shaking. Why is there no warmth from the burning Roman sun, no scent from the spring flowers? Maybe the God of War forbids it. This is his field after all. Ranuccio is a Roman. That must count for something against one of Milan's finest swordsmen, twenty paces away, intent on killing him, ending his sordid life.

Ranuccio steps forward, a tennis player moving like a fat footsoldier encased in a suit of lead armour. He smiles at the thought of the shame on both men. Who is ending whose sordid life? A duel of equals after all. Felicità . .

* * *

The Roman candle all but extinguishes Caravaggio. Now, and for the rest of his days, the face of Ranuccio Tomassoni waits for him in the stillness of the night, in the shadows of empty streets. A cocky pimp, an arrogant nobody seduced by the connections of a family name, a husband, a father, a loved brother. And what is Caravaggio now but a reckless fool, a destroyer of a man's life, a murderer. His freedom, his reputation, possibly his art and almost certainly, as it seems to him in these days after his thrust ended Ranuccio Tomassoni, his redemption, gone.

It is not fear of an ignominious death at the hands of a nobody that disturbs him, but fear of losing his soul. He has already witnessed a Milanese version of Dante's Inferno as a boy. When not confronted by Tomassoni's death stare, he can touch the dark-stained shroud of his father, smell the horses, hear the wooden creak of the cart, see the cardinal as the *monatto,* taste plague in the damp air.

Michelangelo Merisi da Caravaggio is dead already: at least he thinks so. A wounded killer, an exile from Rome, a fugitive from every sword-wielding man in the Papal States intent on justice or revenge. He hides. He waits. He works. He paints his tortured mind on to the severed head of Goliath. Defeated. Aghast at how he has fallen. A man for whom death is not the surprise: it is the absence of forgiveness or salvation, the total darkness that now envelops him. Caravaggio is dead, a Goliath without redemption. Naples offers only an existence of *Purgatorio.* The new commissions, the escape and the refuge there, will not bring him, Caravaggio, son of Fermo, back from the dead. He cannot return to Rome. He must seek absolution elsewhere.

* * *

'You should be asleep now, Michelangelo. It is late.'

'Another story, papa. Please. Tell me more about the crusades and the knights. I want to hear more about the Holy Places and the battles they won.'

Fermo meets his son's wide-eyed gaze. 'Well, as I told you. The knights showed great courage. And about 500 years ago they fought hard to win back Jerusalem for Christianity. Do you remember I told you about the Order of Saint John and what they did?'

'They were great fighters, papa, with their swords and shields and they killed the – I've forgotten the word.'

'Let us just say, Michelangelo, that they are the people who do not believe that Jesus Christ is Almighty God, Our Lord and Saviour.'

'But what about the Knights of Saint John, papa.'

'It is too late, and this candle is losing its flame.'

'Just a few more minutes. Please. You tell such exciting stories. The knights. What about the knights?'

'The Knights of Saint John had to fight, son, but in the beginning, about fifty years before they helped to recapture Jerusalem, their purpose was to care for our Christian pilgrims to the Holy Land who became poor and sick.'

'What are pilgrims, papa?'

'They are just people like you and me, Michelangelo; people who are on a journey to heaven. We call them pilgrims because they also make a special journey to where Jesus lived and died and rose again.'

'Did the Knights of St John not fight, papa?'

'Yes, they fought to protect the pilgrims. They built hospitals and castles too. As I told you, their crusades were about making Jerusalem and the Holy Land Christian again. But then, in the city of Acre in the year of our Lord of One Thousand Two Hundred And Ninety One, the Knights of St John and other Christians were surrounded by the Muslims and they were defeated. Those that survived were the last Christians to leave the Holy Land. So, sadly, that's what happened to the brave Knights of St John.'

'That's no good, papa. You haven't told me a story. I don't want to hear how they lost. Was that the end? Were there no more battles?'

'That's enough for one night. And look at this candle. We are almost in darkness.'

'I can still see you, papa, and I promise to go to sleep after you tell me one more story.'

'One more, then. In fact, that was not the end of the Knights of St John. They had to leave the Holy Land, as I said, but they did not give up. They still fought to defend Christians much closer to our home, south of Milan and south of where the Pope lives in Rome. At first they gathered on the Greek island of Rhodes, but then they made another island across the sea from our land their stronghold. It is called Malta. More than two hundred and sixty years had passed since that dark day when the Knights were forced to leave the Holy Land. The Knights of St John built a great fleet of ships to keep the infidel – '

'The what?'

'Infidel. It's a word we use to describe the Turks, or the Ottomans as they are sometimes called. They are people who don't believe in Jesus as Lord and God. Anyway, the ships were built to protect Malta and Christian lands across the Mediterranean from being invaded by the infidels. Then something happened, something that no-one could believe was possible. But shall I blow out this candle and tell you about it tomorrow?'

'No, papa! Now. I'll be afraid of the dark and will not sleep if you do not tell me. Was it something terrible?'

'Quietly now. Lie down and I will tell you. Settle down. It all started when the ship of one of the most famous Knights, an able sailor and brave fighting captain, attacked a big, slow Turkish cargo vessel on its way from Venice to Constantinople.'

'What was his name, papa?'

'Well, it's a bit of a mouthful, Michelangelo Merisi da Caravaggio! The Knight was called Fra Mathurin d'Aux de Lescout Romegas. Even more remarkable than his name was what he did. Some think of him as the greatest Knight who ever lived because he always captured or sank any infidel ship that he came across. Some say that God Himself protects him. Once, when a storm destroyed the Grand Harbour of Malta and all of its ships in one night killing all of the sailors, he was found alive the next morning floating under the upturned hull of his ship.'

'But what about the cargo ship, papa? What was special about that?'

'Well, Romegas captured the ship and found that there was precious cargo on board worth 80,000 ducats. The Turkish Sultan, Suleiman – '

What's a Sultan, papa?'

'He's like an emperor, and under Suleiman the Turkish empire grew and grew, putting more Christian people and lands far beyond the Holy Places under threat. Anyway, Suleiman was very, very angry at the loss of his precious ship. He was angry, too, because he had received letters from an important Turkish lady whom the knights were holding as a prisoner on Malta. So Suleiman decided to destroy the Knights of St John on Malta once and for all.

'To rescue the lady?'

'To be honest, I think he was more concerned with his pride and the loss of his ships. You have to understand, Michelangelo, that the Sultan and all the Turks and all the Muslims see *us*, the Christians, as the unbelievers. We are the ones who need to be conquered in faith as well as in battle.'

'I don't understand.'

'Later. It's too late now. The key thing in the story is that Suleiman had had enough. He ordered this big attack on Malta. And a little over ten years ago, on May 18th One Thousand Five Hundred And Sixty-Five to be exact, the attack began. The Sultan sent a huge armada of nearly 200 warships loaded with cannons and 30,000 troops. Can you imagine, Michelangelo, what a terrifying sight they would have been? But on Malta, the Grand Master of the Order of St John, whose name was actually Fra' Jean, let's call him the Chief Knight - he only had 6,000 men to defend the whole island. Some were fighters from

Spain, some from Sicily, some from the Kingdom of Naples, and others were armed Maltese. Many were not well trained in how to use those axes on long poles called pikes, or swords, or even firing cannon.'

Fermo pauses, even though anxiety over his son's wakefulness at this late hour had passed. Fixing his eye on the cracked wall's weakening shadows he thinks of how he had gathered the details of this story over many years, remembering and writing down the accounts he had been given. It was too important to forget. Michelangelo should know the sacrifices made for him and one day, God willing, he would take his son to Malta. He strokes the boy's tousled black hair and turns away from him to face the candle drowning in its own wax.

'Are you still awake?'

'Yes, papa. Please go on.'

'Many hard battles were fought on the island. The cannon fired. Boiling oil was poured over the invaders from the walls of the forts. The Turks fought and fought to capture the island, beating their loud drums. They threw weapons like small exploding cannon balls which stuck to armour. The Turkish galleys sailed in close to the shore, too, to bombard the defenders. Thousands of the invaders were killed by the brave Maltese and their allies who joined them in battle, but the Turks did not leave. May. June. July. August. They besieged Malta because they believed that sooner or later, the Maltese Knights of St John and their untrained soldiers would run out of food and fresh water; or that they would simply give up hope, fearing a horrible death. But do you know what, Michelangelo? Fermo whispers, leaning down towards his son, observing that the sleep-inducing work of the candle is almost done.

'No, papa.'

'God gave the Knights courage and help from other Christian ships out at sea. They stopped the Turks' own supplies of food and water getting through. On Malta the farmers poisoned the wells with hemp and burnt their own crops. Can you imagine? The sacrifice they made, all so that the invading infidels could not survive on the land they conquered. And God sent very, very hot weather that summer. The Knights were prepared but the Turks suffered from fever, even plague. That's how the Siege of Malta was won and – '

The candle crackles its last and the darkness envelops father and son.

* * *

Truth? What is that? Caravaggio asks Pilate's questions over and over again, his own judge and executioner. Oblivious to the rising and tumbling of the felucca or the billowing of her square-set sails, he is immersed in the sea of his own thoughts.

Truth? What is that? What will be my judgement on Malta? There is no case to condemn me. The case is sustained only by the jealousy, no, the revenge, of others. Have I not already atoned for my sins, enduring the pain from wounds. Not from the flawed swordsmanship of Ranuccio Tomassoni. Not by him, but the brother, the toy soldier Giovan Francesco Tomassoni. Had Petronio not intervened, my own life would have been spent. I am the victim. I suffered the injustice. I am the one who has suffered the greatest loss: exile from Rome; the life of a fugitive; the loss of the Church's patronage. I am the one who has atoned for my orgies. It's there on the canvas. I will tell the Grand Master as I fall prostrate before him. Cross the Mediterranean, I will say. Find Scipione Borghese.

50

Ask him for my painting. Then look into the face of the beheaded Goliath. See there my gruesome history, my pain of murder and malevolence. Look into Goliath's eyes. Whom do you see? It will dawn on you. Like the Supper At Emmaus. Is that not a painting of recognition also, Grand Master, where all that went before counts for nothing in the presence of the Risen Lord? And how, tell me, might I commit The Seven Acts Of Mercy in one altarpiece for the penitent faithful were I not so much in need of mercy. Tell me that.

There is your truth, Grand Master. My works speak of the faith deep within me. Were not some of our most revered saints, Francis, Augustine, or dare I mention even the great crusader knights; were they not men of vice and pleasure before they found salvation through conversion and service? I am no saint as well you know. But I ask you to consider who I have become since I plunged my sword into the thigh of Ranuccio Tomassoni. I might as well have driven the bloody blade into my own heart. Can you not see? I am a humble artist who seeks forgiveness. And for all my folly, for all of my contemptible conduct, I am still a child of the most revered Order of Saint John. My earliest memories are of my beloved father's bedtime stories. In the dim candlelight of our humble home he carried me to Jerusalem with him, to the castles, to the hospitals and battlefields where the Knights of Saint John fought for Christianity, fought for our sick and wounded pilgrims, fought for our holy places.

I held his hand, Grand Master, as we relived the divinely inspired courage, the Christian sacrifice of your fellow Knights at the Siege of Malta. Not only them, but the population of this whole island. You see. I understand what the Order has endured. How they must have suffered. It was as though my father was there. At the Siege of

Malta, I mean. At the great sea battle of Lepanto, too. It captivated him. I was too young at the time to understand how he could have obtained so much knowledge. After his death I learned of his obsession. No travelling Knight of St John within twenty miles of Milan was safe. Nor was any sailor captain or oarsman who served on our ships in those days. He didn't even have to have been at Lepanto, only know another who was. My father had his web of informants in place across the city and beyond, ready to tell him when he could surprise his unsuspecting prey.

All I can tell you, Grand Master, is that my father never tired of night-time tales of bravery and leadership from the Siege, from Lepanto, from the crusades. Lepanto especially. He believed in the knights of Malta as the saviours of Christendom. This was his way, I don't mind telling you, of expressing his high hopes in me, by telling the stories over and over. One day I would bring honour to our family, our home of Caravaggio, by fighting to defend the faith. Was that what he thought? For you see, Grand Master, I was born in the same year as the Battle of Lepanto.

Thus occupied with such conversational gambits for his imminent audience with the Grand Master of the Order of St John, the felucca's embrace by the walled arms of Valletta's harbour fails to register in his troubled mind. Lepanto would be his masterstroke, his best strategy for disarming an old man, for disabling any opposition from an archaic monument, one who nevertheless could bestow redemption. The old man would not see a helpless, desperate painter with a sordid reputation. That was not the Caravaggio that Fra' Alof de Wignacourt, Grand Master of the Sovereign Military Hospitaller Order of Saint John of Rhodes and Malta, would meet. This he knows for sure.

***

As he did the day before and the day before that, Caravaggio takes his seat on the stone wall in the garden courtyard of the Grand Palace of Valletta. Far from being an uncomfortable perch among the dry foliage and tumescent flowers, the stone seat is fashioned like a throne with a smooth high back, the finely chiselled stonework lost over time to the sun and rain. Caravaggio dozes in the heat, waiting for the moment when some or other aide of the Grand Master would nudge him to say 'I'm sorry, His Excellency is too busy to see you today. Return tomorrow.'

At first, when the words sound in Caravaggio's head, he dismisses the voice. He had been studying the courtyard murals of the bloody Siege so intently he must have been imagining one of those Knights addressing him in his heat-induced reverie.

'I am honoured by a visit from the esteemed artist Michelangelo Merisi da Caravaggio.'

It seems odd for a Knight to divert his attention from the threat of death and the slaying of Muslim invaders to speak to him. Awake and asleep, he sees the spume of Tomassoni's blood, his blade thrust into the Roman's thigh, its shaft catching the fading light. He looks at the impaled, mortally wounded Turk at the feet of the red-caped Knight pleading for mercy.

How can that voice so intent on death be so assured, so commanding, so specific calling him by name. Is this hallowed sanctuary still home to the Knights of the Siege, phantasms gliding through baked courtyard arches, never seen, always announcing themselves to –

'You should stand when the Grand Master addresses you.'

Caravaggio stumbles to his feet.

'Most Reverend Prince, Sovereign and Lord, Grand Master, I, I was not expecting you to come to the courtyard to greet me in person. Forgive me.'

In the slow arc of his bow, Caravaggio sketches the outline of his host, feeling instinctively that the time for painting this holy sovereign, on whom his life depends, will come. The patrician air of entitlement, as scented as the *buttuniera* that blossom on this outpost of Christianity, still does not mask the carriage of a soldier. Had the metal straps of a daily helmet stretched and pinned his ears so firmly into the side of this pointed head. The shorn iron-grey hair remains pressed-on, as if the helmet had only just been removed. The beard, its source flanking the steep forehead and trained to converge on a single point at the base of its owner's jaw, is also reminiscent of armour. Though betrayed by years of indulgence, the stocky strength of this once great warrior Knight is discernible in his neck, in his arms and in his posture most of all. A harsher judgement on the fugitive seeking redemption, Caravaggio thinks, if the Grand Master's portraits make the bulbous wart on the right side of his nose as prominent as it is. If he is to make a deal with God and his representative on Malta, the face has to be fashioned anew. Cast it in a new light without blemish, a high white forehead framed by an oval of the clipped greying bush of hair, ears tidy but not flattened, the sun-wrinkled lines and bulging betrayals of years of idle living, replaced by an undiminished greying Christian soldier. Take off his silk finery and put him in armour. That will make him happy.

'The Order of Saint John welcomes you to Malta, Signor Caravaggio, and we rejoice to hear you ask for forgiveness in your first entreaty. But come, it is hot and you need refreshment. Out of the sun and in the cool breeze we can talk. As I am speaking to an artist of such distinction it is distracting for me to address you as Michelangelo, so allow me to address you as Caravaggio. It is simpler.'

'Of course, as you wish, my Sovereign Lord.'

'Enough of the Sovereign Lords, Caravaggio. Grand Master will suffice as long as you do not forget that I am indeed your Sovereign Lord and master of your future on this island. In fact, your whole future depends entirely on me.' Wignacourt makes a Christ-like gesture with his arm beckoning his overheated guest to rise and follow him.

'Grand Master, you have already shown concern for my fate by granting me this audience and by your action in protecting our small flotilla from Naples.'

'You flatter yourself, Caravaggio. The flotilla carried much more precious cargo than you. There is more at stake than your precious talent. If the Muslim galleys had overwhelmed our garrison at Gozo or stolen our supplies from *your flotilla,* slaughtered sailors, knights or even any artists on board, 'Allah is with us' they would cry. 'Let us now avenge the deaths of our beheaded and mutilated Muslim brothers whose blood ran on Malta fifty years ago. We shall kill every Maltese infidel, man, woman and child.'

They reach the shaded balcony on the upper floor. The host occupies his customary velvet seat whilst his guest takes the only other option, a narrow wooden bench against the cool outer wall of the palace.

'I did not mean to imply', Caravaggio replies in the most conciliatory tone he can muster, 'that my arrival was more important than the safety of this island. When I was a boy, night after night my father told me stories of the God-given courage in the Siege of Malta. As we came within sight of the Grand Harbour for the first time, I set eyes on the fortress of Castel Sant'Angelo. Until then, only in my mind's eye had I ever seen its five hundred troops and fifty knights, the batteries of ten or more eighty-pound guns, all commanded by your heroic predecessor, Jean de la Valette. Until now, only in the dim light of my imagination could I see the desperate defence of St Elmo against wave after wave of Turks. I thought back to my father's stories trying to imagine the brothers, the peasants, the farmers, the Christian soldiers and Knights from across the Christian Mediterranean – standing shoulder to shoulder using every possible means to repel the invaders.'

Wignacourt's nod of approval encourages Caravaggio to continue. He senses the opportunity to deliver his rehearsed passion. 'Fire throwers, the cascade of boiling oil, the homemade hand bombs, earthenware pots stuffed with explosives and fuses. My father told me, too, the story of Fra Abel de Bridiers de la Gardampe – how could I forget him with a name like that and because of what he did – of how, when mortally wounded, a brother rushed to help him. Go away, he cried. Don't think of me as alive. Your time is better spent helping others. And with that last command he crawled away to die at the foot of the altar in the chapel. To think that I am now here on this sacred isle under your protection and but a few moments ago I could almost be present at these scenes gazing upon the courtyard frescoes.'

Wignacourt raises his arm signalling for Caravaggio to stop.

'Please. Spare me your self-justification. You were asleep when I found you. Walk with me and I will show you what it means to be a Knight of Saint John. Presuming you were awake at first, you have only witnessed a small part of the Siege of Malta.'

With Caravaggio put firmly in his place, *Sua Altezza Eminenza* Wignacourt turns and walks into the palace.

Flanked by two escorts, a soldier and an assistant, he strides purposefully towards the porticoes that frame the palace's central courtyard. Still sweating and humbled, the more hesitant prospective Knight of Saint John, trails behind him, trying not to be cowed but focused on his goal. The only course: to do this Frenchman's bidding. There are no better options, no faster routes to papal pardon, to acceptance, to art, to survival. The indefinite exile from Rome, the murderous agents of the Tomassonis, the lawful killing of 'the murderer, Michelangelo Merisi da Caravaggio' by any man in the Papal States: all threats and punishments extinguished if this veteran of Lepanto and Defender of the Faith, sees fit to intercede for him with Pope Paul V.

To be a Knight of the noble Order of Saint John, he ponders; to live in the shadow of death and be lifted up to the light of Resurrection and surely then to be reunited with his father. His fate is in the hands of Wignacourt and the sacrifices he demands. Prostrate himself before him and the brothers, begging forgiveness. You shall not kill. You shall not commit adultery. You shall not covet your neighbour's wife. You shall not. You shall not. You shall not be accepted into the Order. You are not of noble standing and your deeds betray the faith you are supposed to profess.

Wignacourt interrupts Caravaggio's thought. 'In the same year I was fighting on the galleys at Lepanto – '

'And the year of my birth,' Caravaggio interjects, it being a key objective of his visit to make that point.

'And the year of your birth', Wignacourt repeats, 'the Grand Palace was constructed. At first it was intended as a command post for the Knights. Over time it has become a treasury, a place to celebrate the victory of Christianity over usurpers of the true faith. These Gobelin tapestries that you see, the bronzes, Chinese vases, gilded ceilings and paintings, bear witness to our superiority.'

Are you not embarrassed by these riches, these spoils of war?' Caravaggio asks.

'Is this all that you fought for in Jerusalem and Rhodes and Malta? These trophies.

I had thought I would find a more noble Christian spirit on Malta', he says, inhibitions and focus leaving him simultaneously. 'I am fleeing for my life because I killed a man in Rome, running to escape those who would see me executed, not out of any sense of justice. They want me silenced because I shout out the truth about their hypocrisy, their greed. Go to Malta, I told myself again and again. Prostrate my vile and sinful body before the noble Knights of Saint John. For they are the lights that shine for all the world to see. The lamps that sit proudly on the lampstand in the middle of the Mediterranean, holding back the powers of darkness, the lights Our Lord and Saviour gave us to follow. What army could be greater, nobler, brighter than one ranked with these soldiers of Christ? With God the Father Almighty on their side who could be against them?'

Pointing at the tapestries, Caravaggio is in a battle scene of his own now, raising his voice, the darkness falling in his head. 'Even when they endured their own crucifixion in the Holy Land the flame did not burn out. Butchered, tortured, beheaded and bloodied crusaders at their feet in Jerusalem, in Acre, in the holy places, the Knights of St John are still standing. They should have been dead men. Dead men in a dead Order. Defeated and crushed. Two hundred years of care and protection of holy pilgrims, of hospitals paid for with toil and death, of castles and struggles against the godless, blown away like the sand in the desert. My father once told me that the Knights of St

John should have been there on the night they came to arrest Jesus. They would not have run away, he said. I remember his exact words because they amused him so much and he repeated them often, 'They would have done much more than cut off the high priest's ear.' My God, Grand Master, what a picture that created for me, the Knights of St John encircling Jesus, facing down his enemies, swords drawn.'

Wignacourt raises an eyebrow and a hand to prevent any more taking of the Lord's name in vain. Caravaggio isn't even looking at him.

'For those Knights to be driven from the ground on which he walked. For those knights to re-form and rally once more in as remote and unlikely an island as Rhodes and then to this barren rock. Night after night my father took me out of Lombardy and placed me on the best vantage point. Was it here, here that I stood, an invisible child observer of a siege where Christian courage and faith were redefined? Here that Jean de la Valette shouted commands at his Knights and the poor Maltese not to yield?

I have never forgotten my father's dramatic retelling, his swishing gestures of swords cutting through flesh, of his lowered tone when he reached the end of the Siege and counted the losses. Briefly, just briefly, Grand Master, while I baked in the courtyard, the Siege frescoes carried me in the other direction, back in time and place, to Milan. I was back in my bed, wide-eyed, looking up at my father.'

Caravaggio imitates a deeper, mock serious, older voice. ' 'Have I told you the true story of the brave, brave Knights of St John and the Siege of Malta?' ' Tell me again, papa', I would almost shout back at him. 'Start when the fleet is first sighted.' I am awake now, though.' '

The visitor leaves the battlefield as quickly as he had entered it and stands, hanging from his shoulders with the bearing of a man awaiting execution. 'I know where I am. I see all too clearly where I have arrived and what has brought me here. This palace speaks of material wealth, the looted spoils of war, not of redemption or forgiveness. This island, this Order of the Knights of Saint John – what have they become? The galleys of the Turks are a constant threat in Maltese waters, but what do I find in Valletta? Knights in mock combat, testing sword strokes and defences, strengthened just possibly by the sacraments and the prayers of the Maltese around them?'

Rallying to his oratory once more Caravaggio continues, holding Wignacourt in silence as a captor would subject his hostage to his distorted beliefs. 'Only a blind man could fail to notice the mighty fortresses and military intent fortified by churches for eternal reward in this limestone citadel for Defenders of the Faith. You have your gallows in full view and the letter of the Grand Master's law is proclaimed, but even a blind man can taste and smell and hear what is around him. The night holds no fear for him. So he walks, listening, feeling his way, expecting the streets to be empty. Surely the Masses have been said and the Knights must rest for their day of training and preparation for defending this bastion of Christendom.

Instead, the blind man struggles to hear the calls of migratory birds he expects in the stillness of the night. Not a time either for his search for the light that has eluded him. There are too many voices for that. English? Was that a Germanic tongue? That one's definitely an accent of Provence. There, Castile or Aragon maybe. Babbling together, stale drink common to the breath closest enough to his face, spilling out of the *auberges*.

The blind man has been here before, it seems to him. Rome or Naples or Milan, probably all three. Christian cities all, where piety and decorum are reserved for the hours of daylight. But when the incense has drifted up to heaven like a sung Te Deum and the church doors are closed, a new belief controls men's hearts.

Do you know what that belief is, Grand Master? No? I'll tell you. It is the belief that whatever they do in the hours of darkness can be atoned for in the hours of daylight. A Knight – he must be a Knight because of his accent and strength – grabs the arm of the blind man. Come, he says, we are leaving the *auberges*. Tonight is not the night for showing you the brothels either, for the revered Sicilian Knight, Giacomo Marchese, is holding a party and newcomers are welcome, even blind men like you.

Are the Knights not bound by laws of poverty and chastity, the blind man protests. 'Discretion, my friend', is the reply. 'No brawls. No cavorting in the streets. No drunken orgies and you will be spared a trip to the prison of Castel Sant'Angelo. Drink as much as you like. Have as many women as you want. The Grand Master will turn a blind eye, if you'll pardon me for putting it that way.'

Oblivious to this outburst, or so it appears to his noble and servile attendants, the Grand Master's gaze settles on a distant horizon. Not for the first time in his service are the servants required to observe an obtrusive silence. Caravaggio stops, realising the lack of challenge. The silence between the two men hangs in the soft sea breeze.

Vincenzo, personal valet to Wignacourt, looks to the same horizon as his master. Experienced enough to leave a small part of his consciousness alert to a new instruction, yet able to fill the silence with his own imagination. He is once more on the galley at Lepanto, standing up in a line of crossbowmen, concentrating through his feet. To be a level firing platform he shifts his weight, forwards, back, balancing, swaying with the rocking galley, using the dead weight of the wooden crossbow to steady himself. Ready for the command to fire from the Knight of St John at the end of the line, fixing on a target that will rise out of the sea.

He steals one glance, then another at Brother Alof de Wignacourt, resolute in plate armour, a steady hand gripping his pike, standing on a mountain top, not the same rolling sea. Now commands to the twenty-five banks of rowers are shouted, signals given. Concentrate, Vincenzo. Balance. Steady your arm. Popping flashes of fire from the arquebusiers of the closing Turkish galley rip into the sails. Two crossbowmen in Vincenzo's line crumple and tumble into the foaming sea.

'Prepare the cannon'. Wignacourt does not flinch, does not crouch, does not shout. His command carries clearly over the screams and flames. 'Rowers, ramming speed.' The scimitar-wielding Turks are clearly visible and audible now. The arquesbusiers are lining up a second round. Above the thrash of crashing oars and wailing warriors, Wignacourt again so clear 'Crossbows ready. Pick a target. Check bolt. Wait. Hold – '

Wignacourt turns to his valet and issues a new instruction.

'Vincenzo, please escort our guest out of the palace.'

Chapter 3

THE VISITATION

'Francisco. Francisco.' The gentle calling of his name penetrates the thick wooden door. It is the voice of an owner searching for a lost cat, soft but insistent. Zurbaran wishes to be found, as he always does, alert. Ten seconds will elapse before the rusting metal latch will be lifted slowly out of its notch by her turning the iron ring. It is enough time to pull himself upright, plant a paintbrush in his hand, put on an expression of thoughtful creativity.

Rays of fading sunlight stream past and through the woman whose outline frames the doorway. His wife is wearing a Virgin-blue jacket-bodice and a worn petticoat of washed-out pink. Waves of radiant curled brown hair flow down neatly below the shoulders from her centre parting, the delicate filigree of the Sacred Heart-shaped earrings he knows are hanging, hidden. Gold matters to Leonor. Gold first drew him to her at Mass when his head should have been bowed in prayer or fixed on the back of the priest.

All of the parishioners of La Magdalena parish in Seville he knew, the daily communicants and the less ardent faithful of Sundays and feast days. He has long since committed faces, features and frames to memory, some to appear on canvas at a later date. Not this new vision of devotion, solitary, composed, gold necklace glinting in the red, yellow and blue light filtered through the stained-glass windows. How to look and look, and not betray such a joyful distraction to his son, Juan. Images remain with him longer than words in every circumstance, except that now he recalls Petrarch seeing his beloved Laura in church for the first time. *S'amor non è, che dunque è quell ch'io sento.*

Francisco need not have worried about his son. Juan may have accompanied his father to Mass, but paid no attention to his father's devotion. Father and son had not spoken in any meaningful way in the two years since his sister, Maria, had been given a dowry of 2,000 ducats for her marriage to the merchant, Joseph Gasso. Not that Juan resented Maria leaving nor his father's generosity. It was more the fact that, father and son, left to themselves, had nothing to give each other. The great Zurbaran who brought the celestial to earth could not bring himself to make any revelation of his own. Or felt no need to share his feelings, Juan could never decide which. To his son he seemed as far removed from real life as the glorious mysteries on his paintings for which he was so revered in Seville.

Not once had Juan witnessed his father sobbing over the loss of his stepmother, Beatriz, who had raised him; still less his own mother, Maria, of whom Juan had only the faintest recollection. The paternal embraces, the candid, unprompted assurances about his talent, the treasured father and son dialogues about life and love – all remained in his imagination. The most animated moments in their relationship occurred on those frequent master-to-pupil occasions when his father could not disguise his disappointment over a detail, or worse, display a dismissive disregard for what he had chosen to paint in the first place. Always present in these fractious exchanges though never expressed, Juan believed, was his father's conviction that the reputation of the great Francisco Zurbaran would be diminished by the emergence of Juan Zurbaran, a painter of still life. In spite of such maturing tensions, the habit of attending Holy Mass together continued, allowing time every Sunday and feast day for the arguments to cool and settle.

Francisco responds to the divine light flooding his workshop. 'Leonor, *mi amor,* I am sorry. He puts the false paintbrush down and stands to embrace his wife. 'I am sorry. I did not hear you calling me. I was lost in thought. Sometimes it's better for me to take more time before I start sketching.'

'You don't have any pigments ground up and ready to use either, Francisco,' she chides. 'Did Marcos not come up to do that earlier as I told him to?'

'Yes, yes he did. He's a good boy, but a clumsy one. And you know how easily bored he gets, so I told him to go out and play in the sunshine with his friends. After he knocked over an easel last time he came in to my workshop, I wondered whether we should wait until he is at least ten before involving him in my work, however helpful he might want to be.' In trying to recover his senses and make reasonable conversation, the response he has mustered merits a rebuke.

'So we leave behind our friends, the maids and servants whom we know and trust in Seville. We say goodbye to every single person who can help us cope with five children. Agustina is still only three years old, Francisco, and Eusebio, five. Marcos, being helpful is not a problem, believe me. José and Micaela are harder to control. 'I'm grown up now', Micaela says to me. 'I'm thirteen years old. I don't need to do children's chores any more. And José? He is heading the same way, knowing he can say the same by this time next year. Don't look at me like that, Francisco. You know it's true, and please don't say to me that everything will be fine when you are paid for those commissions from Lima of years ago. There's no sign of the money coming yet, is there?'

'No. Not yet.'

Leonor is not finished. Not by any means.

'So? We've left Seville. For what? We just abandon the parish of the Sagrario? All of my friends are there, Francisco. All of our children were baptised there. For what? So that you can sit up here daydreaming, leaving me to run our household and sell jewellery. We are supposed to be in Madrid so that you can re-build your commissions, your reputation; so you can earn respect from the king and the wealthy orders; so we can live and give our children a future.'

Zurbaran offers no resistance, puts up no defence. He accepts the verbal lashing and fears confrontation more. He cannot put into words how sorry he is. The sacrifices Leonor makes, the love she has for him, are more than he deserves. If only more commissions and payments had come through. Not just from Lima but Mexico, Guatemala too. Buenos Aires. He had been such a fool to trust. Why couldn't he have been a goldsmith like Leonor's father? Simple transactions. You make, you sell, you always know what money you have. But then, if Leonor had met him twenty years ago when he was handsomely rewarded for – well, what does it matter now? – the Charterhouse of Jerez, the monastery of Guadalupe. Still treasured by the monks perhaps, but the man who painted these works, what was his name again?

'Francisco, are you listening to me?' He has not moved, not looked up at his wife.

'Look at you,' she says, and kisses him tenderly on the crown of his bowed head. Standing behind her husband, Leonor places her palms flat across his hunched shoulders. 'You are so tense and pale. You look as though you've seen a ghost. I know it's hard for you too. To leave Seville where you were so well-known and respected.'

'Not any more,' he hears himself saying. 'It will be Juan's anniversary next year. I can't believe it's ten years.'

'Is that what all this is about, Francisco,' she asks gently, 'your locking yourself away up here and not working?'

'No, no, it's just you going on about Seville and the Sagrario, and – '

'Hush.' Leonor turns to kneel in front of him. She puts a finger on his lips. 'Don't think for a second that you should have loved him more or even been a better father to him. You taught him all that you knew, didn't you? Gave him every opportunity. Maybe you would have grown much closer – '

'Had I better protected him from the plague, you mean' he says, more defeated than accusing, removing her finger and clasping her hand.

'Tens of thousands died in Seville, Francisco. You cannot blame yourself. We will never know why it claimed the young and strong as well as the old and weak.'

'God knows.'

A silence falls between them, the implication too difficult to comprehend, that God knew and yet allowed it to happen. The just and the unjust taken alike. Men like Juan, not given time to correct their youthful mistakes, to mend relationships, to fully become themselves. Who is to say that Juan's still life would not have evolved into a new form of painting, or that the king would not one day have selected him as the new court painter of choice? There is no explanation, adequate, divine, rational or otherwise. Leonor knows how the memory of Juan haunts her husband.

Francisco lifts his head. His eye catches the glints of gold beneath her hair, and smiles for the first time since Leonor entered the room.

'The wooden kneelers are bad enough,' she says, pressing her palms on to Francisco's knees to push herself to a standing position. 'But I won't be able to walk if I kneel for any longer on your stone floor. Anyway, we have no time to discuss Marcos now, or Agustina's accident for that matter. Nothing that can't be mopped up.'

'Nothing that – what? You're not saying that – '

'Nothing you need to worry about, Señor Zurbaran; but you might want to wash and smarten yourself up. Look at your hair and those tired eyes. We have a guest.'

'A guest? But who knows we are here? We are still so new to Madrid.'

'He says you were apprentices together and met in the studio of Pacheco. It couldn't be – him, could it?'

'I'll get ready,' he says with fresh urgency. Leonor is framed in the doorway again made more beautiful to him by the shafts of sunlight. 'Leonor', he calls after her. She stops and turns, and this time the heart-shaped earrings catch the light. 'Thank you,' he says.

* * *

How often she repeats the matrimonial lines of Ecclesiasticus to herself Leonor Tordera Zurbaran cannot be sure. As often as she prays the sacred mysteries, passing the beads of the rosary through her fingers perhaps. That would mean daily. She recites them again now, quickly, silently, in the few moments it takes to follow her husband into the kitchen where their guest is waiting.

The grace of a wife will charm her husband, her understanding will make her stronger. A silent wife is a gift from the Lord, no price can be put on a well-trained character. A modest wife is a boon twice over, a chaste character cannot be over-valued. Like the sun rising over the mountains of the Lord, such is the beauty of a good wife in a well-run house.

If this guest is who she thinks it is, the visitation could not be less timely. She draws a sharp breath at the thought of the greasy earthenware pot where she had not long before cooked eggs, standing, as unwashed as the white plates around it and knives stained yellow. Leonor knows the garlic and pimento would combine with the ground remnants of the copper pestle and mortar. The spicy sulphur would be hanging in the air, clinging to clothing as tobacco does, drifting into the carafe of tepid water left on her old wooden table. Please, please, Lord and Saviour, quench his thirst. Put temptation to pour a cup of water out of his mind. It is a kitchen scene to shame her.

And what of the common view? The one spread through gossip in the market-place, in the streets of Madrid and Seville, in her own home. The view that says Diego Velazquez, whom she has never seen, never met, who so captivates her king, her husband, whose reputation as *confidant*, as counsel, as curator, exceeds his role as painter to the king, is a more trusted adviser than Olivares ever was.

I know Velazquez well, Francisco had said. 'We grew up together as apprentices in Seville. We have a bond. Now that he has the king's trust, the power, the influence and – *do not forget, mi amor,* – the king's purse to commission paintings for the royal palaces, he will not forget me. Wait and see. One day I will take you and all of the children to El Escorial where you can look on my paintings with pride.'

Velazquez. The visitor who never arrived, whose royal messenger never stood at the door of Seville's greatest painter, Francisco Zurbaran, with a summons. The childhood friend, the brother apprentice, the one certain source of reviving and sustaining her husband's career, never once, never, never requested the presence of Francisco Zurbaran. The great friend Francisco talked about to the children. Never once. The friend whose absence spoke of indifference, whose silence confirmed it, year after year.

I will not give you my name, the unexpected arrival had declared. Let it be a surprise. Pointing the joined fingers of his right hand to the floor he made a broom swishing motion, signalling her to leave and retrieve her husband. Velazquez or not, she can barely tolerate to be treated in such a dismissive manner in her own home. Though, on this occasion and much to her own surprise, she acquiesces to the gesture without complaint, nods and withdraws, already preoccupied with the possible reasons for this mysterious visit. Velazquez might only just have learned of his old friend's arrival in Madrid and had long considered commissions for him at the king's command, and so the perfect moment had arrived. Or, if not Velazquez, the most esteemed graduate artist of the Pacheco school, who was representative of his class, sent to reassure Zurbaran that the drought was over. They would rally round him and open doors of the best connected *Madrileños*.

Leonor still would have hoped for a more resplendent and gracious ambassador. The rudeness does not necessarily betray a condescension, she tells herself. It is all part of the act, the performance needed to entice and surprise their dear Zurbaran whose reputation and fortune they now want to restore. Not to her liking, but that must be the explanation. It could not be the alternative which she had experienced in her apprenticeship of her father's jewellery trade: men well regarded in society for their public kindness and integrity; but who placed their private conduct, in the presence of young women especially, in a different moral sphere. Leonor had placed such male visitors to the jewellery workshop on a pendulum, swinging between a rude but harmless lack of courtesy to a harmful lack of decorum. She had considered words other than decorum, but preferred it as it suited her religious sensitivities. Lack of decorum was a better way, she told herself, to think of the assortment of comments, indiscretions, stares and other unwanted attention that she did not wish to dwell upon.

Her lot, her childhood, adolescence and marriage, for the most part, measured against that of the women of the parish in Seville, was a happy one. She could not and would not complain, repeating to herself, whenever tempted, the instruction of St Paul to the Corinthians. Do not rejoice in wrongdoing. Make allowances. Trust. Hope. Endure whatever comes.

Leonor only knew respect and discipline from her father, nothing more. An answer to her prayers would have been more, much more of his loving tenderness. What more could a father want than a daughter whose obedience as a child, whose responsible nature even as a teenager, whose desire to love and learn from him was never in doubt. She grew up yearning for his affection, an acceptance of her need for affirmation; a reassurance that it did not matter to him how clever or dutiful his 'smart Leonor' could be, he would love and cherish her however she turned out.

Only after his death did Leonor grasp how his behaviour succeeded only in achieving the opposite effect. She presented to him without fail a profile of competence, the emotional and physical complexities of a maturing young woman hidden from him. To his delight, she possessed the gifts of anticipation, judgement and appreciation of jewellery as a commodity. From the moment he realised that his smart Leonor had become such an able, willing apprentice he was blinded from ever seeing her again as his little girl in need of love and protection.

By puberty, every conversation became a consultation, one business partner to another. Leonor began to manage the business finances, at first in small expenses. Seeing how quickly she learned he schooled her in his beloved double entry book keeping system, made holy he told her by virtue of it having been perfected and described by the Franciscan friar, Luca Pacioli.

She observed negotiations and responded to her father's request for her counsel on how a better deal could be struck the next time. Smart Leonor was not a silly little girl at all. Not vulnerable, a head not turned by gold or silver or boys; a good girl in whom a father could be proud, about whom he need have no worries.

Leonor never complained, never confronted him, never wept. She feared his disappointment more than any possible retribution. Over time their relationship only grew in terms of business, two associates living under the same roof, each complementing the ability of the other, one compensating for the other's failings, the senior partner increasingly relying on the efficient energy of the junior. That was the irony. Leonor's quiet industry, her complaisance, her competence, all contributed to an aching loneliness as a young woman; the joy of achieving success, making her father happy, discovering her business talent, suppressed.

Not insensible to this cold truth, Leonor understood how well her apprenticeship had come to serve her and

Francisco. Negotiating skills took male counterparts unawares, blinded as many of them were by prejudice. She sensed the dilemma they faced in one-on-one trading intercourse with a woman: a weaker vessel to be easily, quickly outwitted in the transaction and be done with; or one to be slowly charmed and exploited at will during or after the negotiation.

Instinctively, Leonor reads the attitude of her husband's visitor. The pendulum swings decisively towards lack of decorum. He had observed her closely, she notes. Not with a lecherous eye, nor a lazy one, but an eye practised in capturing her most feminine details, seeing through and around her whole being. It is invasive. It is, she decides, a calculating eye, searching for, and finding answers to her age, health, wealth, child-bearing and class.

Leonor had been the subject of a similar study before. The first time she became aware of this furtive assessment of her was not in the company of a jeweller, though the parallel of examining a gemstone had crossed her mind. Appreciative, admiring even, until a flaw could be found, a value reduced, a judgement of worth.

The first time, then as now, the wandering eye gathered in dimensions, qualities and blemishes, processing them in a matter of seconds. Then, as now, Leonor froze, defenceless, motionless, as if framed in a painting. Then, as now, she realised she was in the company of an artist, only this time one whose eye is not fully focused. If this is indeed the fabled Velazquez, he is not as she expected him. Except for his dark deep-set eyes everything about his head above a shapeless cloak was grey. Rogue ribbons of grey locks fall loose and curled, as untidy as the grey moustache adjoining the strip of grey beard beneath his lip, are neat. Where is the poise, the black silk elegance of a courtier, the *fanfarone*, the chain that had become such a male statement of style and affluence? Abrupt and rude he may have been, but this is a man who has seen a ghost, who is haunted by something, who has lost his way.

Released and swished away to retrieve her husband, she pauses out of sight in the shadows between the kitchen and the stone stairwell. Riled by the stranger she, the wife, the mother, the accountant and keeper of the household, had said nothing, had issued no challenge. A friend of your husband's from the art school of Pacheco, he had said. That was at least forty years ago. Her gut tells her that this artist or whatever he is, had witnessed a life not always informed or illuminated by his engagement with art. Places he had been, people he had met, actions he had taken, choices made, betray him now. How different from soft, gentle Francisco. Leonor senses the malady disguised by rudeness. He unsettles her. A discomfort she quickly resolves to hide from her husband and this unknown.

* * *

If Francisco Zurbaran does not recognise the figure whose grey head rests on his hands, elbows outstretched on the wooden table, he does not show it. As Leonor had often seen him do in Seville with parish or local acquaintances whose names he could not recall, Francisco resorts to 'My Dear Fellow' and in one bound embraces the surprised nameless guess slowly rising to his feet. The two men laugh together. That hearty empty laugh, Leonor judges, when strangers don't know what to say to each other, needing those extra few moments of recognition, time to construct a conversational gambit, one that does not give away uncertainty or awkwardness. Francisco's embracing, laughing gambit, if that's what it is, pays off, for the other speaks first.

'Who would have believed that Alonso Cano and Francisco Zurbaran would meet again more than forty years after apprenticeships with Pacheco and that other fellow you were with. Who was it again?'

'Villanueva. It lifts my spirits to see you once more, Alonso. I feel young again. You are most welcome. That you should come to visit here in Madrid gives me great pleasure, and especially when we are so new to the city', says Francisco still holding Alonso at arm's length.'

'I am very happy to do so, my old friend. I have thought about you often over the years, but time or circumstance, which is it, I'm never sure, maybe both, have prevented me from seeking you out.'

Unobserved, forgotten in the doorway, Leonor watches this warm exchange, reminded of those salesmen of jewellery of questionable origin who preface their pitch with mundane observations and flattery.

'Never mind that, Alonso. You are here now. I am the same anyway. We all have our ups and downs in life that keep us busy or distracted. You must stay and have supper with us.' Francisco releases his companion gesturing to the door. 'You have met my wife, Leonor?'

'Yes, yes.' Alonso turns and bows his head in Leonor's direction. A hollow show of deference, an empty gesture made in front of her many times before by men whose lack of decorum could not be disguised. Nevertheless, she tilts her own head and can hear herself say, 'Yes, *mi amor*. Señor Cano and I have met. Let me clear this table and bring you both some bread and wine so you can talk and find out what brings Señor Cano here.'

Satisfied with these introductions, Francisco bids Alonso to be seated.

'Yes, Alonso, I am keen to hear how and why you found me. I have heard your name, of course, many times over the years. In praise I might add, for your paintings and your sculpture in particular, but also the success you have had as a mentor to a new generation of young artists. I do commend you on that work especially.'

Leonor admires her husband's subtlety: you are welcome but what I really want to know is whether you have been successful or are you well-connected enough to identify or source commissions for me in Madrid. Watching Alonso Cano, his body language, his smile, stretched and held for too long, she knows that this visitation has nothing to do with rekindling a teenage friendship, and most definitely is not about presenting Francisco with new opportunities to resurrect his career. He has a different purpose entirely.

'And who hasn't heard of your achievements in Seville over decades?' Cano responds in kind. Zurbaran smiles at the acknowledgement. Leonor wonders whether Francisco also notes the brevity of the praise, a politeness possibly concealing a lack of knowledge, or is it a statement about Francisco Zurbaran, a Sevillian painter in exile whose work is no longer commissioned by anyone of any importance.

'I confess that I know nothing of the path you have taken in life, my friend, other than the reputation of your work. As Leonor will tell you, news passes me by. I am hopeless when it comes to who said what to whom. Marriages, children, successes and failures, I am out of touch on pretty much everything. Selfishly or stupidly, you might say, I become too absorbed in my own thoughts and work and family, so I am usually the last to hear what's going on.

And I don't know if you are aware, Alonso – or maybe that's why you are here – but we have only just arrived in Madrid. So, you must stay and have supper, and tell me all that's happened to you since we last saw each other in Seville. When was it, 1617? 1618?'

'A bit later, I think', the visitor replies. 'You remember, I only joined Pacheco's workshop in 1616. You had started as an apprentice a few years before me.'

Leonor wants to hear more, to see where this odd encounter is leading, but it seems the right moment to intervene and repeat her offer.

'Señor Cano, please make yourself comfortable. I will bring wine with bread and cheese and olives, so you and Francisco can talk more.' Surprised by her presence in the doorway Cano nods his assent, resentful, she feels, that she has overheard any of their conversation at all.

On her return, the rediscovered friendship of the boys who had grown as apprentices together had vanished. As she enters, the two men seem tense, leaning forward, voices lowered. They do not acknowledge her as she places the victuals in front of them, suspending their animated dialogue until believing she had withdrawn. Concentrating on listening as they resume conversation, assuming that she had left them, Leonor hears one word that confirms her suspicion. One word, spoken with reverence. One word, the invisible bond that unites Alonso Cano and Francisco Zurbaran. Of course, she realises, that is why Cano has come. Nothing at all to do with friendship or interest in Francisco. It isn't about business. She cannot be sure, but Cano probably isn't even looking for help himself. It is something much stronger, much more important than either of them. One word changes everything. Velazquez.

* * *

Cano bangs his fist on the table. 'Caravaggio?' he shouts. 'Who says that Caravaggio is the greatest painter of the modern age? That philanderer. Murderer. Even if only half of his reported crimes are true, Saint Francis of Assisi himself would still struggle to intercede for him.' Naturally enough, conversation had returned to the dreams of their youth, the simultaneous gratitude to Pacheco for the talent he brought out in them, and their desire to seek out other influences, different styles of painting, not celebrated by their teacher.

Leonor hadn't finished pouring the first cup of wine when her husband's response to Cano's question brings a swift end to any small hope she has of the visit's purpose being of one brother in art caring for another. Cano's sudden outburst makes her and the cups jump. In that moment, the stories she had heard so many times of the techniques of the inquisitors come back to her: no time to waste on establishing the truth from the subject of their enquiry. They knew the answer already. The only real question was what it would take to lead the witness to the predetermined truth. Clearly, Caravaggio was not the answer Cano expected or wanted.

'It's fifty years since he died a shameful death, Francisco; surely time enough to forget the misery he brought to those so unfortunate to cross his path.'

'I thought you were asking about the gift of his art, Alonso, not the purity of his character. Is your question not one about whose work will live on, who will influence artists of our generation and those still to come? I had heard that when Rubens made his tour of Madrid he talked about the miracle of Caravaggio.'

'Ha! The only miracle Caravaggio could claim was to stay out of fights and women's beds long enough to work on a canvas. You are mistaken, Francisco', says Cano, his voice softening to the earnest barely audible tone of a confessor, a voice whose gentle authority could not be mistaken. 'Not Caravaggio, but someone with whom we share a common bond; someone who needs our help.'

'And that is why you have made this journey to see me after all this time?'

'It is. We have a divine opportunity, Francisco, to crown the God-inspired life's work of our friend Diego Velazquez. The king has nominated him for the most holy Order of Santiago and we – '

'A divine opportunity, you say. God-inspired work. Though we seem to know so little of each other, Alonso, neither of us is ignorant of the path Diego has chosen. True, his painting of the Madonna, the crucifixion and Joseph's Coat are widely known and praised, but for a man who has had the luxury of not one but two extended visits to Rome, as I understand, as the court painter of the anointed king of Spain and her Empire, he has precious little to show that is what you call God-inspired. Just think of the energy and enthusiasm you or I would have to bring more of sacred scripture and God's Word to life in our art after being this close.' Zurbaran surprises his guest with the sudden-ness of his movement, pushing his chair back and leaning across the table till he is close enough to smell the cheese and wine on Cano's breath. Leonor, too, wonders at this quick animation of her husband. She has not seen him like this before.

'This close I tell you, Alonso; this close to what you would really call God-inspired brushstrokes of Raphael or Michelangelo or Giotto; true artists who made the truth of Almighty God's intervention in the lives of mortal man real for us. Caravaggio too, even a scoundrel like him. Whatever man he was – a philanderer and murderer as you say – his works reflect the inner struggle and darkness of our faith. At the same time they present us with the radiance and glory of God. That's why, Alonso, I think of

Caravaggio as the most gifted painter of our age. It's not for us to know how or why he had this gift but I can think of no other who matches his skill or intensity.'

Zurbaran's attempt to mollify Cano fails.

'How can you say that', Cano responds, on his feet again, 'when our friend and companion Diego has been raised so high by the King of Spain? Not on a whim, Francisco. Not so he could commission another flattering portrait of himself. He's the king for God's sake. He can have whoever, do whatever, he likes. You should really think carefully about what you are saying, Francisco. You talk as though Caravaggio was told by God in a dream what he had to do. Was he like Joseph, is that it, Francisco? 'You are a mere mortal, Michelangelo Merisi da Caravaggio, with the devil within you, but you will have this gift from me. Your art will be shocking to the Pharisees of your time, but it will speak to my people, giving them fresh understanding, renewed faith.' '

'Really, Francisco, Cano continues, his voice reaching every corner of the house. 'Is that what happened, a dream? Because God either didn't know that his chosen one was spending most of his time hopping between beds and brawls, or that his art would always be one big act of confession. 'Please, please forgive me'. That's what I think Caravaggio is saying in most of his paintings. We've been brought up to think of him as this great original. Was he not just a deeply disturbed man putting himself on the canvas? I don't think it's being great or original to be bound by the belief that art has to serve only the Church. More powerful than any sermon, more effective than any Grand Inquisitor, it is the ultimate manipulator of the masses. That's what I think, Francisco. 'Believe! Believe', Caravaggio's art cries out, 'or you will face eternal hell and damnation like me.'

'That's the difference, Francisco. Caravaggio was never freed from his demons or the Church. Never knew what it was like to paint without needing redemption. I accept he wasn't anything like those Flemish old masters that Pacheco used to go on about. Of course he was different. A new style, a clever use of light and darkness to draw us in to every painting, to make us feel as though we were there. That is his gift, God-given or not, but I cannot accept, Francisco, that he is the greatest of our lifetime.' Finally, Cano pauses for breath.

Zurbaran tries once more to find common ground with humour.

'Don't misunderstand me, Alonso. I cherish the memories of Pacheco's and Villanueva's workshops, though I too can't understand why we spent so long on the techniques of the so-called Flemish greats.' His forced laugh does not bring about any change in the expression of his vocal guest. He persists in a conciliatory tone.

'I think of you and Diego as old friends. We discovered our talent together, and however modest we might want to be about it, Pacheco recognised it too in each of us. He understood more, I think, than anyone else I have known what makes great art so arresting, so compelling. I am still embarrassed now to think of how much we ridiculed his paintings that he showed as examples of technique. So ordinary, so out of date even then. The master of technique, the expert in Christian icons, our revered teacher, could not transfer what was in his head into his own paintbrushes. And we, yes, you, Diego and I, made fun of his failing behind his back. I suppose I shouldn't be too hard on us. We were just boys then, full of confidence, or arrogance might be a better word.'

'I remember', Zurbaran goes on, warming to his monologue, 'that old Pacheco really did have an influence on Diego's style, at least to begin with. He was listening, absorbing, imitating. I know what you're going to say, Alonso; but no, I don't think it was just because Diego was attracted to Pacheco's daughter. Like us he made fun of the old man, of course, but I do believe he needed Pacheco's guidance to discover his path. And, as you know, Alonso, after he obtained his licence as an artist he started out painting religious subjects. When I saw his *Adoration of the Magi* I was jealous, I admit. Barely twenty years old and yet the work of a true master.'

'There, you said it,' Cano interrupts. If you can say that of Diego at the tender age of twenty surely it is even more true of him now as a man in his fifties. A man I might remind you, Francisco, who has commanded the trust and confidence of the king as court painter and curator of the royal palace. Whatever successes or handsome commissions you or I or Murillo of even any of the younger generation like Pedro Atanasio Bocanegra or Juan de Sevilla, whom I trained, ever had – not one of us has the achievement of Diego Velazquez.'

Zurbaran bursts out laughing. 'Speak for yourself, Alonso.' The tension between the two had been rising and Leonor is relieved by her husband's humour. For the first time since their reacquaintance they did not seem to her so strained, their shared laughter not so empty. She steps into the kitchen, fills their cups and they seem to forget about their disagreement, exchanging anecdotes of apprentices' mischief, and taking turns to enlighten each other on their own most comical achievements.

Stories told, goblets re-filled, the reprieve still does not last long. Leonor senses that the renewed teenage bond, strengthened by the wine and laughter, also stiffens the resolve to be more direct. She wonders again what is the purpose of this visitation. The rudeness with which she was first greeted, and instinct, tell her that Cano wants something from Francisco. He isn't going to give anything either, certainly not a commission for Francisco, one that would balance the family budget. She shivers again at the thought of recent expenses: the move to Madrid; the town house Francisco insisted upon in a central district; the markets where street sellers charge ten per cent more than those she had tamed over many years in Seville. In every context she has no currency here. Only she seems to be aware that Francisco's next step in reviving his career has to be a profitable one for all of them. Take the wrong step now, when they are so financially vulnerable at the wrong end of Francesco's painting life, and the children would suffer most. It doesn't bear thinking about. Mercifully, Francisco, who normally couldn't function in any way after more than three cups of wine, had not yet succumbed. Though she winces at his truthfulness in front of Cano, whose purpose and character she still does not know.

'I grant you, Alonso, that Diego was taking a risk to leave Seville for Madrid at such a young inexperienced age. Maybe that's what set us apart. We all had a unique talent as old Pacheco kept telling us. Had he stayed in Seville, Diego would, I am sure, have won many commissions from the Church. Ha! I should thank him then, as should Murillo and Ribera and all the rest. It's ironic, isn't it. The man they call *El Sevillano* didn't make his name in Seville, didn't look back, didn't share his good fortune with those of us who played no small part in making him what he was.'

Cano had slumped forward, forehead resting on folding arms. Too much drink, Leonor thinks. Too much emotion. More likely, she decides, a ruse to let Francisco bare his soul before unveiling his own true identity.

'What I can't determine is how much was luck and how much design,' Francisco continues. 'We all knew how ambitious he was to make a name for himself. And – let me remind you, Alonso – we all rallied around him when his first attempt to ingratiate himself at the king's court ended in failure; when he came back from Madrid tail between his legs.'

Cano raises his head. He sits up, body stiffening, confirming Leonor's belief that he had been listening intently all along, waiting for the moment to reveal his true purpose. She can see more than frustration in his eyes and posture. A bull, whose rage aroused could see nothing else around it, only the source of its ire. Incapable of ignoring the challenge, it had no other option but to respond. Deeper, slower breaths, stamp the ground. Judge the right moment to charge. Leonor fears what would follow.

'But he went back didn't he, Francisco?' Cano shouts, waving his arms wildly. 'He knew he was destined for greatness. Pacheco saw it too and that's why he used all of his influence and money to give Diego the opportunity he deserved. That's the difference. He had it in him.'

'What, Alonso? He had what in him?' Zurbaran replies in kind. 'A talent for portraits of the king? A gift for painting buffoons like Pablo de Valladolid? That's my point. When you think of the opportunity he had to restore the faith and divine inspiration of the king and, by royal decree, the whole Spanish empire. Our decline is there for all to see. We've had more than three decades now of this Philip. We can talk about the successes of his reign if you like. His leadership in court theatre maybe, or his championing of Spanish playwrights, the de la Barcas and the Lope de Vegas'. You might want me to point to the undoubted greatness of his art collection assembled in large part by our friend Diego. We should not forget the Titians, the Raphaels, the Giottos that now adorn El

Escorial. Modern talent hasn't been forgotten either, I am told. There's Nardi for one, Carducho, Gonzales, and many others like them – all painters who have flourished under the king's patronage.'

'Bullfighters too, Alonso. Since the king declared his passion and established the bullring in Escorial itself we have lived in a golden age of bullfighting, have we not? It's just a pity that we haven't had the same rate of success in killing the Dutch or the French as we have had with bulls. The successful re-taking of Breda in 1624, the victory captured on canvas for the king by Diego, you say. A proud moment, I agree, and still in those early years of the king's reign did we not all believe his policy of dealing with the Dutch threat would reassert the authority of Spain?'

'But as we know, Alonso, all he succeeded in doing was to irritate Louis. Philip couldn't defeat the Dutch quickly enough and create a powerful alliance with the only other great Catholic power, but he could make war with France inevitable.' Zurbaran pauses, though not long enough for Cano to intervene. Leonor listens to her husband extend the chain of thoughts further, wondering how long he had been rehearsing this speech in his head. She is beginning to understand now why his long periods of solitude would pass without resulting in finished paintings.

'So we've had more than twenty years of that now with no end in sight. Perhaps, as I have heard, Philip spends too much time following astrology or with his mistresses, or adding to his palace of entertainment, to be too concerned with decisions of state. If rumours are to be believed, maybe we are where we are because the king is too indecisive and listens mainly to the advice of his court painter.'

The wooden chair scrapes and clatters as it topples back on to the stone floor. The sudden movement of the apparently half-drunk Cano takes both Zurbaran and Leonor by surprise. By nature a rabbit in the face of danger, Francisco freezes, open-mouthed, as Cano thumps the table with his fist. Through the shaft of fading sunlight the specks of dust dance in the air. Zurbaran's cup could not withstand the shock to the uneven wooden surface. The tide of thick red liquid encircles Leonor's carefully arranged bowls of fruit and plates of bread and cheese. In that second, to Leonor it appears like spilled blood, gushing from a wound. The bowl and plates slow its broad advance, funnelling and forcing it into one long thin column. Leonor sees a finger of blood pointing to the place where Cano had been sitting until a moment ago.

Taking two steps around the oblong table, Cano pounds it again.

'And what would a failed provincial painter from Seville know about running the Spanish empire?' Leonor hears herself shout 'Señor Cano' but the figure towering above her husband ignores her. Waiting for the first blow to land she has only one thought: this is not the first time, is it, Alonso Cano, not the first time you have flown into a rage at the slightest provocation, not the first time you have been so out of control, so violent.

'Who do you think you are, Francisco Zurbaran? You turn up in Madrid expecting Diego to open doors for you, or maybe you had a profitable commission from the king in mind. And you have the nerve to criticise both when you know nothing about either. You have absolutely no understanding of how the court works or of the immense achievement of the man I am still proud to call my friend, Diego Velazquez. You obviously don't. No wonder he has let years pass without seeking you out. I understand why now. He's a good judge of character and *you* don't have one.'

His fury preventing him from saying any more, Cano clasps his fists tightly together and bangs them on the table. Then, only then, Leonor sees in his face the realisation of his conduct. Before any more can be said, Alonso Cano stands upright, turns and marches out of the modest Madrid home of Francisco and Leonor Zurbaran.

Chapter 4

THE ORDER

Thirty years have passed since the victory at Lepanto for the Order and Christianity, seven since the election of Alof de Wignacourt as Grand Master, and seven of Vincenzo at his command, serving his knight's novitiate.

Apart from his palace duties Vincenzo is required, as all Knights are, to work one day a week at the Sacred Infirmary. Mercifully, he thanks God, thus far he has escaped any major outbreak of disease or influx of casualties as a consequence of any sea skirmishes with the corsairs. In the routine of the Infirmary, the beggars arrive at regular intervals for their free medicines. Doctors, surgeons and nurses tend to the sores and crumbling skin of lepers in their separate clinic as well as the rows of bedded patients in the Infirmary's great ward.

Even in the less bellicose period of his novitiate, Vincenzo counts 340 occupied beds. Patients who can walk or suffer minor ailments are cared for in a different clinic, tended by another group of doctors, nurses and novitiates. This military operation extends to the delivery of care and medicines to the old in their homes.

Mealtimes prove to be the high point of Vincenzo's day. The Infirmary's staff select the meals according to the relative strength of each patient, vermicelli and chicken for the weakest, whilst most often game and wine are presented to the strong. What incentive is there to leave the Infirmary, Vincenzo often wonders, when such nourishment is served daily on a silver dish by no less than the servants of the Grand Master, himself the servant of the Servant of God. Why leave with such service, especially on the days when it comes from the bailiffs or the Grand Master who rolls up his silk sleeves to work in the Infirmary on feast days.

As his masters and fellow novitiates expect, Vincenzo displays the necessary black and white armour to merit the accolade of being a Knight of Saint John. The novitiate who is not of noble stock aspires to become a Knight of Obedience. White is for piety, purity and good works. For sustenance, expect only bread and water. Take these vows of poverty, chastity and obedience. Love Christ in other Christians. Visit the sick every day and obey their orders. Black marks dedication to the one true faith. The Order of Saint John has divine authority confirmed by a continuous line of Successors of Saint Peter and no less a figure than the Cistercian, Saint Bernard. That divine authority permits the bearing of arms to stop and even kill those who threaten the very existence of Christianity.

To be a Knight of Obedience is a shorter pilgrimage to eternity, conferred by the Grand Master and confirmed, as Vincenzo liked to think in his own adaptation of Saint Paul's exhortation to the Ephesians, to put on the armour of the day. Vincenzo's armour of each day is to be black or white as the Grand Master commands. The armour defines who he is, the purpose of his life. It guarantees his eternal reward. For every Knight of Saint John says

Vincenzo, amused by his own reverential Pauline humour, there are all kinds of service to be done, but always to the same Grand Master. It is he who is the Sovereign Lord of the Order of Saint John. He who is the Order's Light, who decides what is right and what is wrong, who is worthy of giving his life as a Knight and who is not.

It is he, Grand Master Fra' Alof de Wignacourt, who remembers the fallen and wounded, even the crossbowmen who fought alongside him at Lepanto. This Grand Master is the man who is understanding of the Knight's weaknesses and shows them compassion. This is the French Grand Master whose faith and love of Malta is so deep that he makes his case to the Successor of Peter for a feast day in commemoration of Saint Paul's shipwreck on Malta. The Sacred Infirmary, the network of water viaducts, the defence of Christendom, the creation of work for old, limping has-been crossbowmen like this one, giving them reason to live and to serve – this is the Grand Master.

Vincenzo is not so naïve to believe his loyalty is shared across the island, and not so blind to the Knights whose arrogance, and worse, is unchecked. Anonymous on the streets and harbour paths of Valletta, he is used to hearing the grumbles of the Maltese.

'Why does the Grand Master need so many slaves?'

'I hear he has as many as 100 in his palaces.'

'No, it's 200.'

'And why do we have to call him Serene Highness now? Has he not got enough power and palaces, or enough slaves to call him that?'

'It's because they made him a Prince of the Holy Roman Empire, whatever that's supposed to mean.'

'Well, it certainly doesn't mean cheaper grain or spices.'

'Or wine.'

'Give him some credit. The Order's re-building Valletta.'

'They've been re-building it since the Great Siege over 40 years ago. Oh yes, it's lovely to have our neat chessboard of streets with little gardens and fountains but maybe, just maybe, if Wignacourt didn't spend so much time on building his Court and furnishing his palaces, we'd all be better off.'

'Do you remember? When our French nobleman became Grand Master he pledged to bring the Order back to its former splendour and greatness.'

'Who cares about that when the crops fail, or when Eastern traders are allowed to charge double for spices?'

'Or when the Knights think they have a divine right to take any Maltese woman, loose or not.'

'At least most are protected by their long black stoles and covered faces. Most still adhere to the old traditions and do not converse with men.'

'Sometimes they have no choice when drunk Knights approach.'

'You think they need to be drunk to lust after our women? You've been out in the fields for too long.'

'They would not be like that, these so-called Christian Knights, if Wignacourt laid down the law about how they behave.'

Vincenzo holds his tongue in the streets, never reports what he has heard. Discretion works both ways. In the palace he need not be so discreet. Here, his compressed reflex devotion guides his action and now ensures the abrupt dismissal of Caravaggio. No-one and certainly no painter, whatever his reputation, has the right to insult the Grand Master like that. Not to his face, anyway.

'When can I see Wignacourt again? The brusque arrogance of the question takes him by surprise; confirmation if any more were needed that this self-absorbed ingrate has no judgement or understanding of respect. They had reached the courtyard and are within sight of the palace gate, when Vincenzo pauses.

'If', the word weighted heavily and hung out as a barrier between the two men, 'If His Serene Highness, the Grand Master, requires your presence once more you will be summoned. You will remain a guest of the Order in the *auberge* assigned to you until then, signor.'

Caravaggio turns away from his escort, suddenly realising that he is back in the courtyard of his earlier daydreams. 'Who painted these frescoes of the siege?' he asks, his back to Vincenzo.

'D'Aleccio. I can only say that the Grand Master took pity on him and gave him refuge.'

'Because he was an artist?'

'I cannot say, signor, at what point d'Aleccio suggested painting these frescoes of the siege. The fact remains that His Excellency and the Order showed him compassion and gave him a second chance in life.'

'So he's not above admitting artists, even those with stains on their character?'

Caravaggio's sudden change in tone from impatient inquisitor to vulnerable refugee momentarily makes Vincenzo forget that he is supposed to be leading an unwelcome guest away.

'The Grand Master is forgiving even in the most grievous of circumstances', he says. 'I can also assure you that, being an artist and becoming a member of the Order of Saint John are both possible. The Order, and this Grand Master in particular, see the glory of God in art.'

'You speak very freely for a servant', Caravaggio counters.

'Secretary. You misunderstand the nature and privilege of serving the Order and the Grand Master, signor.'

'You think so? Where does it state in the Order's provenance that a man must blindly serve in poverty, obedience, celibacy, whatever, at the expense of his own talent, to neglect the gifts Almighty God has given him. Eh? Tell me that. I wonder whether he scorns every Hospitaller, every Knight. Perhaps what he sees is their arrogance in believing they have a foot in the eternal kingdom. He is looking upon men who have gained the whole world, or let us just say have gained the admiration of the whole of the civilised Christian world. He prepares to make his judgement on them, not on their so-called greatness as valiant Christian soldiers and defenders of the one true faith, but as men whose souls have been lost to humility, men who have forgotten that the first must be last. Place no other gods before me, my dear Vincenzo. Thou shalt not kill. Thou shalt not commit adultery. Thou shalt not steal.'

'And when you are in the Grand Master's Palace thou shall not take the name of the Knights of St John the Baptist in vain.' Spontaneously, unexpectedly, the two men laugh together.

In that instant this latest and least likely character in Caravaggio's drama, dispels his dark mood. Would that more Vincenzo dell'Antonellas could have thus intervened to arrest Caravaggio. How he had needed the Tomassonis or the Pasqualones to laugh him off. It's just Michelangelo Merisi da Caravaggio going through another one of those tempests in his mind, they should have said. Ignore these aggressions. He'll lash out at anyone, cruel, nasty, vindictive. Let it pass. He can't help it. Doesn't mean it. Tolerate his weaknesses for argument, for women, for fighting. They will pass. Just stay out of his way until they do. Don't provoke him and eventually he will go on his way and return to his beloved painting.

* * *

Fermo's son is never going to become a Knight of the Justice of the Sovereign Military Hospitaller Order of Saint John of Jerusalem, of Rhodes and of Malta. Nothing to do with his rudeness to the Grand Master, Fra' Alof de Wignacourt, in their first encounter. He is in fact disqualified by virtue of his nobility, or rather his lack of it. Only those of proven ancestral noble lines can take the religious vows of poverty, chastity and obedience. In essence, he knows all too well, what stands between Caravaggio becoming a Knight of Obedience and being ordered by the Grand Master's decree to leave Malta, is Caravaggio.

His only hope of amnesty, his only means of papal rehabilitation, his only path to redemption, is to become a Knight of Obedience of the Order of St John. Even then, this requires the approval of the Grand Master and the personal blessing of the pope, as it would do for any candidate not of noble lineage.

He is not to know how much Wignacourt admires his work. Even greater than the Grand Master's admiration is his desire to match the splendour of the courts of France and Spain and Rome, and his recognition of the opportunity to do so through Caravaggio. Wignacourt petitions Pope Paul V, more than six months before Caravaggio disembarks from the galley captained by Fabrizio Sforza Colonna. Pride and politics prevent him from appealing exclusively on Caravaggio's behalf. The French nobleman chooses another Knight, explaining how both men have exemplary virtue and merit. 'Your Holiness, give me, I implore you, the authority for this one time only to adorn these two men, filled as they are with the desire to dedicate themselves to this Order and its Hospital, of which I am its most humble servant, with the habit of a Magistral Knight. I vouch for their devotion to obedience and the noble Order of Saint John.' Paul readily agrees to Wignacourt's impassioned plea. Ignorant of this knowledge in the days of anxious waiting for a further summons, Brother Michelangelo Merisi da Caravaggio, as he wants to be, imposes a discipline of greatest surprise to himself. His first occupation would be casual, polite enquiry of those Knights - and those he knows to be in the Order's service – whose path he would purposefully cross in the market, the osterias and, helpfully, in the home of the Sicilian Knight, Fra Giacomo Marchese, who entertains him. What kind of man is the Grand Master? What are his appreciations, his leanings? Wisely suspicious of his intent, Knights prove to be less than forthcoming. Idle gossip and the names of its authors have a habit of rising on the wind up to the hilltop palace where judgements would be made. Only Fra Giacomo is less guarded, unsurprisingly, as he has made a statement in welcoming his notorious guest.

'Make the Commendatore your ally', he says when the two men find themselves alone on his balcony looking out across the harbour. The silence between them is awkward, not helped by Caravaggio's belief that his host belongs in antiquity. Fra Giacomo is a tall, thin man whose careful deliberate movement reminds him of the Greek hoplites adorning ancient pottery. Though lightly armed for battle they attack with precision and ferocity. Only a fool would underestimate their guile and valour. They are not given to sharing information, Caravaggio imagines, that is not strictly necessary.

'The Secretary, Vincenzo dell'Antella?' Caravaggio looks up, the question presented as if to express his own dim perception.

'He is modest.'

'And that's a good thing?'

'He was received into the Order years before Wignacourt became Grand Master.'

'And what does that tell me?'

'Cavalier Fra Vincenzo, as he was then, illustrated a book on the history of the Order with a drawing of Valletta.'

'I see. So I should be aware of the Secretary's artistic skills.'

'No.'

'What then?'

'The Order's history was written by Giacomo Bosio. Giacomo and his brother, Giovanni Ottone Bosio were friends of dell'Antella. Over 25 years ago Giacomo and Giovanni murdered the brother of the Viceroy of Calabria in the Vatican Palace.'

'What happened to them?'

'Giacomo and Giovanni were cultured men as is dell'Antella. The Bosios were poets, historians. Their father was a scholar, an archaeologist. They were respected. Had many connections in Rome.'

'And you are saying to me that Vincenzo dell'Antella was sympathetic, might even have helped them?'

'I cannot say for sure.'

'So?'

'The pope pardoned them.'

'And Wignacourt?'

'The Grand Master trusts his Commendatore completely. He will accept his advice even if it flies in the face of the guidance of the Council and Knights of the Order. He will listen to his Secretary and stand by him whatever happens.'

* * *

Wine usually loosens the tongues of the less noble, on the other hand. Yet even in a more garrulous state most find it difficult to heap opprobrium on their lord and master. Talk to him about viaducts, say some. He's done more than any other ruler on this barren rock to make sure people and farms have enough water. Saint Paul, say others. He knows the Letters better than any man on the island. Did you not know that it is Wignacourt who persuaded the pope to make the Wrecking of Saint Paul on Malta a feast day on February 10th every year? That's it. Talk to him about Paul on Malta, or the Siege, or the Battle of Lepanto, and you are sure to have his undivided attention.

One vanity of the fugitive artist's vanities, only truly recognised by him, is his gift for extracting information when he needs it most. What other artist could mix so easily with the ordinary, so far below him, he tells himself. Who could imagine any of the great artists now, or at any time in the past, engaging in bibulous exchanges with peasants and street people for the sake of their art, making laughter and stories and opinions flow as readily as the wine, so that they cease to care whose company they keep. He, Caravaggio, is the master of disarming even the most wary of ordinary folk, being one of them, becoming the eyes and ears of their indiscretions.

'Tell him about the secret marriage of that Knight from Naples last year.'

'Better not, he might blurt it out in front of the Grand Master.'

'Tell him anyway', pipes up a third, throwing his head back with laughter and simultaneously banging his fist on the table. The cups and dust dance together for an instant in the corner candlelight. Unless a punch is thrown or sword drawn no-one, not in this back-street tavern of Valletta, will give this group a second glance. No-one notices the finer cloak of the small unshaven man with dishevelled black hair in their midst.

'What's the latest count on the number of brothels we have?'

'Three.'

'No, it's definitely four. You're forgetting the new one run by that dragon from Crete.'

'You have personal experience, do you?'

'Make fun of me, would you, Aaron, a poor farmer like me, with barely enough to feed my children, with – '

'Easy, Gomu. I'm only joking, but it's the Knights who like a good tussle, especially the young ones, eh?'

'With the whores or the dragon?'

'That's more like it, Gomu. Careful, though,' says Aaron, pointing at his two companions. 'We shouldn't give our friend from Milan the wrong impression, should we? You wouldn't find any veterans from Lepanto going to a Cretan whorehouse like that.'

'No, they couldn't make it up the hill.'

'Excellent', Aaron roars, slapping the farmer on the back. 'That's more like the Gomu I know.'

Caravaggio laughs as he is expected to do. The third man does not, he notices. He is younger than the other two. His short, blonde hair, blue eyes, pale skin and soft hands suggest he has fallen in with these two gnarled, sunburnt Maltese more by default than design. He is all but a page boy in manner and frame, hardened only by the company he keeps. Caravaggio cannot tell whether the lad is embarrassed by the musings on male deviation because they are too close to his own truth, or because he has another predilection of which he can never speak. At any rate, Aaron and Gomu do not seek his comment. He continues to stare into his cup of wine as if willing to turn it into water.

Cups filled and re-filled for Aaron and Gomu at least, further inhibitions are abandoned. Any lingering respect for the sacrifices of the Order that governs their lives are swept away in a free-flowing river of wine. Observations of the arrogance, corruption and groping weaknesses of the Order's warrior caste are mingled with recollections of their own grinding routine of survival. Due deference for the relative peace and prosperity the Order has brought them, the outsider reflects, will return with sobriety. They dare not sustain resentment in public. They cannot live in denial of what had passed between their forebears and the Order in defence of their island forty years before.

Aaron, Gomu and thousands of Maltese like them had lost fathers, grandfathers, aunts, uncles in the Great Siege. Kith and kin had fought valiantly, primitively, armed only with the farm tools Gomu still uses today. They had stood alongside the imported holy Knights, men clad in iron armour, trained to kill. Their land scorched, wells poisoned, sheep slaughtered, whole families bound by blood and the thin soil of Malta, butchered, beheaded, mutilated corpses thrown into ditches or left to rot for the children to see.

The girls became women dressed in black, obedient, submissive as the law required. The boys became men: farmers, shopkeepers, traders of indulgences and weaknesses, drinkers in the osterias, erasers of childhood. Aaron, Gomu and their silent companion can share memories in the presence of a stranger. They would tolerate him, let him see what little they have. He is paying for the wine after all. They are flattered by his attention, the interest in who they are, the desire to know more, not so much where they have come from, but what they have come through. Each has his own anecdote of the Siege, or some Maltese-accepted fact, once told, then re-told, and finally over the decades credited as gospel truth.

The Great Siege of Malta? Algerians, Berbers, Turks, the elite Janissaries – as many as fifty thousand besiegers in all, carried to Malta in a fleet of two hundred warships with hundreds more cargo vessels and transport ships for their supplies, gunpowder, cannon and horses. Fewer than five hundred Knights faced them, aided by over one thousand mercenaries from Spain, Sicily, Lombardy, Venice, Naples and the papal states.

'And take note of this. Remember, my friend.' It is Aaron who raises his hand to halt the flow of facts and figures from Gomu and the blonde third man, animated at last.

'There can be no doubt that Malta would have fallen without the fearless fighting of three thousand Maltese militia defending their homes.'

'What happened to them?' The artist's question instantly changes the mood among his informers. The blonde boy looks at him directly for the first time.

'They couldn't find all of the bodies. They say that as many as seven thousand Maltese men, women and children perished.'

The inquisitor waits for what he thinks is a respectful silence before resuming his quest.

'And what of the Grand Master, La Vallette? How is he remembered?'

'All grand masters want to be remembered as true warriors, defenders of the faith', says Gomu, the two other heads nodding in agreement. 'But La Vallette stands head and shoulders above the others. Even the way he carried himself.'

'What do you mean?'

'He wore a thick shot-proof breastplate. Over the top of that, like the tabard of a herald, a sopravest of interwoven cloth and gold with a great white Maltese cross on its front. Only the Grand Master's was white, not red like the other Knights. He carried a sword and dagger and wielded the hand buckler.'

'Which is?'

'It's a small, spiked shield for hand-to-hand combat. If it wasn't for him – ' The blonde boy's voice trails away.

'At first it looked as though Malta's and our families' fate was sealed,' Aaron continues. It doesn't matter who you are on this rock, Signor, you don't forget the dates when the lives of our parents, relatives and friends hung by a thread. May 18th 1565: the day when the ships bringing death and destruction were first sighted. May 25th: the day the Turks started firing their heavy cannon at our little fort of Saint Elmo. That day the Grand Master put Fra' Pierre de Massuez Vercoyran in charge of St Elmo, but gave him only two hundred mercenaries and fifty to sixty Knights to defend it. What was that against the 80 pounders of the Turks, their sappers and merciless janissaries. They wanted St Elmo so badly because it would have given their ships an entry and perfect protection in Marsamxett. The Grand Master sent in more troops. We still tell our children today how the defenders of St Elmo fought.'

Aaron is interrupted, and the three Maltese vy to provide their guest with some lurid and vivid detail of creative defence. Boiling oil. Pots packed with explosives. Circles of fire: large hoops bound with inflammable wadding, then set alight and rolled at speed down the hill into the Turks. But the Turks kept on, too great in number, too determined, too fearless.

'June 8th,' Aaron goes on, 'the day the Grand Master was presented with a petition by Fra' Vitellino Vittelleschi, signed by fifty-three of his brother Knights in St Elmo saying that unless they were evacuated at once they would walk out of St Elmo to face the Turks and certain death.'

'And what did La Vallette do?'

'He responded by sending them more troops and ammunition, so they remained and fought. The Turks attacked in the night, too. Always the drums beating. Cannonballs of iron, bronze and stone smashing St Elmo to pieces. They say that as many as four thousand arquebusiers were trained on the rubble of the fort. Any movement, any sight of our brothers through the gaps and they were dead. Just one more date for you, Signor Caravaggio: June 23rd, the eve of the feast of St John the Baptist. On that day, four chaplains heard – '

'No, it was only two', the blonde boy interrupts. 'Do not exaggerate for our Milanese friend or he will never believe anything we say. Later, he will only recount our stories as the drunken talk of Maltese peasant farmers, simpletons. Isn't that right, Signor? No offence.'

'Very well, then' says Aaron. 'Two chaplains, but not a man round this table is a simpleton. Now, the table by the window over there, that's another story.'

Surprised at the success in making his companions laugh so heartily at his joke, Aaron takes up his story once more, cheer in the group restored.

'It was midnight, the first minutes of the eve of St John, when two chaplains heard the confession of sixty men who were left in the chapel of St Elmo, the only building still standing. In the Mass they then celebrated, every man could receive the Body and Blood of Christ. Every man. The priests then buried the chalices. They burned the altar cloths, vestments, anything sacred that could be defiled. Through the night the priests took turns to toll the bell, till daybreak. It is the eve of the feast of St John the Baptist, remember.'

'And I don't want you to forget either,' Gomu cuts in, 'that many of these sixty defenders were already wounded and starving. For the Turks, not being able to capture this one small fort on the island was unthinkable. Go on, Aaron.'

'When the attack came at dawn they sent in their galley to pound the fort first. Then, wave after wave of sappers, *arquebusiers,* from every angle. And the bloodthirsty janissaries. They would show no mercy, such had been their humiliation at the hands of so few in this struggle over St Elmo. How long, Signor Caravaggio? How long do you think the Knights and brothers could withstand such an attack? Think on that for a moment while I tell you – '

'Shall we re-fill our cups first?' Gomu again.

'About just one of the defenders.'

'Yes, ask anyone on Malta today, who Colonel Mas is, and they will tell you – '

'Thank you, Gomu. That's what he's known as, but his actual name is Fra' Juan de Eguaras. By the time of the final attack he had lost so much blood already from his wounds that he could no longer stand. Colonel Mas insisted on being carried in his chair to where the Turks would be most likely to break through. Imagine that, Signor, sitting, bleeding to death, readying to fight for certain death.'

'He was the first to die?'

'When the Turks swarmed over the rubble one survivor says Colonel Mas jumped out of his chair wielding his pike before one swing of a scimitar took off his head. That's why, Signor, it took the Turks four hours to gain control of St Elmo. A handful who had fought so valiantly escaped, swimming underwater to safety. It is only because of them that we know what happened on the eve of the feast of St John the Baptist. The priests? The other knights and brothers of the Order of St John? All dead.'

Aaron pauses and looks at each of his two companions before turning to Caravaggio.

'You ask us about the Grand Master? You want something from him? Let me tell you that the man whose shoes he fills addressed the Knights and brothers of the Order on that fateful feast of St John the Baptist. By then he knew the worst. The devil's grip of the Turks was so tight – 'Overcome with emotion, Aaron empties his cup and wipes his sleeve before composing himself.

'So tight, that they took the heads off all of the Knights. On the naked chest of each they hacked out the shape of a cross with a scimitar; then nailed each man to a cross and pushed it out on to the bay. When La Vallette gave his sermon on St John's Day he asked all of the Knights and brethren to renew their vows. By the time he spoke every man present had seen four of these crucifixes washed up on the shore. The Grand Master's words that day will never be forgotten and will be passed down from generation to generation.

What could be more fitting for a member of the Order of St John than to lay down his life in defence of the Faith. The fallen of St Elmo have earned a martyr's crown and will reap a martyr's reward.

To our parents and relatives who fought alongside the brethren, he said,

We are all soldiers of Jesus Christ like you, my comrades.'

'It was just the beginning of the Siege, Signor. But La Vallette, Fra' Jean, would not yield. He stood firm, defending Maltese men, women and children when he could. The cry often went up with each Turkish attack, 'Remember St Elmo.' For months, malaria, dysentery and countless repelled attacks did not stop the Turks. Again and again', Aaron bangs his fist on the table', 'killing, slaughtering, mutilating. I lied. One more date for you: August 20th1565. On that day, no fewer than eight thousand – did you get that? Eight thousand – were beaten back from St Michel. I have heard – we all have – that of the forty thousand Turks who laid siege to Malta in 1565, only ten thousand survived, their pagan tails between their legs.

Caravaggio is nodding, unexpectedly moved by the storytelling from these unlikely raconteurs.

'We owe him our lives, Signor. Nothing less than that. We don't know what your business is here, but it seems you want to know about Grand Master Wignacourt and the Order for some purpose of your own. If you need to impress, then any reminder of what Jean de La Vallette did and what he preached on St John the Baptist's day after the horror of St Elmo, will serve you well.'

* * *

Vincenzo dell'Antella stands, perspiring. He dabs his forehead, shifts weight on to his left foot hidden by the trailing black cape of the Knights of Malta, emblazoned with the seven-pointed white Maltese Cross. He takes a step forward feigning a curious look as if attending to a detail out of place. It is a step to release the silk of his undershirt from a sticky, sweating back. Wignacourt notices the movement. Enthroned on the left of his Commendatore he looks up momentarily, breaking his study of the slow procession. It is the first day of December. No heat is in the air. The Oratory has overpowered the smoking perfume of incense with its scent of damp wood, strengthened by the late November rains. There is no reason to sweat. The eyes of master and servant meet. No

105

message passes between them. It is too public for any nod of understanding, too awkward to give any member of this solemn assembly reason to believe that the Grand Master and his Commendatore know more about the ignominy brought on the Order than they have shared.

Across the open rectangular space under the flat wooden roof of the Oratory, a caped file of mature men, some shuffling in bent decrepitude, others erect, virile, enter from the sacristy. Vincenzo watches the head of each pass below the immense altarpiece canvas which fills the shorter wall at the opposite end of the rectangle. He knows every man. Each defines what the Order has become. Among their number are Knights of compassion, men who have realised their true vocation in caring for the sick of the Infirmary, riddled with disease or plague or leprosy. For the dying these Knights have become the bridge to eternal life. They shuffle in front. Behind them, at the end of the snaking trail are the Knights of brothels and braggadocio, whose cockiness is unmistakeable even in the flickering candlelight.

In between are the Knights of fire and fury, the battle-hardened campaigners, survivors from the distant glory of Lepanto, the embarrassment of the Armada, the bitter struggle in the Dardanelles. Vincenzo thinks he can see more than age in the heavy step of these warrior Knights. It is, he believes, an awareness of the mortality that will embrace them, as it did their fallen brothers-in-arms who died during the Great Siege and who now lie only footsteps away in the cemetery on the other side of the Oratory wall. How each man must contemplate the judgement he will receive, standing before the Almighty proudly asserting his right to enter Paradise. It has to be so. He is, after, the Grand Marshal, or the Grand Hospitallier, or the Castellan of Emposta, the illustrious Grand Master of here. How each man must defend his title, be he so deluded, deceived or indoctrinated to believe that his place is so assured.

'*Grant me a fair judgement, Almighty God and Eternal Father. Though I was not martyred in defence of your faith, see the habit in which I was buried. Grant me entry into your kingdom. I have failed many times, but this habit is a mark of your protection and forgiveness. Let it be enough. Please. Let it be enough. Allow me to enter.*'

Which of these if any, Vincenzo ponders, doubts the right to be with the Lord in Paradise, if not this December day in 1608, then one day soon, that the wearing of the habit, the membership of the Order, the seven-pointed star have given him.

Vincenzo's reflection is broken by one of the priors, the Prior of Champagne, who twists his silver head upwards to take in the vastness of the painting looming over the procession. You won't find the signature in the bottom corner if that's what you are looking, Vincenzo whispers to himself. No. Look to the left. You didn't look too closely at this Beheading of St John when you saw it for the first time four months ago, did you? It is not a clean killing. As a Prior you might not have witnessed a man's head being hacked off before. Look in front and behind you at the oldest warriors and think for a moment about what they witnessed here on Malta. You see the executioner reaching for his knife. The sword hasn't done the job. The head has to come off. Herod is waiting. The debt must be paid to Salomé. See. The executioner and the gaoler and the women are surrounded by darkness. The killing is in the light. John beheaded, is bound and trussed like a sacrificial lamb. You have found the signature now. There, in the pouring out of blood, *f.michel*. Fra Michelangelo da Caravaggio who joined you as a brother with this painting. You see that, reverend prior? The blood. The name of the man you are here to put on trial written in blood above your head. Or should I say the man whom you have already condemned. He's like St John, Prior. St John is only set free from the rope that binds him to the wall. Look. See. There in Caravaggio's darkness – released for a blunt beheading without trial. Only this time, and you are not to know this, holy Prior, it was a rope that set your brother free. Dropped. No, dangled. Ten feet. More. What does it matter now? The rope disappeared into the darkness of that hole in the rock of Castel Sant'Angelo. Who put it there, I cannot possibly say, not to you anyway, Prior. Yes, take your seat. What's wrong with you and your stony-faced brethren? Have you seen a ghost? You stare at the stool on which his habit has been so dramatically placed. Not folded. Not arranged as vestments awaiting the priest in the sacristy. Look at the habit, Prior. It is a coiled heap as if the cloth was forced over the occupant's shoulders and pulled down to his ankles, stripped for trial. As an Order, as a Church, we don't lack for theatre or symbolism, do we, Prior? You stare at his habit as if he had just stepped out of it and stood as an apparition before you. And you, all of you, are about to pass sentence on this man, this ghost, or his habit at least. Let us get on with it, then, this beheading beneath a beheading. Lepers aren't given trials, just cut off before the infection spreads.

The sound of shuffling feet and settling on wooden benches having finally ceased, Vincenzo dell'Antella, happily released from his thoughts, nods his assent to the burly Lord Shield Bearer poised at the lectern to the left of the seated Wignacourt. Vincenzo is bemused by the arm-waving and wild gestures of the storyteller for the prosecution. The brothers are transfixed, he sees, transported by the gravity of events. He looks around the assembly for the hint of a smile when the Bearer places his open palm to the side of his mouth and steps out in front of the lectern, taking great strides to the left and right, shouting,

'I, on behalf of His Highness and our noble Order of St John did personally summon Fra' Michelangelo da Caravaggio once, twice, thrice and a fourth time in our public places of this island's capital city of Valletta, and never did he appear.'

Nor did there appear a single smirk nor a wry smile, no single look to the left or right, only rapt attention. The outcome of the vote this Brother Prosecutor is about to call for is not in doubt.

There is to be no testimony from novices, the wide-eyed apprentices of the Order not used to thinking for themselves. These same novices had quickly learned the art of misleading their instructors in faith. Petitioning for time of private prayer in the Oratory, their true purpose to ask questions of their brother suspended above them as he painted the wall-sized canvas. From older masters and mentors they could expect tales of self-justification, of heathens crushed, of blood running down both sides of a sword carrying out God's work, of Christendom defended. From the crusty infirmarians they could brace themselves for every colour of disease and bile, as vividly described as the ministry of Christ-like care. The least earthly of these *hospitalliers* could be relied upon in every instruction, to make a boast of hastening his own occasion to reap an eternal reward, by touch, and by breathing in the air of death.

From Fra' Michelangelo the novices could be certain of not having to endure either extreme. Among themselves, they would joke about the irony of the Milanese painting death in the second most important killing in history, whilst conversing with them about living life to the full, the good and the bad. Whether it is because the feet of the novices are planted firmly on the stone floor of the Oratory while Caravaggio is at a safe distance on the platform above; or whether it is simply because his back is turned towards them, they are not afraid to pose questions, personal and probing. Most are prefaced with 'Is it true . . ? or 'They say that . .' To be drunk. To be in a brawl. To be in a swordfight. To be with a prostitute. To be in Rome. To be in in the presence of the pope. To imagine the face of Christ and paint it.

The artist brother above them responds and sounds as an oracle would, faceless, ambiguously candid, honest, speaking truths about life that the novices cannot obtain anywhere else. It is a sacred space after all, one where answers must be sought and found. They are not over-awed, not deliberately daring to show less reverence, but find inexplicable courage in this seemingly unique opportunity to make discoveries about life as it is beyond the Order, beyond Malta. In the pronouncements of the oracle they find both light and darkness, responses that ring true, convinced as they are that their source is a life experience of struggle and weakness. In him they find a common humanity.

The verdict of the assembly on Fra' Michelangelo da Caravaggio will be unanimous, each voter so deluded, deceived or indoctrinated to believe he is making God's choice through the Order. The statute will say nothing of how this Knight of Obedience's entry was bought and paid for with a Beheading, only that he was 'deprived of his habit, and expelled and thrust forth like a rotten and fetid limb from our Order and Community.' Only six months before, the paint on his portraits still fresh, the Grand Master, had addressed the same Knights in the Oratory.

'Whereas it behoves the leaders and rulers of commonweals to prove their benevolence by advancing men, not only on account of their noble birth, but also on account of their art and science whatever it may be . . .And whereas the Honourable Michelangelo, a native of the town Carraca in Lombardy called Caravaggio in the vernacular, having landed in this city and burning with zeal for the Order, has recently communicated to us his fervent wish to be adorned with the habit and insignia of our Knightly Order . .Therefore, we wish to gratify the desire of this excellent painter, so that our Island Malta, and our Order may at last glory in this adopted disciple and citizen with no less pride than the island of Kos (also within our jurisdiction) extols her Apelles; and that, should we compare him to more recent artists of our age, we may not afterwards be envious of the artistic excellence of some other man, outstanding in his art, whose name and brush are equally important.'

The democratic defrocking definitively decided, Vincenzo gives a second nod of assent, this time for the Knight of Disobedience's habit to be removed from the stool. He takes no notice of the final symbolic act of expulsion, nor of the trail of Knights threading slowly out of the Oratory through the sacristy.

The king, for that is what Wignacourt is in all but name, should have known from that first meeting that he would have as much control over the behaviour of Caravaggio as he did over the Order's warrior Knights after dark. It wasn't as though the artist had no history of fighting or killing people. If it hadn't been the assault on the *Cavaliere di Giustizia* there would surely have been a brawl or worse with some other Knight, some time, somewhere else.

The truth is, King Alof – a name Vincenzo can only use in his thoughts – had already decided Caravaggio's acceptance into the Order before he set foot on the island.

Those letters of intercession sent to Rome were still not enough. King Alof even instructed him, Vincenzo dell'Antella, lowly Commendatore, to write as a double guarantee. This artist of divinely gifted talent would, so the narrative went, reflect his glorious light of brilliance on the Order, and therefore the Church, inspiring all of the faithful across Christendom. Caravaggio would give the Order art as majestic as any city in Europe, the Grand Master assured Vincenzo. All Wignacourt needed was the papal Bull of Reception and then he could do with Caravaggio as he pleased. And, as he pleased, Vincenzo reminds himself, meant admitting the painter of the Supper at Emmaus as a Knight of Obedience.

He is a serious man, Wignacourt. Humourless, some would say in the shadows. He didn't see the – . Well, he didn't see it. Nothing about Caravaggio is obedient. Not the way he paints, not the way he lives, not the way he responds to authority. Nothing. The very idea of making Caravaggio a Knight of Obedience, within the body of Knights of Justice, King Alof didn't see. He did not see the absurdity of it. The conversation had gone nowhere.

'Grand Master, a Knight of Obedience?'

'Yes. That is what I decree. Why do you look at me so, Commendatore? You think I cannot see the challenge through your polite request for clarity.'

'It is only, Your Highness, that we have both seen Caravaggio's attitude to anyone of influence and power over him. Humility is not his natural state. His gifts may well enhance and strengthen the reputation of the Order. His weaknesses are also well-known. Are we to overlook these?'

'We have embraced our brother Fra' Michelangelo in a spirit of forgiveness as has, take note Commendatore, the Holy Father, who has acceded to our request. It is not for us now to question the wish of His Holiness. He has read and interpreted our request fairly. Why do you raise this objection now, Commendatore when we have spoken for the Order? What else would you have me do with him?'

'I mean no disrespect, Your Highness, to you or the Holy Father. My intention is merely to illuminate your decision.'

'We have a long association, Commendatore, and a bond of trust forged in battle. We have defended the Order with our lives, but do not forget who is speaking to you now. Be careful of what you say.'

'Your Highness, as a Knight of Obedience, there is no need for Caravaggio to live by vows of chastity or poverty or obedience.'

'Yes, Vincenzo, not even obedience – '

'He is free to continue as an artist – '

'Yes. So why do you object? As long as he paints, he will make the Order the envy of Christendom.'

'I understand, Your Highness. It is also incumbent on him, for his and the Order's sake, to carry out many good works.'

'And be seen to do so, yes, Vincenzo. As a Knight of Obedience he must serve in the Infirmary and serve the poor and his fellow brothers through other good works.'

'You have asked for no other proof of his heritage, Your Highness?'

'Your probing is tiresome, Commendatore. We have no need of proofs. You surprise me. We cannot be sure if the friendship you appear to have built up with Fra' Michelangelo in these past months means you would rather see him exiled from this island and the Order to save him and us from betrayal, knowing him better now as you do. You seem to have little faith in the power of conversion.

You, of all people, who has spoken to us so many times of St Paul. You, the passionate advocate of commemorating his shipwreck on this island of Malta. He has been here, touched this very isle with his example, and yet you think our brother, because of his many faults, cannot be converted.'

'I do not doubt the power of either St Paul or of the Order to inspire a new faith, Your Highness. Fra' Michelangelo has spoken to me of his pained childhood, his losses and the anger he struggles to control. It is only in painting that his energy is well-spent.'

'Long may that continue. We are thinking of the glory and sanctity of the Order of St John, Vincenzo.'

'So you will not ascertain whether – '

'Enough of this. Enough. I will hear no more about it. Suffice for you to know that we have the papal authority to make Michelangelo da Caravaggio the most generous offer of refuge, and redemption, if you will. We have no need to show any proofs to you or any other Knight. We are certain of his nobility.'

PART 2

Chapter 1

THE INQUISITION

'I was born fifty-six years ago in Agreda, Señora Zurbaran.'

'Leonor, please.'

'You do not need to call me Abbess or Reverend Mother, or any other such title of importance. Sor Maria will be sufficient. It is what I prefer. I should warn you at the beginning that, either because of who or what visitors think I am supposed to be, they allow me to talk and talk. So do interrupt me. It is not good for my throat anyway. I become so parched in summer and winter.'

'Of course. I understand. Agreda was where you were born and brought up?'

'It was a humble frontier village then, as it is now, almost hidden among the foothills of the Moncayo range of mountains. My family name is Coronel. Our ancestors were also of this place. Here in our family home on the Road of the Knights my mother, Catalina, gave birth to me. In time, I became the eldest surviving daughter out of eleven children. She was, she would agree, a very mature woman by the time of my birth, a mother of thirty-nine years.

My mother radiated joy and generosity, her vocation, to bring children into the world to love and praise Almighty

God. My mother's father, Don Francisco de Arana, you may be interested to know, as you are talking about noble lines, was a Basque from a village near Bilbao. As for my grandmother, Maria of Orobio, she came from a noble family of Agreda. Divine providence smiled on my father, too, with rich and gentlemanly parents, though it is true that they did die at an early age, leaving my grandfather and younger brother to manage the estate as best they could.

As proof of *our* lineage – which I underline for your benefit, and for the avoidance of any doubt, you understand – on my father's side, my great great grandfather made a decorative certificate of our family's nobility. Where you come from still matters. My great great grandfather, still on my father's side, his name was Diego Coronel. He married Maria Luis de Pulgares. Well, Diego Coronel was a fighter on horseback for the king and queen, Ferdinand and Isabella, at Toro against the Portuguese. In the battle he lost not only his horse but also four fingers on one hand. He survived nevertheless, as you can see. That was in 1476, clear evidence, the fingers, the certificate, you would think, of my family's loyalty to king and queen and country.

The Inquisitors were not interested in these facts. They were obsessed with two things. First, Agreda's tolerance was an immediate source of suspicion. It is, everyone knows, often called the Village of Three Cultures. A village where stones are not thrown at Jews or Moors was bound to harbour families and inter-relations without pure blood.

Secondly, they fixated upon Coronel as an ancient noble family name, but one tainted by an extraordinary association. An instrumental figure in the funding of Christopher Columbus' voyage to the New World was the Chief Tax Collector of King Ferdinand and Queen Isabella.

His name, as Jewish as he was, Abraham Senior. When the Edict of Expulsion was issued in the name of Ferdinand and Isabella in 1492, Jews were instructed to leave Spain. Those Jews who wished to remain became the *conversos*, adopting the Catholic faith and Christian names. This, in 1492, after Columbus' discovery, Abraham Senior became Ferrandez Perez Coronel at his baptism. Was he a direct ancestor of mine, you are wondering. Whether he was or not is of no consequence. My ancestors were among the most devout Christians, Jewish though they may once have been. Look at these books behind you by the Venerable Luis of Granada. A Dominican. A theologian. A man who, I do not doubt, drew on both the Jewish and Islamic traditions to inform his vision of God.

You have made the journey here to plead for your husband for fear he will be eclipsed by his rival and former friend, Velazquez. If I can summarise. The case for Velazquez is that he has been loyal to the king. He has endured and outlived Olivares. He is the court painter who has the ear and confidence of the ruler of an empire, much to the annoyance of the king's advisers.

The case for your husband is, well, what exactly? What do you want him to do? It is a question of loyalty and sacrifice. Why come to me if it is jealousy that drives him and if it is jealousy that is in your heart also? You seek a restoration of your husband's standing. The proper order needs to be restored, you might say, where the man who paints the ecstasy of Saint Francis of Assisi, the man who paints Jacob, who paints Reuben, Simeon, Levi, Judah, Dan, Naphtali, Gad, Asher, Issachar, Zebulun, Benjamin and, of course, Joseph, all of his twelve sons, is given his rightful place. You see, I do know the work of the great Francisco Zurbaran. It is Zurbaran who reflects the faith of his king, educating subjects across his empire in the

Old Testament, the gospels, veneration of our Blessed Mother and the lives of the saints.

Zurbaran is not the painter who places ordinary people on canvas as witnesses to his talent. And yet, it is Velazquez whose ambition is greater. Not restoration in the eyes of men, but resurrection to see the face of God. Perhaps his spiritual understanding is greater than your husband's. How are we to know how the Lord speaks to Velazquez? He is obsessed now, is he not, with acceptance as a Knight of the Order of Santiago. It is not for us to stand in his way if that is the Lord's calling. What if Velazquez had sought to use his influence with the king to seek another direction, to grant a favour after years of service? Wealth? An upgrade to a position as government minister? The new Olivares? After all, who knows better the mind of the king? You should ponder these questions, these possibilities, before asking for my help. Don't look so surprised. Anyway, I warned you I would talk and talk.'

Unexpectedly, the abbess laughs, smiles warmly, places a maternal hand on the arm of Leonor Tordera de Zurbaran, simultaneously reassuring and relaxing her. Leonor knows now that she can speak her mind. Abbesses of convents, mystics even more so, were, in Leonor's mind at least, supposed to be distant, detached, without feeling, other-worldly. Instead, she finds herself warming to Sor Maria and ready for a rare woman-to-woman conversation, albeit one where she must listen to exceptionally long monologues.

'You may look at me as impoverished by choice. My cell. These austere surroundings. This rough cloth encasing all but my face. How can a woman live without jewellery?' She smiles once more, oblivious of the contrast of her greying teeth against the starched white wimple, and leans across to touch the gold necklace around Leonor's neck with her coarse fingers.

'I am struck by the possibility', she says, 'that Señor Velazquez may in fact be seeking a communion with God that I, in all humility and gratitude, can say that I was given as a child. You don't believe me, again, Leonor. I can see it in your eyes.' Leonor checks her posture and expression. Uptight, attentive, serious yet receptive is what the situation demands. She attempts an apologetic smile. The abbess taps her hand and settles back into her chair.

'My father rose at three in the morning while the rest of us slept. He practised the Exercise of the Cross, carrying a large cross on his back, praying with great fervour and tender sighs. My mother followed the example of Mary's meditative prayer and often spent three or four hours at a time in the evening practising various spiritual devotions. When I was a child, I would watch her put on a Franciscan habit, stretch out on the bed and place a skull over her face so that she could better understand our mortality and the eternal nature of our soul. This is not an isolated example, a moment of despair, but a regular occurrence in our home to which I was witness.'

'As you say it', Leonor interrupts, 'I can see my husband's painting of Saint Francis of Assisi. He gave Francis the same vision.'

'What Saint Francis felt as God's presence as a young man, I experienced as a child having observed the daily practices of my parents. I was only a child, Leonor, when I received four clear insights. I can only describe each one to you as a moment of the purest and brightest light when God's presence filled my mind and understanding. In this light I knew God to be the creator of everything, of the universe. He is the cause of all effects. In this light, God also revealed to me the power of his love on the human heart. I saw clearly the unity of three persons in one God. Lastly, I saw the extremes of good and evil, of light and darkness, of grace and sin.'

'When I was a little girl', Leonor responds, 'my only experience of God was at Mass on Sundays and Holy Days. My parents were dutiful rather than religious. God for them was a landowner to whom rent should be paid and deference shown. As long as there was sufficient light in their lives from the income of my father's jewellery business, we did not worry too much about the darkness. Paying God his due was more of a guarantee against the darkness. I cannot imagine how you could be so, so – ' Leonor waves her arm and looks to the ceiling for an answer. Sor Maria does not finish the sentence for her.

' – so holy, so aware, so , so, full of understanding. How is it possible? Could you not just have been imagining it? Before I was ten years old all I wanted to do was play with a skipping rope or dress up putting on the gold necklaces and rings that my father showed to me. I dreamed of wearing fine gold as a matador on horseback, of the crowd thinking this was another brave young noble until the bull was slain. Only then would I raise my head, the crowd cheering, and remove my cap. They would gasp in amazement at the woman before them. How can this be, they would say. A woman? A noble woman at that. A matador? Such skill. Such bravery. Such elegance.'

'Ah, but to think your glory would have been so short-lived. Pius V would have had you excommunicated. You still would be.' The tone of the abbess is not severe or chastising, more sad for pointing out the reality, even in good humour. She changes the subject. 'And what did you dream of at Holy Mass?'

'At Mass?' Leonor repeats, half-laughing as if she is about to grasp the humour in a joke, but then realises. 'I am sorry. I didn't mean.' Sor Maria waves away the indiscretion.

'At Mass I didn't understand what was going on. The stream of Latin from a man whose back was turned away from my face did little to nurture faith within me. For a long time I thought the priest speaking was the voice of God through him; that what he uttered was literally and spiritually so far above my head that I wasn't meant to understand. Only the spectacle of it all captured my imagination. I watched the people, the jewellery they wore, their efforts to match the gold on display in the vestments, on the altar. The incense, the incantations, the inexplicable responses, all made an impression on me as a girl. It became, it is true, Reverend Mother, a part of the fabric of my life without ever adding any real meaning to it.'

Throughout this brief confession, the abbess listens without expression. 'Who can know or understand the mind of God, Leonor?' she says softly. 'Why you should be in his presence in the sacrifice of the Mass and not be touched with the early fervour of faith I cannot explain. Nor can I say why you were so bewildered by faith as a little girl, whilst I was so captivated by it that – and you will find this harder to believe – that my parents prepared an oratory for me in our modest home. An oratory, Leonor. Can you imagine? My mother went round the local churches and convents to see what statues she could find for me. Christ, Our Blessed Lord At The Pillar Scourged was one, St Michael the Archangel another, and Saint Francis of Assisi too. All featured in my oratory. By the age of eight I was too ill to continue attending the girls' school in Agreda. At home my parents created a rota of daily devotions which my sister and I had to observe.'

'But why?' Leonor cannot help herself. 'Why cut you off from other children? Surely God's will was not for you to suffer the loss of childhood for his sake. I am struggling to think what your life as a girl would have been like, not learning and playing with your friends. So little exposure to the world – or at least to Agreda, especially when you tell me that is a place where people of different faiths and cultures live together peacefully and with tolerance.'

'Usually, Leonor, when visitors here meet me for the first time they are more guarded, but with you it's the opposite. The words tumble out so quickly. You say what is on your mind.'

'Reverend Mother, I am sorry. I should have been less candid.'

'No. Do not apologise. It is refreshing. I know my childhood seems strange. I know it is difficult to understand, to see the goodness in my parents; easier to think of them as austere, humourless people, absorbed by their own virtue. On a selfish quest even, to ensure that for them and their children the journey would end in eternal life. Yet that is not how they seemed to me.'

'Were they of noble birth?'

'As I have explained, but, even for you that is a very direct question? You are asking not from curiosity but from a desire to seek my counsel. When I received your letter I thought about where our conversation might lead. Knowing of my influence with the king, you are seeking to improve your husband's status, to restore him, is that not so?'

'That's not why I am here, Reverend Mother.'

'You have not come for spiritual guidance, have you?' Sor Maria asks in a softer tone.

'No, Reverend mother. I see an injustice. Through his art my husband has given glory to God and served the Church throughout his working life. More than that, he has honoured the king, educating and enriching the lives of his subjects. In fulfilling a lifetime of commissions he has painted for a king and an empire guided by the divine order: the divine at the highest level, mortal man beneath, and below man the worlds of nature and objects. He has not wasted his time or his talent on the ordinary. He has not been distracted by – what shall I say about those other paintings – the less meaningful.'

'And you think the king should show his gratitude by commissioning him to decorate more of the chapels of royal palaces or invite him to court alongside Velazquez.'

'That is not why I have asked for this audience with you.'

'Nothing as crude as approaching me as a means to restoring your husband's reputation and fortune. I can see that. But it is what you long for. You have only recently moved to Madrid you said in your letter after years of living in Seville. With how many children at home?'

'We have five children.'

'Your husband, Francisco, has not brought his family to Madrid because he has secured commissions of such value and duration that they merited this upheaval?'

'No, Reverend Mother.'

'Then why are you here?'

The question hangs in the still, silent air of the convent. It is not a rebuke, not the voice of a woman looking down on her from a higher spiritual plain, not that of one who – as she knows – had once taken a lesson from the harsh interrogations of the Inquisitors. It is weighted with compassion, tenderness. Even so, Leonor cannot speak at first. She allows her mind to wander, resting in the knowledge that the abbess is a woman used to waiting for an answer. Sor Maria of Agreda dedicates her whole life to it, firm in the belief that an answer will come. This is the life she has chosen, or perhaps any woman whose parents created an oratory for her at home had no choice at all.

In Sor Maria's thinking, fill a day with enough silence, enough reflection on the answer you are expecting and then eventually, eventually you will convince yourself. The answer is real. It is here. You cannot see it or touch it. You simply know because you have allowed it in, to come to you. Once you have the answer, the acceptance, you cannot deny the peace that it brings. Sacrifice. Suffering. Pain. Loss. This woman has known them all. She thought she knew as a child that she was called to know the answer, to wait for it. Others. Zealots. The self-righteous. Some indoctrinated. Some deceived. Some deluded no doubt, seeing in signs and statues and rituals what was not there. This woman is not one of those. She accepts me. She knows. I have said nothing. Nothing. Nothing about the faults I find in the Church, in the lowly places women occupy, in the wealth of the Spanish empire for the privileged educated few. Nothing of my faults, my weakness for gold and jewellery, my readiness to put prosperity first. Not like Francisco. Not like him at all.

'I am here because my husband, Francisco, will soon be asked to give an answer. In many monasteries and convents of this land, not as humble as your own, Reverend Mother, there are bishops, abbots and prioresses too, I am sure, who would rejoice to see Francisco Zurbaran, the most spiritual and pious of painters of our age, given the reward and recognition he deserves. He, more than any other, merits the king's blessing, an acknowledgement of his noble calling.'

'You have come to me in Agreda, then, because the question he will be asked does not require an answer that says 'Tell the king and the Council of the Order that I humbly accept their invitation.' '

'If only, if only, Reverend Mother, that were the question. If only that could happen. He, we, could then put behind us the pain and poverty in our lives these last fourteen years of our marriage balanced only by the blessing of our five children. The problems started even before then. After his second wife, Beatriz, died, he struggled for years to collect payments owed to him for commissions in Lima. That he should have had to accept such work when there are thousands of monasteries and wealthy patrons here, is still beyond me. Then there was the dowry of two thousand ducats for his daughter Maria's marriage to Joseph Gasso – '

'Slow down, Leonor. Calm yourself. Was Maria the only child from his earlier marriage?'

'No. No, she wasn't. He had a son. In his twenties when I first met him. Juan. A painter. In every way like his father: thoughtful, observant, kind, generous, idealistic. And in every way not like him at all.'

'What do you mean?'

'Francisco mentored his son. He taught him the basics, everything from the mixing of pigments to the choice of brushes, matching the position of the canvases with daylight in the studio. Obviously, I was not there to see the father and son bond grow so strong. Francisco told me about it much later, the hours they spent together. Francisco looking over Juan's shoulder, pointing, advising, cautioning, occasionally frantically scraping away his son's most clumsy brush strokes. He told me. That's what he did. At least, he did until Juan was big enough to push him away.'

'Take your time, Leonor. Are you telling me that Juan did not wish to become a painter like his father, or that he pushed him away as sons often do to their fathers when they become young men with a mind of their own?'

Leonor straightens her back and presses fingertips to her ear-rings as she does when she is nervous and storytelling. Assured that she remains presentable with them in place her family tale unfolds at the same breathless speed.

'I don't know of anything Juan wanted to be other than a painter, Reverend Mother. The problem was that he was not interested in painting religious subjects. You can imagine what Francisco thought of that. It was a bitter blow to him. Francisco had envisaged – I know because he told me – a future enterprise together, father and son, sharing the work given by the princes and shepherds of the Church from far beyond Seville. They argued. What were once only playful exchanges of opinions between them gradually became heated debates, then evolved as full-scale arguments. That's what Francisco told me.'

'About what?'

'Juan's artist's eye - if I can call it that – only saw still life. He did not like it when Francisco would criticise his technique. At first, Francisco did not know Juan was prepared to forego the more profitable commissions from the Church in pursuit of perfection in still life art. So, as I see it, for a while Juan just humoured his father, out of respect and, I would assume, to avoid confrontation.'

'Is that what Francisco is like too?'

'Yes, he would do anything to avoid an argument or confrontation if he can. Some, like me, would rather have it out, arguing, shouting if necessary, and then the air is cleared. It is quickly forgotten. Not so with Francisco. It is as though it destroys his inner peace. What he calls home,' Leonor points to her head, 'is burnt down. It takes him a long time to rebuild it again; and while he is doing that, he can't paint. So he avoids confrontation.'

'Juan's patience didn't last?'

'I wasn't there, so it's difficult to say. Eventually he told Francisco, I think, that he did not need him any more. There was nothing new he could teach him, nothing that would help his technique as an artist. So he left home in Alcazar Street in Seville.' Leonor pauses, breathing faster, the emotion welling up inside her. Sor Maria, not uncomfortable in the stillness sits, hands clasped on her lap, a rosary intertwined with her fingers, waiting, not embracing or consoling. Leonor is grateful for the distance, the space, the time to compose herself and wipe away her own tears before continuing her story.

'I think Francisco was so hurt. He felt he was losing a son and his legacy at the same time. He could have lived with the decline of his skills as an artist and his popularity if he thought that in some way Juan would take his place. Even in the earliest days when Francisco was courting me, days when he should only have been thinking of romance', Leonor looks up and finds the abbess smiling with her, 'he shared his hopes for Juan, the introductions he would make, the influence he had.'

'Velazquez?' the nun asks.

'No, never Velazquez. He would talk about the fathers of Seville as he called them, the city elders who had bestowed on him this great honour as *de facto* painter to the city. He mentioned the Jeronomites, the Dominicans, the Carthusians, but never Velazquez though they had effectively come of age together as apprentices under the influence of Pacheco.'

'Was Velazquez then not a natural choice for your husband? The king's painter and master of the royal collections at Escorial?'

Leonor shakes her head as much as a gesture of disbelief as rejection of Sor Maria's suggestion, as much again to hide the flow of tears falling on to her cheeks.

'This. This, Reverend Mother, is at the heart of my grief, my fear for my husband's response to his invitation. You see, Juan so admired the painting of Velazquez. At first Juan knew of him only by reputation. When he finally saw his works for himself at the court in Madrid he would not stop talking to his father about how Velazquez captured street life, people living ordinary lives. Juan even liked those paintings of the king on horseback.' The women force another smile, in mock horror.

'Sorry. I do not mean to cause offence or be disrespectful. Other paintings too, whatever it was by Velazquez, portraits of Don Juan of Austria, Olivares, or The Surrender of Breda – you see, I even know the paintings myself, he went on about them so often – Juan found in them a quality that was less, less – ' Leonor looks around her and up to the dark corners of the ceiling, in part searching for the word and giving the abbess the impression that she is fearful her husband is hiding in the shadows.

'Stark', she says finally. 'Less stark. Less black and white. More to reflect on in life, more to admire, more to learn. What he took from his father's paintings', she hesitates again, 'and Juan never said this to me, Reverend Mother. After all, I was not his mother, still less an artist, so what would I know. I loved him as a mother. You understand that, don't you?'

'Of course.'

'In his own way Juan loved his father, respected him, and he knew, he knew for certain, that all of his passion for painting came from him. It had to. Juan had so much to be grateful to Francisco for, it's just that he didn't want to follow in his footsteps.' Leonor stands up and steps towards the green shutters holding back the heat and light of the day. 'Or be anything like him. Not in art. Not in temperament. Not in love. Not in faith. I cannot even say it to your face, Reverend Mother.'

'Come sit down, Leonor. God is full of mercy and compassion. God loves Juan exactly the same as he loves Francisco. He loves each of us with a love so strong and so deep we cannot begin to understand. Isaiah tells us so. See, he says, your name is carved on God's hand. He will not forget you.'

Leonor leans against the cold stone wall, weeping. The sound of her sobbing passes through the shutters on to the street below. An old man, grey, unkempt, bent from age, released from the restraints of reserve as befitting an elder of Agreda, a citizen under no compulsion to humbly respect the incarcerated holy sisters of the town, stops at the wailing. 'Let her go', he shouts up at the closed shutters. 'Why make the rest of us miserable? Why do we all have to endure her suffering? She doesn't want your god, or to be shut up all day. What's the point? Let her go and live her life as she wants, so we can all have some peace.' When neither shutters nor the gated door to the convent yield a response, the grey figure wanders on.

Within, the abbess has risen from her unforgiving wooden seat, laid her hands on the shoulders of Leonor Zurbaran, turned her round, and clasped her tightly. Opening her eyes, Leonor notices the rosary wound around the nun's hand and is almost hypnotised by the cross dangling freely. 'Come,' the voice says. 'Sit down and tell me more.' Neither conscious nor awake, or so it seems to Leonor, she is once more seated facing the abbess. She sees the nun's lips move.

'You were going to say what Juan took from his father's paintings. What did he learn from them?'

'Learn? Learn?' She speaks slowly, numb, barely recognising the words, repeating the question as mothers do in response to mourners' condolences at the funeral of a child. In that moment at least, inhibitions, polite reserve are replaced with a blunt, bold honesty that is out of character.

'He learned he never wanted to be a painter like his father. He learned that there was more to art, more to people, more to this country and empire than some foolish, naïve idea that you either choose to live in the light of God's presence or you live in darkness. Juan kept saying to Francisco, 'Why must you see art only in these terms? Why must there always be this hierarchy in your paintings of divine over mankind over nature?' Hardest of all for Francisco, Juan used to say 'Look at The Temptation of Saint Thomas Aquinas or Saint Anthony Visiting Saint Paul The Hermit. Even his Coronation of The Virgin looks more real. That's what he learned. He would say to his father's face that being some kind of Spanish Caravaggio only meant that he was out of touch with how people were living or how the Church was behaving. It meant he was blind to the beauty around him, he said. In the simple. In the ordinary. Caravaggio at least mastered that.

Up until fifteen years ago Francisco, Francisco Zurbaran, brought honour and prestige to the great city of Seville. For the fifteen years before that, he had repaid the faith the city elders had placed in him. You are the most accomplished of Seville's apprentices they had once told him. Leave Llerena. Make Seville your life and you will be remembered as one of the great artists of this Golden Age of Empire. You are divinely inspired they told him.

I can only tell you what I heard in Seville, the comments made to me and my own reaction to the paintings that I have actually seen. The Sevillians, it is true, came to think of him as the greatest of painters, one of their own. For them Francisco stripped away all of the trappings of the Church. He laid faith bare, Reverend Mother. Like here. Like your life. He created on canvas an intensity of personal faith that until then had been so private, hidden behind monastery walls, in convent cells.'

'Did Juan not see that?'

'If he did, he did not want to acknowledge it. About 20 years ago the Jeronomites commissioned Francisco to paint eight pictures for their monastery at Guadalupe. Soon after we met, Francisco took me there to show me his finished work. Before entering the great chapel where they hang Francisco whispered in my ear, 'The abbot's only instruction was to commemorate the ways in which his Order of Jeronomites kept the spirit of St Jerome alive.'

'What did you see when you entered?'

* * *

Sor Maria knows well that the Jeronomites wield great power and influence. They have been given no less a responsibility than the blackened statue of the Virgin of Guadalupe, the same Madonna visited by Christopher Columbus before his voyage to the New World. Our Lady of Guadalupe, the same Madonna, Virgin Mother of Christ, who beheld the Conquistadors before they too set sail. The same Madonna, the Virgin Mother of Jesus, her saviour, her Lord and God, to whom she had given her life, body and soul.

The same Madonna, subject of her eight volumes, *Mystical City of God,* an account of a cloistered nun's visions of the purest life ever led save that of her son, a biography written in faith over eight long years, burned in an instant by her own hand. Then, ten years past – how long ago it now seemed – only the king knew of her anguish, her fear of the Inquisition. Sor Maria will not forget his word or the date of his letter, December 29th 1648, 'I do not doubt your pain at the mention of your name in the Hijar case because I know how foreign such things are to you. Please be assured of my complete confidence in your character, for I know more than others how God favours you.'

What she does not know is how copies of the *Mystical City of God* volumes ended up in his hands. Nor can she ever be certain that the king had followed the threat of the Inquisition's first enquiry about her in 1635. The Lady In Blue, as she had become known to the native Indians of the America, she cannot understand herself, how she could have appeared to them time and again over four years proclaiming the Word of God. Yet the nomadic Jumanos tribe and their trading neighbours, insisted they had seen and talked with the Lady In Blue, Maria de Agreda, a nun who never left her convent in Spain. In different languages they could understand her and she them until, in 1623, she tells them that she can no longer visit. Go further on your summer trading expedition and seek baptism in the church of Saint Anthony in Isleta, she tells them.

Jumanos, Rayados, Xumanas, Choumans, all asserted that they had met the Lady In Blue on at least five hundred occasions. They followed her instruction and presented themselves for baptism every year at St Anthony's for more than six years and were turned away each time. Sor Maria describes the details – the people, the *pueblos,* the countryside, the conversation, the climate, the mountains, the customs, the food, of all the New World areas she had visited, to her confessors. One of these, Padre de la Torre, an Inquisitor himself, a man who believed in her integrity, advised her to cease.

He could, would, have protected her had he lived. With him by her side she would not have had to endure the fifty, sixty, seventy questions and more of Padre Inquisitor Antonio del Moral, not a Dominican, not a Jeronomite, but a Trinitarian. The *Calificador de Trinitarian* who interrogated her in the same cell where she now sits with Leonor Zurbaran knew, as she did, that the plot of the Duke of Hijar against the king was only a pretext. What the Inquisition truly wanted to determine was whether the multiple reports of the levitation and bi-location of Sor Maria de Agreda, the Lady In Blue, were the Devil's work or signs of delusion, a wilful deceit or the hand of God on a true mystic.

Events in question have taken place a quarter of a century before the *Calificador* finally questions the abbess, time enough for the seeds of a reputation to grow. Devotions and reverence for a woman whose holiness may have been based on a wilful or deluded fabrication were more dangerous. More destructive, in fact, than any correspondence with the Duke of Hijar or alleged favourable comments about him to the king. Before he set foot in the convent of Agreda, del Moral understood that Sor Maria had only been a pawn whom the duke had used to advance his favour with the king. Unwilling or unable to make his knowledge explicit in his interrogation of this known *confidante* of the king, the Inquisitor interrogates her nevertheless. The truth already known to him is that no, she was not aware of Hijar's plan to remove Don Luiz de Haro so that he could take independent control of Aragon, a power grab that would divide the country.

In del Moral's eyes, the exoneration of Sor Maria, of complicity in the Duke of Hijar's manoeuvring, did not resolve the issue. It came as no surprise to him that the king's correspondent, his most trusted spiritual adviser would not face the same burning fate as the duke and his circle. Less surprising to him were the doubts expressed by no fewer than four of his fellow *calificadores* who had interrogated the so-called mystic of Agreda. They did not share the king's confidence in the abbess' naïve kindness shown to the duke. Nor did they fall under her spell when she recounted the details of her unnatural powers. Inquisitor Antonio del Moral would make up his own mind, but would not brush aside the memorable conclusion of his brother inquisitors on the subjects that would frame the majority of his questions. In essence, his brothers found it very difficult to convince themselves that it was God's doing and not a passive or active illusion. An illusion, they concluded, given greater weight by, as del Morales recalled in their report, a 'credulity on the part of those who governed her.'

Nor did it matter to del Moral that he was visiting a woman barely propped up in a chair, carried down from the infirmary to the library by the nuns, a woman sick with fever whose treatment, bleeding with leeches, continued. The nuns place the *prie dieu* in front of Sor Maria's chair. Del Moral waits. Slowly, struggling to keep her balance, her senses dimmed, the abbess reaches out to grip the raised shelf. Her legs obey finally resting after a few seconds on the hard wooden kneeler. Del Morales can begin.

'Abbess Madre Sor Maria de Jesus, I enjoin upon you to swear an oath to God and the cross which represents his law, that you speak truthfully and completely concerning all that you know and are asked. You must swear to hold and guard secret all that transpires between us, on pain of complete excommunication in conformance with the order of our superiors.'

Sor Maria barely registered these words. Regaining her senses, she soon realises that del Moral had, like his predecessors, only a passing concern for the Duke of Hijar's plot. Of far greater significance, the claims of her miraculous appearances in the New World without leaving her convent in Agreda.

'On the first occasion of your travel to the New World did you tell your confessor on your return?'

'Yes. I did. I had just entered the religious life then. I was eighteen. I had learned to show all of my interior life to the Church and to obey.'

'What exactly did you tell him?'

'At first, before speaking to my confessor or anyone else, I was anxious about the good of those souls. Then I experienced some light and knowledge that helped me to understand that divine mercy shone on them with compassion.'

'On your way to being transported to these kingdoms', by which the Inquisitor means the lands of the native American Indians, 'did you know what places you saw along the way?'

'I could distinguish very large areas, but only briefly. Mainly, though, I realised the multitudes of people in the world and how few knew the Gospel. With this knowledge, my heart came undone. It was not the purpose to know the names of the places, but the perdition of souls.'

Not satisfied with this answer, del Moral persisted, searching for a clear explanation of the physical experience.

'Answer this,' he asks. 'When carried to those kingdoms or when you were there, did you get wet when it rained – you or your clothing – and if so, were either you or your clothes wet when you returned to the convent?' If such an empirical question in the quest for divine presence surprises the inquisitor in the asking, or the nun in the answering, neither alters their appearance.

'The light of the lord was so abundant and fertile that usually I did have some awareness of the effects of the elements. In some places it was raining. In some, only drizzling. Regarding being wet myself, if it rained, Padre, forgive me, I don't remember.'

Satisfied or not with this response, del Moral notes it and moves on to the next question on his list.

'If the Indians asked who you were, and from where, how did you respond to them?'

'I said that I brought them news from very far away and that I had come to advise them in the faith.'

'But when you were first questioned in 1635 about these appearances, you said you brought them more than news, didn't you? By your own account you carried rosaries, even a monstrance, didn't you?'

'It is true, Padre, that the missionaries I encountered were often low in spirit because they were unable even to say Mass. They had no monstrance to hold consecrated communion hosts. When I told my confessors of this, I was asked to bring a monstrance to them. But for my part, I was afraid to do that, touching the monstrance where Our Lord had been. I returned it to its place. Somehow the nuns could not see it or find it and must have thought I had taken it with me.' Sor Maria leaves del Moral in no doubt about the rosaries, however.

'On one occasion I gave the Indians some rosaries. I brought them with me and distributed them among the Indians, then I never saw the Indians again.'

The Inquisitor dutifully records this miraculous reply and moves on to a more substantial matter, namely what persuaded the Indians to convert. No other question returned the Lady In Blue to the tee-pees, the simple dwellings of the Jumanos all gathered expectantly around her, as this one. She could see again trusting, sun-wrinkled faces turned towards her, some standing, some seated, the buffalo hunters, the elders, mothers, sisters, children, too, those hardened by years of dependence on the fickle bounty of the plains, and those still learning their secrets. All fearful of the Apache, the warrior tribe that has progressively driven them farther south, away from the better farming land, further from the trading posts. No amount of pottery or wooden bows could stop them. Believers only in their capacity to adapt and survive, trusting in their ritual dances, *catzinas* they called them. Sometimes they were not passive, would not listen to her, the occasions she noted when they made a collective preference to consume the pink fruit of a small fungal cactus, peyote. Peyote, a realm of sticky pink juice that would dribble off chins, take away any other thought or threat of hunger, of the Apache or disease. When peyote had finally drained the Jumanos of delusions, they would be more receptive.

'I understand I will be doubted on what convinced them to convert because there is no-one else to verify it. Yes, I preached to them, but it was a dialogue. They asked questions. We discussed the theological virtues of faith, hope and charity which would give them the light to understand God, which would give strength and comfort, I reassured them, not to be so attached to earthly things.'

Del Moral has too many questions on his list to explore how the frail nun seated before him had related to the Jumanos the mysteries of the nature of the Holy Trinity, the miracle of Mary's immaculate conception and the redemption of all of humanity through God's only son. Nevertheless, tell him she does, pausing only briefly between wheezing breaths. Del Moral does not interrupt to ask how these nomadic plainspeople reacted to her message, so far beyond their life experience, so completely unimaginable.

The Inquisitor had become so absorbed in his effort to write down the nun's exact words that he does not notice the silence at first. She had stopped, not as he first supposed, out of fatigue. The abbess looks at him, the instruction in her eyes to put down the quill and listen. She would speak only this once to him, so listen. Del Moral's fleeting thought, before resting his quill, that Sor Maria would carry the same aura, the same fearlessness, the same conviction that she spoke the truth into the moment when the fire was lit beneath her, spurning a last opportunity to recant. His power to condemn or grant absolution, his authority as representative of the Inquisition, his decision on whether the abbess of Agreda abided in God's radiant light, in two places simultaneously, in preaching to savages, means nothing to her. He can see that.

He considers another possibility, that this woman's out of body experiences, her levitation, her visions, are as true as Saint Teresa of Avila's encounters with Christ tied to the pillar. Sor Maria's life, as starkly Franciscan, as pure in poverty, chastity and divine light as it was possible to be. The possibility, therefore, that he is in the presence of a saint, a second Teresa of Avila, a woman who knew the physical pain of sacrifice, who persisted in telling her story of what a life without darkness could be like, who offered a sight of the eternal. Light. Only light. Why would the king's most trusted spiritual counsellor lie? Look at her. She has no desire to leave this confinement. She has nothing to gain, kneeling before him gripping the *prie dieu* held up only by her will, holding on to her conviction of truth, of the light that guides her, holding on to all that she has worked for.

Or could she be imitating her mother, not a voice telling her this time to establish one more convent, but another? Convert the Indians who have never heard the Gospel. A vivid imagination all that is needed for this deception. Something to tell the king, a colourful story from a life without event, a reason for the king to prolong his fascination. Ever the question mark in the king's mind that Maria is his reign's Teresa. That's the seed this abbess is planting, sowing the seed of mystery disguised as mysticism. And yet, to disguise mysticism in this elaborate way, knowing, as she must have done, that suspicions would be aroused, belief suspended until after a thorough investigation. No, she is deluded. Deceived herself in the darkness between wakefulness and sleep. For none of the other simple souls within these walls could have filled her mind with such tales. Whatever else she may be to the king, to the memory of her parents or to the nuns here, there is no guile in this woman. Del Moral sees the evidence before him. No, she must be deluded.

'How long were you there?'

'I was never there a day and a night, nor was it necessary.'

'Then answer me this. If time passed so quickly as you have indicated, how could you tell them so much about all of our sacred faith and principal beliefs in such little time?'

'I never noticed the passage of time. If it seemed as though I was there for a longer time it also appeared as though they gave me some shelter and sustenance. And whatever hours there were they seemed to be enough.'

To Del Moral, it was an extraordinary thing to say, 'seemed to be enough'. What could possibly be 'enough' for savages? There was more to probe, but these questions could be kept for other days. For each interrogation he would make the abbess kneel, three hours in the morning, three in the afternoon. If she wouldn't tell the truth on this first day, she would on the second or third or the fourth, day after day for eleven days, allowing only for a day of rest on Sunday as the Lord would wish. Time and again, del Moral tests the impossibility of her claim, never kindly, never softly. Abbess Maria of Agreda must be left in no doubt that her whole existence in this life and the next depends on it.

'Answer under oath. At what locations and in what situations did you preach to the Indians? Tell me. How did they assemble to listen? Did they set up a pulpit for you or a prominent place where they could all gather to hear you?'

'I still cannot say whether I went there physically or not, but I can say that I did not preach from a pulpit because I am not that important a person. Nor did I summon them or try to make them join me. So, sometimes more Indians came to listen and sometimes they were fewer but, as I see it, the Lord arranged the means to suit the end he desired.'

'Yet how is it possible with people in these provinces who are said to be barbarian, that you could communicate clearly, instruct these people, and for them to comprehend your words? They are, are they not, a people who do not know how to speak, only how to grunt?'

If Sor Maria is offended by this remark she does not show it and responds as though she were describing visitors to the convent from a foreign land.

'Their way of speaking was certainly very different from what we have here. Sometimes we used external gestures. Other times, I cannot explain. Perhaps God used an angel to speak through me. It felt good to my soul despite the mystery of how it was happening, so that I never once felt anything was contrary to the faith or truth.'

'Were you occasionally missed in the time you ascended from the convent to the kingdom of the Indians?'

'I don't think I was ever missed, Padre. That would be impossible to hide among women together so closely.' She actually says this looking directly into the Inquisitor's eyes, betraying no ridicule of del Moral or the Inquisition he represents. There is nothing in her look that says, 'You declare yourselves to be acting for God's justice and judgement, but in fact you have no understanding of his ways at all.' Instead, she raises her eyebrows in mild surprise that her statement is not challenged with outrage or a laugh.

'Who remained in your place if there was no sense of your absence?' He asks in a measured tone. 'An angel possibly? Did an angel come to take your place as an abbess, to sit as you in the choir at matins, or even to be you in the middle of the night, sitting in your chair and writing in your room? If that did happen, how could the angel do so without the other nuns realising that you were different?'

'No, Padre', she says. 'Even though I myself was very engaged with what was happening, feeling completed, diverted and suspended, this all took place in my first three years as a nun, so I was not yet the abbess. Also, while sometimes it was a physical presence, the visits were sometimes intellectual, sometimes imaginative.'

For six hours on every one of the eleven days of interrogation Sor Maria, Abbess of Agreda, holds fast to the *prie dieu* and to the story of her visionary encounters with the Indians. These include witnessing battles between the tribes, and between the Indians and the colonists in Texas. Del Moral reaches the rational conclusion that she is deluded, not of sound mind. It is an extreme case of self-deception. It is not wilful, with the desire to be praised or declared saintly. Each time he reaches this conclusion, he ponders and returns to the simple fact that no-one, not a soul in her limited life of Agreda, no book, no visitor, could have related such fantastical detail. To say that she had been indoctrinated would lead to his own interrogation. What this Lady In Blue says she has done is nowhere to be found in the doctrine of the Church.

Whether the nun is deluded, deceived or indoctrinated, del Moral finds no evidence against her. From the moment at the start of his questioning when she was sick and feverish, he accepts that her intention was to make him understand and believe what was at the heart of her conviction - for the simple reason that it was what she herself believed. Not even the king could have saved her had his, del Moral's ruling, the *de facto* ruling of the Inquisition, found her guilty of ridiculing the Church. Time and again del Moral plays backs in his mind words whose source could not possibly have been the devil.

'I told the Indians that the way out of darkness is through the church and baptism in the spirit. I told them and they were eager for baptism.' And what about her life after the conversions, how had she used it, he also recalls asking her.

'After, I prayed for the removal of exterior influences, the light became stronger and brighter. Now everything is made clear to me through the light of the Lord. It guides my duties as abbess and increases my compassion for the needy. With all the poverty and hardship, I believe that priests and nuns can do much to soften the suffering in the world.'

***

At first, Leonor sits as she would in a confessional, knees together, hands joined and pointing on her lap, head bowed in reverence, but not so low that she cannot see in front of her. The minutes pass, how long she cannot tell. Several times she dares to look directly at the abbess who is still, eyes closed. Leonor thinks that she should feel honoured that this woman of God, this spiritual guide for the king, has entered into a deep contemplative state. It can only be on her behalf, a prayer, a supplication, a direct communication. For Leonor, God is to be trusted, relied upon, prayed to, touched only briefly in the sacraments. Never like this, never in His presence, never taken so wholly out of time and place. She imagines words from the abbess flowing from her lips into the ear of the Almighty.

Give me the wisdom to guide Leonor and Francisco Zurbaran, as once you guided Solomon. There is a decision for Francisco to make. You know what it is, how difficult it is for him, a decision that is of the greatest importance to your servant, the king. It is a decision that may lead the only other person in this world whom he trusts as much as me to the certainty of his eternal reward with you.

Leonor dare not interrupt the abbess' silent entreaty of which she is certain. She waits. Wait. Let the abbess find her in prayer when she opens her eyes. Prompted by this thought, Leonor eases herself out of the wooden seat and keels on the cold stone floor in front of the nun. No sooner has she done so than she feels a firm hand on her arm.

'Sit up, Leonor. Not a single one of my sisters of Agreda, nor any woman need ever kneel in front of me. I will not allow it. Now tell me what you saw on entering the monastery at Guadalupe.'

Leonor stutters. 'At first my eyes took in the glint of gold at the opposite end of the monks' chapel, an altar of gold, protected by golden pillars. In between them, framed in the wall was a painting. 'That's Saint Jerome', he said, 'but I didn't paint him. Look around you.' Stupid of me, I know, Reverend Mother, but I remember thinking that the black and white marble floor was like a giant chess board. I noticed the gold-flaked pillars evenly spaced the length of the chapel leading your eye to the grand altar, each one decorated with angelic figures entwined with green and red coloured vines.'

'Did you not see Francisco's paintings there?'

'Yes I did. Maybe it's why I remember the gold and colours on the pillars around the paintings and the altar because I wasn't prepared for what I saw. Francisco had told me that the Jeronomites had commissioned him to paint eight pictures that were to keep the spirit of Saint Jerome alive. I don't really know what I expected. Scenes from his life perhaps, or something imagined by Francisco that would please the abbot, something that would illustrate the Order's influence within the Church through the intercession of Saint Jerome. But that's not what he painted, nothing like that at all. I looked at each painting, and in each one I saw my husband repeat a message. I should only have seen what I was meant to see: monks of the Order at the moment of their encounter with God. Visions. Apparitions. Miracles. The clear evidence on display for all to see that the men who had given their lives to the Order of Saint Jerome were authentic. Such true believers that God makes his presence known to them at the most unexpected or defining moments in life and death. Each painting verifies and confirms the Order's strength and influence because, if God speaks to them directly, the Church, the king, patrons, benefactors, the people, should always enrich the Order of Saint Jerome.'

'Are you telling me this, Leonor, to show you understand why the monks would have been satisfied with Francisco's paintings?'

'My husband is not a jealous man, Reverend Mother. He doesn't envy the riches of others whether they are merchants or aristocracy. He's not like me. Francisco doesn't see beautiful clothes and jewellery and wonder what it would be like to wear them. It's not in his nature. Then again, he is hopeless with money and nowhere near as firm with the children as he ought to be.' Leonor smiles and laughs at the same time, turning away, embarrassed by her tears.

'What do you mean, Leonor? Why do you say that?'

'I'm just trying to tell you that Diego Velazquez is my husband's friend. It doesn't matter that it was thirty years ago when they were close, not to Francisco. My husband doesn't want to judge him, in spite of the man Velazquez is, or rather the path he has taken. You have to see it from Francisco's point of view. Diego Velazquez has not been a true friend to him. He has not used the good fortune of his years of royal patronage and court influence to share with peers from his youth under Pacheco. In fact, he has hardly painted at all, and when he has, it's been another portrait of the king or a painting of some old woman cooking eggs, or some other work of no consequence. I'm sorry. I didn't mean to be disrespectful to his majesty.'

'I understand', the abbess nods. 'Francisco feels let down by Velazquez, and now in this later stage of life he sees the man he thought a close friend of comparable talent, in a position of wealth and stability whilst producing art that is not – you might argue – inspired. Can I suggest to you, Leonor, that the success of Velazquez at the royal court did not exercise your husband whilst he was receiving his own accolades in Seville. It is only now when, as you tell me, that the once celebrated Francisco Zurbaran has fallen out of favour in Seville, replaced, you might say, by newer and younger painters, that he feels so aggrieved.'

'I understand, Reverend Mother, but as long as I have known Francisco he has spoken to me with great sadness about Diego Velazquez. He accepted and quietly mourned the loss of his friendship and the opportunity, as he put it, to 'inspire each other' in depicting scenes from the gospels, paintings that would meet the needs and wishes of the Church and Empire, sustaining the greatness of both. The opportunity, too, at least as Francisco saw it, to learn together in perfecting a technique they so admired in the work of the Milanese, Caravaggio; painting characters as if the sun or even the radiance of God himself shone on them, against a background of shadows and darkness.'

'But Velazquez took no notice of him?'

'No. As the years passed, Velazquez' star rose in every possible way. As long as Francisco received plaudits and commissions for his work for the Jeronomites and other Sevillian patrons, I think he could live with the ascendancy of his friend who made no effort ever to engage with him, apart from that one time for the Buen Retiro palace, never mind open doors to the court or the king.'

'And then?'

'Then, by the time I met Francisco it had become almost impossible for him to bear or utter his name. The curator, he called him. The traveller. The philanderer. Yes, word reached Francisco's sensitive ears about Velazquez' second extended trip to the Papal States, the birth of an illegitimate son there and the rumours that the boy's nursing and nannying were paid for by the Spanish ambassador. Though that irked Francisco far less than the thought of his friend, Diego, having the time, opportunity and royal seal of approval to study the paintings of Caravaggio. Francisco would still have embraced his friend from Pacheco's workshop if these trips and privileges had resulted in a full use of his talent or a sharing of insights with his peers or a new generation of young artists like Francisco's son, Juan.'

'Instead?'

'Instead, Velazquez kept to himself. Revelled, as Francisco put it, in the nickname they gave him at Escorial, *El Sevillano*. The Sevillian. The outsider. The small town man who mastered the art of court intrigue to become safer and more trusted than Olivares. *El Sevillano!* Can you not see the irony and injustice of it, Reverend Mother – the man who didn't need commissions from the Jeronomites or the Carthusians or the Franciscans or the Dominicans or any other Order anywhere near Seville to make a living.

'Francisco felt bitter about that too?'

'No.' The hurt and anger in Leonor's tear-streaked face subsides as quickly as it had arisen, giving way to a softer voice of resignation.

'He simply couldn't understand why Diego, having laid his own eyes on the genius of Caravaggio, and all of the art in Rome that has inspired faith in millions across the centuries; why Diego wouldn't then be the most productive, the most evangelical of painters in Spain. Why would he not do that? Why would he be so selfish as to waste that opportunity, to turn his back on friends like Francisco?'

'What are you saying, Leonor?'

'What Francisco found so galling, apart from the fact that Velazquez hardly painted at all, was that what he painted was so ordinary. He seemed to be experimenting or wasting his time on subjects that would not revive the faith either in the Church or the king's empire. He just painted what he saw around him. Velazquez didn't copy Caravaggio. He didn't bring the rich bounty of what he had seen or the great artists he probably met in Rome, back to Spain. As far as Francisco was concerned it was Velazquez turning his back on everything: friends, faith, the Church, the need of the people for divine inspiration in art. He cared only about suiting himself. Sorry, Reverend Mother, I am babbling again.'

'I see why you would want to take the side of your husband, Leonor. It's understandable. Of course it is, especially after your change in fortune and the fall of the Zurbaran reputation; but consider, too, that the king would not think so highly of Velazquez without reason. I am not at liberty to discuss with you what his Catholic Majesty has confided in me in his correspondence. Suffice to say that the king has been profoundly grateful for Christ On The Cross, and paintings like the Temptation of Saint Thomas Aquinas or the Coronation of the Virgin. You see. I can name paintings for the Church by your *El Sevillano*.'

'He's not my *Sevillano*, Reverend Mother' laughs Leonor, evoking the same brief response.

'Velazquez is not, as you describe, Leonor, without a care for the Church or the spiritual needs of Spain. Do not forget either that the King of Spain is anointed by God, charged with a responsibility so great it is difficult for us to comprehend. It might help to think of his burden as another divine mystery on which we need guidance and understanding. We cannot say whether or not Diego Velazquez has been sent by God himself to paint for his Divine Majesty, to counsel and protect him, to minister to him. Try to see Velazquez with the king's eyes, Leonor. Try. Ask Our Blessed Lady to help you.

Go back and talk to Francisco. Talk to him about Diego Velazquez as a modest man, a servant, whose only ambition is to do the king's bidding. See a man who can project the divine presence and strength to the people. See a man who makes the sacrifice not to paint. Yes, not to paint.

The king is not blind to his demands on Velazquez that prevent him from accepting other commissions, from painting day after day. You only see the privilege of the journeys to Rome, the luxury of beholding, even buying the art of Caravaggio, of Titian, of Raphael, of Giotto. What the king sees is how he has made Velazquez busy with the art of other men, making the collections a great treasure for Spain.'

'We see Velazquez making a great treasure for himself.'

'As I said, I cannot share what the king has confided in me; but I can say that I believe one reason he admires his court painter is that he has never been overwhelmed, never overawed, never inferior to the Caravaggios, the Titians, whoever. He has never copied them, never thought of himself as less of a painter because he has only been commissioned by one source, and not the wealthiest of patrons, princes of the Church, or even the Successor of Peter himself. What kind of man responds with Joseph's Coat Brought To Jacob or the Forge of Vulcan? You look surprised, Leonor, that I, a simple nun cloistered in Agreda, should be able to name paintings I have never seen.'

'More surprised, Reverend Mother, that you can describe a man whom you have never met with such warm feeling.'

'How do you know Velazquez has not been to visit me also? You look shocked, Leonor. You should not be. You cannot know. King Philip has his weaknesses as did his father and grandfather before him. You might even think that Philip the IV's weaknesses are even more pronounced, his judgements more questionable, self-control always a challenge.'

Leonor had not anticipated these artistic and worldly assessments from a reclusive nun, a mystic following in the footsteps of Saint Teresa of Avila.

'In spite of his weaknesses, he came to a woman for counsel. I will tell you what this has to do with Velazquez in one moment.

Consider first that from the age of sixteen when he became king, Philip relied almost completely on one man, the Count Duke of Olivares. What did Philip know as a boy? Latin. His prayers. The company of friars. His devout, distant and fragile father dressed in black, always black. The dominance of the Duke of Lerma over him. When the time came to be king, Philip's experience told him that the king's role was to sanction the decisions of his most trusted adviser. Olivares became Philip IV's Lerma for twenty years. Olivares was everything the king was not. Take the lead at home and in war, or be led, Olivares advised him. Conquer or be conquered. Make decisions. Except that all of the decisions requiring the king's signature had first been made by Olivares and given to Philip to approve. The king did not so much know his mind as know Olivares' mind. He did not complain. It was the way he wanted it to be.

As a young monarch, Philip commanded Olivares, or vice versa, to meet three times a day, morning, noon and night. Policy. Appointments at court. War. Always war. Decide now. Sign here, Your Majesty. See the politics in every situation.

'I am not sure that I understand what you are saying', says Leonor.

'Olivares would not allow the king to meet ordinary people outside of court, Leonor. Politically, such a concession would have been regarded as a weakness, the king, coming down to their level. So, they saw to it that the king, a tender, kind man, would never feel their pain or hear their needs. Only Olivares, other nobles acting as political advisers, – approved by Olivares, of course

– court acolytes, and his Confessor could speak to him.'

'And his court painter?'

'Yes, Leonor. That is my point. Diego Velazquez has been the king's painter, his curator, his non-political adviser, his friend for thirty-five years. He has outlasted Olivares. He has outlived wives, survived wars. Think of the countless hours they have spent together uninterrupted, the artist behind his canvas, King Philip in one more regal pose. Imagine where their conversations might have led. The beginnings in Pacheco's workshop. The bonds that Velazquez established there, friendships and rivalries with your husband, Alonso Cano; the falling in love with Pacheco's daughter, Juana, and the joy of two daughters, Ignacia and Francisca, both still infants when Velazquez arrived at Escorial.' Sor Maria pauses, as if allowing time for parental understanding to awaken in her guest, though the apology of the man about whom her confessional correspondent had written many times is not over.

'I am sure you can imagine,' she continues, 'the scene of the Court Painter having to tell his king about the deaths of these same two, one as a child, the other a young woman. Then think of their conversations about Philip's appetite for collecting art, the vision he had of adorning his Hall of mirrors with antique sculpture and the Venetian masters; or of his desire to learn more about the people who live in his empire, for he has only known soldiers and nobles and royalty and prelates.

Can you not see, Leonor. It took Philip twelve, fifteen years or more after he ascended the throne to know his own mind, to wean himself off Olivares. In time, he realised that Diego Velazquez was a better representative of his empire than any other adviser. With his Court Painter he could have real conversations about what interested him: philosophy, poetry, history, architecture, language, mathematics and, of course, the lives of Spaniards beyond the walls of the royal palaces.'

As she concludes her defence, the abbess observes that Leonor's head is bowed, seemingly as disconsolate and defeated as before. Sor Maria's indirect sharing of content from letters she has received over many years is still too much a betrayal of confidences and feelings, too candid for her guest. She lets the silence fill the library once more. When Leonor volunteers no comment, she changes the subject.

'It was fifteen years ago when I actually met the king. He was en route to the Aragon frontier to see his army and decided that he wanted to meet me here in Agreda, in this convent, in this library. Imagine that, Leonor. By that time he had rid himself of Olivares. I am told that peasants, nobles, friars, children – as one Spanish people they lined the route waiting for him to pass. And for His Divine Majesty to be accompanied by a retinue of dozens and not hundreds from the royal court, was unheard of.'

'What did he say to you?' says Leonor, looking up again.

'I cannot tell you directly, Leonor, but the coup to remove Olivares, if that's what it was, had only just happened. By that time his majesty had been married to Elisabeth of France for more than twenty-five years. You will know that they married as children, the king just ten years old, Elisabeth thirteen. Only one son from seven children, a fragile boy, not as bold or as robust as Velazquez would have had us believe, I'm afraid.

'The young prince died only three years after he visited you in Agreda. He must have had some idea when he was here that Balthasar would not live as his heir even if he survived to manhood,' Leonor surmises. 'When he met you in this library he knew his son was unlikely to become the man with whom he could share the burdens of empire in his declining years. I would think he understood, too, that even if he were to have another son - however that might happen - the boy would still be too young to grasp affairs of State or the mind of his father. It would be too late in the king's life to create a meaningful bond that would comfort and console him.'

Warming to the belief that she is now solving the mystery of the king's attitude to Velazquez and how that might provide a guide for her husband's decision, Leonor's logic tumbles out as if fearing her deductive powers will be lost if she does not give them a voice.

'By the time the king stopped in Agreda he was then, in his own mind at least, in a desperate position. The decision-making credibility of his reign depended on one man. That man, Olivares, ultimately alienated the rest of the Court and distanced Philip from other possibly more level-headed advisers. Philip well understood his dependency on Olivares. But, rather than assert his authority, rather than confrontation, he turned to Velazquez, his personal flatterer and most trusted adviser in what mattered to him most, the enduring glory of the Spanish empire and his legacy. Its art, its treasures, its magnificence, not merely maintained at El Escorial, at Buen Retiro, but enhanced, enriched. What was it his grandfather had called it: 'a new Jerusalem'? Philip II never had a Velazquez though, did he? His grandson does and he has been willing to overlook the arrogance, the Roman indulgences. He could even enjoy and talk to his travelling curator about the unthinkable.'

Leonor looks into the abbess' eyes, judging whether the nun had anticipated the unthinkable. She has. Leonor continues.

'Velazquez, as the man whose life rests on the favour of his divine majesty, brings to his patron paintings that would have caused Philip II to have him exiled or worse. Yes, he brings back the mythical and religious masterpieces of Titian and Reubens and the like, but the subjects of more and more of his paintings are just people. Not saints. Not martyrs. Not apostles. Not the Virgin. People. Plain. Ordinary. Living as far outside the new Jerusalem as it's possible to be, and your king accepted them.'

'My king?'

'Your king,' Leonor repeats, 'who turned to you fifteen years ago, presumably to save his own soul. He wanted, no, he needed, to restore the balance in his spiritual account. He was worried about how God would judge him. Philip could not stop a war. He had no power over Elisabeth or his nobles who had conspired to remove Olivares. He had his collections, his new Jerusalem, his Velazquez, but at what cost to his soul?' As quickly as she had spoken, Leonor sits bolt upright, hand over her mouth, her eyes stretched wide in horror as if a ghost had joined them and stood behind the nun.

'Reverend Mother. I'm sorry. Forgive me.'

'Leonor, I am not angry with you. It is understandable that his Catholic Majesty's actions, then as now, should be the subject of ... interpretation. It is widely known he has not followed his grandfather's declaration that all art was to be a call to prayer and devotion. *El Sevillano* was never going to suffer the fate of *El Greco* and be banished from El Escorial. Some might say that it is Philip IV's weakness in allowing the art of ordinary everyday life that is damaging our faith and therefore our confidence in who we are. Others point to infidelities. The second marriage to his niece and the joy of five children notwithstanding, I do not shock you by speaking of what is widely known: the king continues to indulge himself. These aberrations, Leonor, do not make any remorse or search for forgiveness any less sincere. Remember that. Nor do they blunt the joy of a new-born son and heir a year ago. Pray to Our Lord and His Holy Mother, the king writes to me, to keep him for their service, for the exaltation of faith and the good of these realms. He is still a father who believes in prayer and intercession for the protection of his son.'

Whether it is age or the depths of her own thoughts and feelings, so rarely if ever expressed to another woman, Leonor listens. Sor Maria is, she is certain, still mindful of her presence, but no longer looking at her, staring at a place only she can see. To Leonor's perception, the nun is speaking to herself now, repeating previous thoughts and prayers.

'He is a peacemaker, prepared to compromise and find a way to end the war with France. What other monarch or emperor would ask a cloistered nun to correspond with a French court intermediary such as the Duke of Gramont. This is the man who could have been sent to us by God, trusted by King Louis and His Eminence, Cardinal Mazarin. Time will tell whether he is indeed a channel of peace. We cannot know the mind of God or his plan for each of us. It is entirely possible that the endeavours of the Duke of Gramont, our emissary Don Luis de Haro and even my own efforts in a small way, will result in peace through marriage, a Spanish king's daughter, the next queen of France.

We cannot know why God's will was for me to become a nun, for you to become a devoted wife and mother, and more, a woman who thrives in commerce, though I cannot profess to understand why that is necessary. While I am behind these walls, every day writing, praying, for understanding of Our Lady's Immaculate Conception and why he chose Mary to be the mother of his son, you are managing your household, nursing and educating your children, loving your husband. Surely more is not needed for a woman, and if we cannot know the mind of God, Leonor, still less can we know the mind of Diego Velazquez or Francisco Zurbaran or Michelangelo Merisi da Caravaggio.'

'Reverend Mother, do we not know a man – or these three men – by their actions, whatever their gifts as artists? We know that Caravaggio committed murder, lived a life of debauchery and died a wretch. The evidence of Velazquez' choices is clear: a life of self-interest and comfort with no regard for his friends, no consideration of anything other than how he might please his royal patron and protector, and his few paintings reflecting back to us what we can already see in our streets and homes. It is all too clear to see that he is a man obsessed by his own standing. No longer is it enough for him to have outlasted and out-thought Philip's advisers and family. Now he seeks to guarantee his eternal reward through the Order of Santiago. He has made a life of wealth, Reverend Mother, of privilege, of selfishness. He has lived this life in the shadows, showing himself only when his advantage, not the king's, not for the faith of the Spanish, not the endurance of the empire, shone in the brightest light.'

Leonor's accusations rise and rise and fill the dry book-scented air of the library. Sor Maria lets in the silence a second time, allowing Leonor's anger to subside. In each wordless moment the bitterness escapes through the gaps in the shutters, underneath the wooden door, into the cracks of the stone floor. Adopting the calm, quietly authoritative tone necessary for the nuns of the convent of Agreda whose weaknesses and transgressions have been brought before her, the abbess leans forward and takes the wedding ring hand in her own.

'It is possible, Leonor, that Caravaggio repented alone and before God as he faced death. It is also possible, though I cannot say openly, that his majesty and his court painter of over thirty-five years have an understanding. You will be aware that two years ago Velazquez painted for the king a 'Portrait of the Family'. Being here, I have not seen it, obviously, but I know its purpose. In the painting I understand that the king and queen are seen looking down upon the Princess Margarita Maria attended by her maids of honour. There is a dog, a dwarf, and the king and queen again reflected in the mirror.'

'I have seen the painting.'

'You will know, then, that Velazquez himself makes an appearance, working at a canvas that is hidden from our view. He stands in his plain black tunic looking past the painting on his easel directly at us. The whole Portrait of the Family is an illusion. The mirror makes it so. That gathering could not have taken place. Those people were not all alive two years ago.' The abbess pauses, looking straight into Leonor's eyes to be certain she has grasped their significance.

'And which court painter of his own volition,' she resumes, speaking more slowly and softly than before, 'would or could include himself in a painting with the king and his successor, the Infanta, for his son was not then born.

'Reverend Mother, forgive me. I know I said too much in anger, but I do not understand why you are telling me this or what it has to do with Francisco and the decision he must make.'

'Tell me first, Leonor, about Francisco's paintings for the Jeronomites. You said there was a clear message in these paintings of the monks and their encounters with the divine.'

Leonor, feeling instinctively that her audience is coming to an end, withdraws her hand, responds precisely and clearly, controlling her emotion, speaking with her normal composure and confidence. Both had abandoned her when she was led into the library, into the presence of the king of Spain's friend and spiritual counsellor, this bi-locating, levitating nun who had stared down the Inquisition, whose frailty deceived.

'I see now why it is impossible for my husband to testify that Velazquez is descended from nobility. It will be a betrayal of what he believes to be true. He will see his boyhood friend who has made one of only two possible choices.'

'Which is?'

'Francisco's belief, repeated eight times on the walls of the chapel at Guadalupe, is that you are either in God's light or you are in darkness. You have free will, but God will judge you on your choice. His paintings show what it is to choose the light. You serve your own interests or you make choices that place you in God's light. We struggle and make mistakes, but we are given many chances in life to choose what matters. That is his message, Reverend Mother. And Velazquez' Portrait of the Family?'

This time the abbess takes both of Leonor's hands in her own, clasping together like children about to make a promise together.

'It is not finished,' she says.

Chapter 2

THE REVELATION

Alonso Cano knows what he wants. That much at least is clear. Velazquez will reward him for his testimony.

'Yes, of course my good friend Diego is of noble blood. We talked about it many times. I remember one occasion when Señor De Silva actually sat down with Diego and myself. He drew his family tree before our very eyes. He spoke of his pride at Diego's continuation of his noble line.'

'Do you have evidence of this?' the investigators will ask. 'Can you show us where it is written down? When you were in the Velazquez family home did you ever see seals or certificates confirming this claim to nobility?'

'No, they must have been lost during the plague.'

Or maybe Alonso would claim they were lost in the flood of Seville, or in a fire; something equally false but plausible enough to be believed. All that matters to him is the patronage of the Palace Chamberlain, Curator, Court Painter, Gentleman of the Bedchamber, or is it the Wardrobe, whatever title the king gives Velazquez now. Alonso was always someone who would go to any length to get what he wanted. I'll say that for him. He would never have allowed himself to be cast aside so easily by the city elders of Seville, as I was. What would Alonso have done? He's too smart to make idle threats. I've seen the aggressive behaviour, his explosions of temper, but I don't doubt he would control it when commissions and reputation were at stake. He is too calculating for that, too devious. Yes, devious, that's the word. Alonso would have sought out the abbots and bishops most likely to defend him, to plead his case. Promised them something, made some trade, or would he have found weaknesses in the city's elders? Failings? Embarrassments, behaviour unbecoming of an elder, whose reputation rested on good judgement, loyalty to the Church, fingers out of the city's coffers?

That's more like Alonso. He would have found a way to become irreplaceable. Not bumbling on his way out of the city gates about the honour it has been to serve, the meek acceptance of rejection, a life's work so quickly overturned. Could they not have found a way to honour my years, decades of service, and not turn their back on me for Esteban Murillo and his like? The elders could have put in a good word for me with the Franciscans, the Benedictines, even the Jeronomites. They know who I am, what I can do.

Six months in Madrid and I have achieved nothing. Is there a conspiracy against me? First, the conspirators drive me out of Seville. The archdeacon at the cathedral, Dom Juan Federigui, is one of their number. He has to be: commissioning Murillo instead of me for the sacristy paintings; making sure I would learn of his remark that Murillo's Saint Isodore and Saint Leander that adorn the sacristy were 'by the hand of the best painter in Seville.'

Zurbaran doesn't change his style, they say. He hasn't adapted. We have moved on. It's not a question of divine authority any more. People want to see more than God's light. They don't care so much about one person's salvation or the ecstasy of their vision. Painters like Murillo will adapt. Velazquez understood decades ago, before the uneducated of Spain, the illiterate, knew themselves, that they would be happy to see art of the lives they lived, selling, trading, at home in the kitchen.

Velazquez remembers his friends. That's what they say. *El Sevillano* gave Zurbaran his chance, but Zurbaran wanted to go back to Seville. The monasteries and the city elders there were happy to have more of the same, the art of conversion, of cherubim and seraphim, of coronations of the saints and the Queen of Heaven. Live in God's light or live in darkness.

Zurbaran believed it too, didn't he? Thought it was the only way to live, the only way to paint. Men like Cano know better, Velazquez tells him. Diego understands the pain of Alonso on the death of his first wife. He, too, can absolve him, as the court did, of the murder in bed of his second wife of thirteen years, Maria Magdalena de Uceda, his twelve-year-old bride. As for the death of the artist Sebastian Llanos y Valdes, well, dear Alonso, in every duel both men know the risk. He can be so convincing, Diego. Quietly persuasive. These are good reasons, he would have said, to leave Seville and begin a new life, first in Madrid, then Granada.

'These are life's mistakes, lessons to be learned, Alonso. And any man, especially a sculptor and painter can build up debts. So there is no reason either to be ashamed of the time you spent in the debtors' prison of Seville.'

It shows how strong Cano is, that he can keep going after such calamities. How hard it must have been for him to adapt after each tragedy, to face himself in the mirror, to struggle every day with the rage within him, and knowing that his gentle father, Miguel, dedicated his life to the art of making altarpieces.

What else did Velazquez say to Cano when he acted as a witness for the sale of his house in Seville? That his sins were forgiven? That Diego was in awe of an angry man who embraced change, who denied his temper long enough to produce such works of beauty and tenderness.

'Come to Madrid. The king's first minister, Olivares, has need of an *Ayudante de Cámara*. Introductions can be made.'

One word from Velazquez will be enough. I can hear him advising Cano on his arrival. No, wait. It would have been stronger than that. Diego's own reputation was at stake. He couldn't afford for Cano to be talked about in court, a hothead, a gambler, in and out of whoever's bed he pleases.

'Alonso, flatter Olivares. Bend to his will. Carry out his wishes. Forget your opinions. Paint and sculpt as you are asked. Show how well you can adapt to life at court. Don't be like Zurbaran.'

Would Diego have said that about me? Of course, he must have. It's why he turned to Cano and not to me. It couldn't have been anything else. Diego wouldn't have worried about either of us outshining him. But did he dislike me so much, or look down on my style of painting, that he would help to promote Cano instead? Why, Diego? You knew how wild and unreliable Cano was then. You thought that I was so blind, is that it? So indoctrinated in the teaching of the Church, so bound to the sacred mysteries, that I could not change; that I accepted the catechism without question, took it into my art, painting what I could not see or understand, but still held to be true?

You wanted someone in Court who cared far less about individual salvation or God's light or the mystery of the

Immaculate Conception. It mattered more to you to have an artist alongside you whose quality of work you could trust, yes, but who wasn't so . . So dogmatic, so absolutely certain of the saints, of the resurrection of the body, so clear in his mind that Christians, Spaniards would be guaranteed that reward only by remaining completely in his light, no matter what plague or flood or poverty or death they have to endure.

'Don't be like Francisco. You have to be able to adapt, not so focused on one style, one belief. Zurbaran is not nearly as versatile as you. He is not the one who broke with Sevillian tradition to design wooden sculptures and altarpieces of the Virgin and Child. You create without fear, Alonso, without restraint. That is your strength. Your paintings of Saint James and Saint John have such bright and delicate colours. They prove you can be as radical in your painting as your altar designs or sculptures. You are nothing like Francisco who is best suited to commissions from monasteries. They only wish to see the sanctity of their founders or predecessors or patrons. Who knows what Olivares or even the king will ask you to do: some vanity project or family portrait most likely, and most certainly more biblical paintings if only to keep the Church and her princes happy.

Believe me when I tell you, Alonso, that there is only political reality. The king knows it. His ministers know it. There is no mystery in the lives of people you see in the street, at Mass, in the market squares. Having enough food to eat, avoiding the plague, keeping sons from going to war, celebrating feast days so they can drink more and forget their problems – that is what they care about. The only mystery that matters to them, the one they can never speak of, is how they can work so hard and have so little; how they can have allowed themselves to be, first, so indoctrinated, and second, so deceived, to be as meek as lambs, day after day. Their only hope is that their sacrifice, their submission to Church and King will bring them eternal reward. That is why they can face life as it comes, not as it appears in some artist's vision of the angels and saints and the Immaculate Conception.'

I can hear you, Diego. I know why Alonso was your choice. You made assumptions about me. You made assumptions about the ordinary people you were painting. If only it were so simple, Diego, to say that the water seller in the street, the old woman cooking eggs in her kitchen, the buffoons, have no mind of their own. To think of them as good people who have their failings, but are capable of such acts of love and kindness in short lives.

If only it were so easy, Diego, to separate out lives of hundreds, thousands, even millions of people like them who lived before, who live now and the many yet to be born. To separate them, put them in one big sheepfold if you like, Diego, and say 'These people are deluded, deceived and have had dogma drummed so far into them, that they have believed in God without question, his prophets, saints, angels, judgement, the resurrection of the body or descent into hell. Fools to be so easily led. Fools to believe the art of Caravaggio or Velazquez or Zurbaran, that God's intervention shows them the way, the truth and the life to come. Fools to let the fear be sown in them about their fate in darkness and damnation if they fail to follow.

Set apart from these mindless sheep are rational thinkers – isn't that right, Diego? – who question what they are expected to believe, who tell themselves that they know better. It suits their purpose. Some cannot help making the challenge to the authority of Church and King. It marks them out, makes progress in this world at least, so difficult. And what do Church and King do? Treat them like lepers.

Keep them away, burn them if necessary, lest they think they can or have the right to open the gate to the sheepfold, because then there would be infection and chaos. Other rational thinkers, or schemers, choose to wait in the shadows. They are not stupid enough to betray the weakness of faith. They think they are enlightened, ahead of their time, not constrained by the convention of the day, free. They rely on their own intelligence, not prayer, not dogma, not royal decree, not papal bull. They nod politely to those they see as trying to delude or deceive them, and appear to be in agreement. Except that they are not. They take their own path, relying on conclusions taken on the evidence of life before them.

Do you think, Diego, I am going to brand you as one of these, that I have caught glimpses of you through the wooden posts of my crowded enclosure? I can make my confession to you. Let me tell you how jealous I am of your exalted position, your command and control of a king whose gift in this life is exceeded only by that of the pope. I am angry about the freedom he has given you to make any exploration, any purchase you choose of the riches of art in Rome or Venice or Lombardy. You have learned how to achieve your own ends, and made your undoubted talent work to your advantage. You did not let canon law or court gossip or royal whims get in your way. Always bending to Philip's and God's will, as you liked to show, you forged your own path and did exactly what you wanted.

I watched you from a distance, Diego. Word spread about your travels, your titles. No-one needed to tell me about your talent. I knew that already. I waited for you to recognise mine, but you decided I wasn't a free thinker like you. You convinced yourself that I could never think for myself, never take a risk. I wouldn't change how I painted. I didn't have it in me. Alonso Cano was different, wasn't he? You were two sides of the same coin, and whoever heard of a coin with three sides. You abandoned me.

There! I've said it. I have confessed. It's still not that simple, Diego, to think of me trapped in the sheepfold while you roamed freely, making up your own rules. You still think of me as bound by a code of commandments. Thou shalt not think for thyself. Thou shalt live in fear of judgement. Thou shalt obey without question the magisterium of thy Church, the wisdom of thy king. Thou shalt not change. Thou shalt not laugh.

Why has it taken you so long, Diego, to understand that you are not superior? You thought all you had to do was to cut yourself off from people like me. You could put up with the courtiers and the cardinals and the king himself whilst they had power over you. The king's painter, once certain of the protection of his unassailable patron could make his own choices. Select a few, those he judged to be less deluded, more versatile, the Alonso Canos. Separate himself from the many. The confidence of the king was all he needed. Forget Zurbaran. El Sevillano. That's you, Diego. The unknowable man from Seville who couldn't care less about the people there. You wanted to paint what you could see in life around you and yet you wanted no part of it, Señor Gentleman of the Bedchamber, Master of the Wardrobe, whoever you are these days.

See, Diego. Life is not that simple. You cannot separate yourself from me or other witnesses from the sheepfold. The many, the deluded, the deceived, the indoctrinated, the sheep you have judged and forgotten, the Zurbarans you did not need or want, can teach you a lesson in humility. It is you, Diego, who are deluded if you believe we will bear witness to your nobility. We are not kings handing out titles on a whim without a thought for merit or truth.

* * *

Don Fernando tilts his head. Not for the first time he tries to take in the accomplishment of the cathedral's builders. Even in this upper room, administrative and functional in its nature, hidden from worshippers, the stone pillars sprout from the floor to join high above his head in a flowering of arches and decorated columns. His thick-fingered hands resting on his ample stomach, he stands up and, still gazing upwards, walks through the open door. From his vantage point on the wide triforium, Don Fernando observes the full majesty of the vaulted garden, the River Mino below, and beyond it the green fields of Portugal.

The Vikings had eventually been sent back down the Mino whence they came. It had only been after the Moors were repelled that these hardy Galicians resolved to state, in stone, their unshakeable belief in God's protection. Turning his back on the landscape, the investigator appointed by the Order of Santiago contemplates the lives lost in constructing this fortress cathedral of Tuy. Masonry is falling, limbs crushed, Masses celebrated in the open air, indulgences pledged for the workers whose lives have been shortened by this labour. His scan of the vaulted arches, columns and aisles completed, though promoted more by his disturbing train of thought, he steps back through the doorway. Don Diego does not look up.

'Still looking for a way to deal with the king's gambit?' Don Fernando asks.

'I think you always have to consider more than the first few moves. Always think ahead. Look at the bigger

169

picture. Take everything that's happening into account. That is the mark of a great chess player.'

Don Fernando sits down facing his opponent. 'It is a curious fact', he says, 'that the greatest player of all time would frequently deploy an opening other than his own.'

'You wouldn't just be saying that because Ruy Lopez was a Spanish priest and bishop or because Philip II made a gift to him of a gold rook, by any chance,' Don Diego grins.

'No. You are forgetting, Señor Adovcate, that in one of the first books about chess Ruy Lopez described his own opening in detail. A hundred years ago he was also unquestionably the greatest player in the world, too strong for Da Cutri – another lawyer, I might add – and Paolo Boi.'

'Only to be beaten by both, if my poor lawyer's memory serves me correctly, in the first ever major chess tournament the following decade. And who organised that, my friend?'

Don Fernando, looking at his feet, or at least where he assumes them to be, as his gaze could not penetrate his waist, mumbles a response.

'Sorry. I didn't catch that. Can you repeat please.'

'Oh, I see we're back in full court cross-examination mode now,' says Don Fernando.

'No need to shout, there is no jury to hear you.'

'I was not shouting, Don Diego, merely making an observation.'

'Loudly, in an attempt to put me off, I don't doubt.'

'At least we can be certain now that you have fully recovered from your illness. You seemed to be wasting away. I doubted whether we would be able to make this trip and carry out these interviews. If the Lord had allowed it, I would gladly have given you some of my girth.'

'I see, Don Fernando. One moment, an outburst, then

a kind remark – you are a wily opponent indeed.'

'If you still want me to repeat what I said, it was King Philip II who invited the top four players for the tournament at El Escorial as you well know.'

For the three weeks prior to this exchange the two investigators had formed a workable sparring relationship. To any casual observer of their verbal bouts, Don Fernando was the po-faced, self-righteous, holier-than-thou rotund didact, accustomed to his own magisterium remaining unchallenged, his authority at once endowed and authenticated by his status as a Knight of the Order of Santiago. By definition, he stood ready to pass to eternal life when the Almighty summoned him through the approved portal of the Order, approved and anointed as it was by the Successor of Peter and the divinely chosen head of the holy Spanish Empire.

Successive days of short, long, long, short, interviews with a wide spectrum of peasantry and military, some barely coherent, most with a mantra drilled into them by other unknowns.

'Velazquez? Of noble birth, you ask. Of that I am certain. No, I cannot provide details of his actual lineage, but I have no doubt that he is descended from nobility.'

All God's people, Don Fernando tries to tell himself, though this charade among such a poorly educated unsophisticated mass feels like a penance to him, a noble sacrifice even. He smiles at the thought.

'Ruy Lopez's defeat amuses you, Don Fernando?'

'I was thinking about the saints who played chess actually,' he lies, as easily as he recites dogma.

'There is something funny about the saints who played chess?'

'There is a story about Saint Carlo Borromeo of Milan,' Don Fernando's command of facts extends to anecdotes.

'He was playing chess with friends when one of the group addressed this question to the others in turn, 'What would you do if you were told you are about to die and that God is ready to judge you right now?' I would start praying, said one. Go to confession, said another. Find the nearest church, said a third, and prostrate myself before the Blessed Sacrament in the tabernacle.' '

'And what about Carlo Borromeo?' the lawyer asks.

'Well, as you might imagine, the friends all turned to him to hear his answer. 'I would continue with my game of chess,' he said, 'because I started this game of chess for the glory of God. For that simple reason I should continue.' You never thought of chess as a holy pursuit did you, my learned friend?'

'If you wish to beat me you should turn your mind to *Il Calabrese* rather than your sanctimonious Milanese.'

'I will ignore your slur of one of the saints in heaven. You are not seriously suggesting that we have more to learn from Gioacchino Greco, or *Il Calabrese* as they and you call him, than Lopez,' Don Fernando counters.

He can be relied upon – Don Diego knows so well – to take the bait, confident as Don Fernando always was, that he could win any contest of knowledge. The fact that he had now introduced a theological dimension to their regular games of chess before interviews, broke the monotony of their predictable board strategy and exchange of pieces.

'It was thirty years or so ago,' says Don Diego, warming to the topic, 'that *Il Calabrese* made and gave copies of his chess tactics to wealthy patrons including the late Cardinal Savelli, if I'm not mistaken.' Don Diego likes to deploy his lawyer's trick of false humility at the end of each statement where possible, to give the impression that what he asserts is the truth. 'I would suggest, when that cardinal was playing chess it was not for the glory of God. There is a case for saying that *Il Calabrese* is the greatest chess player there ever has been, beating, as he did, the supposedly invincible Don Mariano Morano here in Spain at El Escorial. He became famous for his own gambit and I have heard his manuscripts of chess tactics and matches have now been published.

What's more, you will be pleased to hear, my friend, that he left all of the money he won from chess to the Jesuits, presumably to help them become better chess players, and all *Ad Maiorem Dei Gloriam,* of course.'

Don Fernando rests his forefinger on the king-side bishop before sliding it through the bank of pawns to the centre files. 'It is never a good idea to mock the Jesuits,' he says. 'Even in jest.' Slowly he lifts his forefinger from the bishop and his head at the same time to look into the eyes of his opponent. 'Saint Aloysius Gonzaga played chess as did two of the three great Sant Francises.'

'Let me guess,' quips Don Diego, not put off by the change in tone. 'Francis Xavier and Francis de Sales, but not Francis of Assisi, not all Jesuits, however.'

'Correct and correct. Need I add that our country and empire's divine inspiration, Teresa of Avila, is the patron saint of all chess players.'

'For goodness sake, my dear Don F. Saintly though Teresa undoubtedly is, she was hardly the chess champion of the Carmelites. Is chess not forbidden in the monasteries anyway? And I thought she made only one fleeting reference to chess advocating the sisters to – what was it? Ah yes, to checkmate the Lord, the phrase she used, correct me if I am wrong.'

'Quite so. She refers to chess in her work, 'The Way of Perfection'. She was not a chess player, as you say, and it is true she regarded chess as an earthly pursuit. But – and this is the point – she drew an analogy for the Carmelite sisters between study and preparation required to win at chess, and the need to excel in prayer and devotion. In short, if you cannot resist playing chess, use its method to strengthen your spiritual life.'

Having delivered what he considered to be the final word on the subject, and therefore the most satisfying outcome of the battle of wits, Don Fernando turns his attention to another move. How predictable, he thinks. The threat to bishop leads to an exchange with the black knight. A sacrifice, a sign of weakness, as it would seem to his less worthy opponent. The lawyer would not see that the dominance of black pawns in the middle files was an illusion of strength. However clever the advocate thought he was, it would be Don Fernando's Ruy Lopez strategy that would bring victory.

From Don Fernando's perspective, the steady stream of interviewees throughout the day are, in their own way, as deluded as his chess opponent. The look on every face entering the upper room of Tuy Cathedral said 'I am here to tell you what you wish to hear. You will believe it is true and I have not given a second's thought to any evidence that can prove it.' Some witnesses had been summoned for no good reason. They knew nothing about Velazquez or his family at all, selected by virtue of their geographical correctness alone.

Only one interviewee that day offers anything of substance: Juan Feixo de Naboa, a second lieutenant in the Spanish infantry. To the investigators he conveys the feeling of a man whose past experience of the battlefield consumes his whole being in the present. Whatever bright, eager, tall and proud young man he may once have been, the two men opposite can only imagine. The lieutenant glances anxiously towards the chess board on the stone ledge at the far end of the room.

'You keep looking over at the chess board, lieutenant. Does it bother you?' Don Diego asks.

Speaking to his tightly folded arms the lieutenant mumbles something about his men always playing the night before going into battle as a way to take their minds off what the next day would bring. In the long twenty minutes of the interview other responses are barely audible. Only once are the distant brown eyes raised to meet theirs. He had been garrisoned in Porto, the brown eyes whisper.

'When? What happened there?'

'It must have been about twenty years ago. In Porto, I mean. For months we were part of the town, buying food, walking through the streets day and night, drinking at the inns. You get to know people. They start to trust you. Accept who you are. Not what you represent.'

'So what did you learn from the people you met in Porto who started to trust you, lieutenant?'

'Not that much, just – '

'Go on.'

'They talked about artists, you know, the famous ones. In Porto, just as in any part of Spain, you know, the name of Velazquez was mentioned.'

Before Don Fernando's Hurry Up arm to the lieutenant can find voice, Don Diego simply nods. Continue,' he says.

'That's it. People I met in Porto talked about Velazquez with pride because his grandparents were from Portugal, you know. That's what they said. Velazquez, yes, I'm sure – descended from a noble family, they said. If there's one phrase they used it was "pure blood".'

Suddenly, the bald investigator is on his feet, knocking his wooden chair to the floor, shouting.

'They? People? That's it? Who, lieutenant? Who? Do you not realise how important this detail is? We cannot return to Madrid with vague statements about who said what to whom with no motivation other than idle gossip.'

Like a priest giving thanks before consecration, Juan Feixo de Noboa, shows the irate Don Fernando his open palms. It is all he has to offer. Don Diego gestures to the door. 'Thank you, lieutenant. You may leave now.'

Having turned away in exasperation Don Fernando strides over to the chess board pretending to plan his next move. Touched by the ghost of the handsome, patriotic young man before him, the advocate stands and escorts the soldier to the door. The lieutenant stares, uncomprehending. 'What does it matter anyway? We are still at war with Portugal. Soldiers and ordinary people are dying in the fighting.' Without waiting for a response the witness takes a first step on the spiral staircase and disappears from view.

Sixteen interviewees, three king's gambits, two days and a Ruy Lopez later, the moves of the investigators appointed by the noble and holy Order of Santiago are more predictable. Variations to dominate the centre, bold strikes to eliminate a bishop less frequent, knights readily sacrificed, pauses of a hovering finger over the piece chosen to checkmate the king, all but a memory. Each player had tired of outwitting the other, battle and banter substituted by unspoken, invisible bonds that chained them to this time and place. Prisoners of duty completing a thankless task, interview after interview barely illuminated by coherence, the darkness of ignorance prevailing in all but a few cases.

'We have to accept that there is no substantial evidence of Velazquez's nobility,' says Don Diego, advancing his queenside pawn.

'There are still a few left to interview,' sighs Don Fernando. 'We cannot leave Tuy until they are completed even if it means more pointless exchanges.'

'Do you think we could suggest this as a form of torture

for Portuguese prisoners of war?'

'Watching us play chess?'

'No, though you do insist on pointless exchanges there too.'

'We could replace beatings with interviews. Place in front of each captured prisoner of importance a mindless individual with nothing of substance to say. Bring in a succession of such interviewees and by the end of the day we would know everything, troop movements, cavalry numbers, battle plans. We could end the war in a matter of days.

'Or', Don Diego lifts the advancing queen's pawn and puts his knight on the square it occupied. 'To save time and energy of organising so many interviewees we could simply use you for the most important prisoners. Each would have to listen to your theories of chess. Perhaps you could start each interview with your monologue of yesterday. You remember. The one that started with Pedro Damiano, the Portuguese pharmacist who believed chess was invented by the Persian ruler, Xerxes, and that from his name comes the Portuguese word for chess, *xadrez*. If the prisoner showed no sign of confessing, your next move – if you will pardon the expression – could be to elaborate on Damiano's theories of Giuoco Piano and the Queen's Gambit Accepted.'

'So you were listening.'

'Like a captive, I had no choice. You could be the empire's secret weapon', says Don Diego, waving his finger in the face of his opponent. 'Yes, you are the new *conquistador*, able to overwhelm any of the empire's enemies with the irresistible force of putting them to sleep first. Captain, what do you think?'

The tall, thin angular man in uniform whose soft steps on the spiral staircase had not been heard by Don

Fernando, stoops in the doorway. He is speechless, succeeding only in appearing bewildered, visibly angry with himself for being caught off guard so easily.

'Well, do you think chess theory can teach us anything about defeating the Portuguese?' says Don Fernando, reframing his partner's opening gambit.

'Well, I think – ', the captain stutters.

'Come on, captain, you must have an opinion. My companion here will be extremely disappointed if you don't.'

'Yes, of course. I think that chess – '

'You don't seem so sure, captain.'

'No. I think that chess can teach you to think for yourself; to, to, outwit an opponent, and that's a good thing.'

'Too many theories, though, don't you agree, captain?'

Don Diego, watching this rude welcome by his colleague of the next interviewee, thinks he can see the military man working through his training in his head before he is ready to deploy skills of keeping options in open in unfamiliar terrain.

'There are many different ways to win a battle,' he says. 'Strategies built on a foundation of past success can help, but without good execution they are meaningless.'

'Well said, sir,' responds Don Fernando. 'Now tell me. 'If you were grievously injured on the battlefield and forced to remain on a sick bed for months of recuperation, would you ask for a chess set and worthy opponents so you could master your game?' The bald investigator lets this hang in the air. 'Or, would you ask for books, to expand your mind? Your knowledge of antiquity, say, or great accounts of noble *conquistadores*. The lives of the saints perhaps?'

The length and candour of the captain's answer surprises both investigators. They had become too used to the breathless deference of previous visitors to their nest in the eaves of Tuy; interviewees with nothing of any substance to say, men and women eager only to limit exposure to the light of the investigation. None wanted a further summons to a more public forum where they could be contradicted, trapped, shown up for what they were: uneducated, unsophisticated, broadly uninterested in the affairs or men or the machinations of the Church. Only, this Velazquez, the king's painter, they say. His family came from, well, somewhere near here, so what harm would there be in saying he was of noble stock, if that was what they wanted to hear? And if this Velazquez does have the king's ear he might remember the people who put in a good word for him.

'I am a military man', the captain declares, standing to attention. 'I obey orders, and the consequences of my commands are measured in territory gained, in lives saved, and lost, and battles won. The outcomes are rarely seen in the cold light of day. What takes place in the shadows where men promote their self-interest, where they dress up as actors to win the applause, where they seek status without sacrifice – such men are not, in my estimation at least, worthy of greater recognition. Their deeds and their works count for little when they are finally shown to be mere platforms for elevation. Their final judgement will be harsh, for they have gathered plaudits but lost their very soul. Such men are to be pitied not admired.'

'You are a serious man, I see', Don Diego interrupts what feels to him like a well-rehearsed speech. 'One who is, however, prepared to pass judgement on others without necessarily being in possession of all the facts. Motivations are complex and we cannot always know what lies deep in the hearts of men. We have not asked you a single question about any light you can shed on our investigation, and yet you seem, to my ears as an advocate at least, to be offering a final summary of your arguments. We expect honest answers to our questions, not your philosophical point of view or any treatise on how God will be the judge of men.'

Forgive me. That was not my intention.' The captain bows, chastised, the bull strength of his neck and shoulders discernible. He is a strong man, agile, used to fighting and meagre rations. 'If imprisoned by my wounds, my thoughts would not turn to chess and clashes of wooden armies. I would go to the one place where I am certain of finding the most generous mix of humanity.'

'Ah, the bible then. Very wise, Captain,' says Don Fernando. 'You see the bible as a collection of books, and indeed it is.'

'Let him finish. Is my learned friend right, Captain? Is that what you mean?'

Fully upright once more, staring into the empty space beyond the seated inquisitors, to all appearances a soldier reporting to superior officers whom he dare not look in the eye, Captain Diego de Vegas Hoyos resumes his explanation.

'As I see it, there is but one author – '

'Of course, of course. The one author of us all.' After the succession of mind-numbing witnesses, Don Fernando cannot contain his excitement any longer. Anticipating his partner's desire to leap to his feet and shake the captain by the hand, Don Diego presses his hand firmly on to his shoulder. He has a foreboding of what a soldier's life would be like under this captain's command and needs to hear more before making a judgement on his reliability as a witness. More, he realises. He needs to know for sure that this detached man, a man of responsibility so absorbed by his own thoughts, a man who would by definition of his rank understand the military, imperial and divine significance of the Order of Santiago, is of sound mind.

Deliberately ignoring Don Fernando's intervention or not, Captain Hoyos continues. 'How he lived to become an author at all is something of a miracle itself, his father a surgeon. Not an accomplished one, I might add. He didn't follow in his footsteps and wasn't going in any direction at all as a young man when he fought a duel, survived and had to flee this land.'

Switching focus from the middle distance the soldier looks directly down at the two Council representatives, now rendered speechless by the surreal direction of this encounter.

'You want to leave Tuy with proof that the king's painter has nobility in his blood. Can you imagine, then, what it was like for this man far from home with no trade, no skill, a violent past, turning up in the Papal States and seeking work as a chamberlain for a monsignor? What evidence do you need to provide on Velazquez's behalf? A few signed witness statements?'

'Be careful, Captain', says Don Diego. 'There are reports of other witnesses we can take back to the Council and the king.'

'Is this not more about the Church and State proving that Philip's loyal and beloved painter, to whom he is regularly exposed, is clean, untainted?'

The two Dons rise simultaneously to remonstrate, to no avail as Captain Hoyos speaks quickly now as if he has a limited supply of breath.

'It's the same for the Monsignor,' he says. 'For this new chamberlain to even be offered this position, the Monsignor made him produce a certificate to prove that he was not illegitimate. His prospective chamberlain also had to demonstrate that none of his ancestors had been brought before the Inquisition. None were Muslims, none Jews, none *Conversos*. Only then could he call himself the Monsignor's Chamberlain. Whether or not that put him off working for the Monsignor from the very beginning I cannot say, but a life of service to the Church was not in him. He became a soldier and in the Kingdom of Naples was drafted into the forces that would be revered across all of Christendom for their sacrifice and victory in 1571.'

'You refer to the Battle of Lepanto, Captain.'

'Yes, he survived but at the cost of his left hand which was permanently maimed. Still didn't stop him from fighting in other campaigns in Tunis and Corfu to name two.'

'*El Manco de Lepanto!*' the Dons chime.

'I see where your story is leading,' Don Diego adds, 'but do please continue. I see that you have a relevant perspective for our investigation.'

'You know, then, of the significance of Lepanto. Christianity itself was at stake.'

'It is, however, unwise to insult us, Captain. We may not be fighting men like you, but we are not ignorant of the fact that, had the Turks prevailed, no army could have stopped their march through Europe.'

'My apologies, sirs, please correct me again if I state what is already known to you.'

'Continue.' Don Fernando waves his hand.

'Every man who fought there and survived, especially the wounded and maimed, as he was, should have received care, gold, property – whatever they needed. *El Manco de Lepanto* found himself returning to Spain a few years after the battle forced to look for work. Pirates boarded his ship. Slavery became his fate and that would have been the end of his story had it not been for the kindness of two Trinitarian monks.'

'You see', exclaims Don Fernando. 'The Monsignor was the exception. These men of faith acted to save a man's life. The Church, I will remind you, Captain, is the living body of Christ. In every village and town in Christendom there are men like these monks who are his hands, his face.'

Only his chess-playing partner nods at this joyful outburst, more of an acknowledgement than agreement. What he said was true. It was always true. Don Fernando was incapable of untruth. He never tampered with the sanctity of facts, found in them an uncompromising certainty. He needed them as the cornerstone of his existence without which his life, his faith, would crumble. To hear spoken what he believed to be indisputable filled him with unimaginable joy.

'What did he do when released?' Don Diego asks.

'*El Manco de Lepanto* had spent five years in slavery in Algiers when this happened. His earlier attempts at escape had all failed. When he eventually arrives back in Spain everything else he tries fails too, relationships, work, everything.'

'No care, no gold, no property then? And writing?'

'Nothing. Writing is the only thing left for him to try. In the years after his release he writes and publishes a romance called *La Galatea*. Nobody reads it.' The veteran soldier pauses as if struck for the first time by the remarkable outcome of his story.

'So why then he did not just give up writing I do not know. Well, he did at first and became a tax collector. He failed there too and the integrity of his work was questioned.'

'I didn't know that. Fraud?'

'Irregularities. Nothing serious. Enough to ensure the end of a prospective career, albeit a lowly one.'

'Is this your point, Captain, that this flawed and broken man turned to writing because he had no choice? He had nowhere else to go in life and his name is only known now across the Spanish empire because his principal characters captured the imagination of readers who saw something of their own life experience in them. Exactly what is your point, Captain?'

Dismayed by the investigator's impatience and dismissive summary, the witness delivers the final part of his rationale in short, clipped tones most often deployed to confirm he will carry out orders with which he silently disagrees.

'My point: I would choose Don Quixote before any other book or chess set. I would ask for Don Quixote and Sancho Panza as the guides for my recovery before any chivalric tale. The Captain bows. 'Or, with respect, before any saint's life or history of the Church and its noble orders. Though, of course, he says turning to face Don Fernando whose enthusiasm for his star witness has evaporated, 'had I asked for a tale of chivalry and been handed a *Life Of Christ* by mistake, as happened to Saint Ignatius of Loyola, I would have gladly accepted it.'

The gesture restores Don Fernando. 'So you are not a chess player then, Captain. You are not inspired by our own Ruy Lopez, or fascinated by the saints who saw in chess a mental discipline to approach the Lord.'

'You are speaking of?'

'Saint Teresa of Avila, of course. But also Saint Aloysius of Gonzaga, or the saviour of Milan, Saint Carlo Borromeo. Let me tell you a story about him and chess if you don't know it.'

'Another time perhaps, Don Fernando. I think it's time for us to get to the business in hand and ask the captain about his knowledge of the king's court painter, Diego Velazquez.'

Captain Diego de Vegas Hoyos assumes once more the stiff pose of a soldier called to account by his senior officers.

'What do you know of the painter's family?' Don Diego asks.

'I do not know any member of his family. Nor do I have any personal knowledge of family members known to others of my acquaintance or under my command, born of a noble line.'

'I didn't ask you that.'

'Yet it is what you want to know and it is why I am here.'

'Why are you here exactly, Captain, apart from wishing to tell us the life story of Miguel de Cervantes.'

'I was answering your question. With respect, sir.'

'But why are you here if you can offer no evidence about the validity of Señor Velazquez's claim to be from nobility and certainly, as you put it earlier, to prove that none of his family had faced the Inquisition, none Muslims, none Jews, none *Conversos?*'

'Well, Captain? It's not like you to have nothing to say.'

'As a young man, before the army, I spent several years in Porto. Empty, aimless time, looking for a direction, but too often finding my weaknesses.'

'We may be in a cathedral, Captain, but this is not a confessional. Please say what you have to say.'

'It was over thirty years ago now. The memory plays tricks on you.'

'We know,' says Don Fernando who had been quiet.

'I met this man, much older than me. Short, grey hair, bent with age, a man whose opinion local people sought. I don't know why. I was too young to have any sense to ask. Ha, maybe he too had fought at Lepanto.'

'Who hasn't, according to your recollections, Captain?' The lawyer cuts him off. 'Why would such a distinguished city elder, if he was as you say, take time to speak to a young nobody as you were at the time?'

'I was introduced to him, that's all. My friends told me that he didn't like to see young men wasting their lives in drink and women.'

'And that was you, was it?'

'To some extent, yes.'

'What was his name?'

'Alfonso Rodriguez de Silva.'

'You are very clear about that, Captain, for a brief meeting thirty years ago. De Silva, are you sure?'

'Yes. He told me he told me he was a relative of the painter Diego Velazquez.'

'What?' Don Diego jumps up, eye to eye with the witness. 'Why would he tell you that?'

'Maybe he wanted me to believe that he had influence, that he was someone I should listen to,' the soldier replies unperturbed. Men shouting in his face is not new to him.

'What else did he say?'

'He mentioned that Velazquez's parents were from an old established Christian family. A noble family, he said, that never had to do any work beneath their status.'

Both investigators are on their feet now.

'Nothing else? He didn't say any more than that?'

'It was thirty years ago. If he did I can't remember. It just stuck in my memory because he was talking about Velazquez. Even I had heard of him.'

'Captain, you have an extraordinary capacity to surprise. This is important evidence and yet you seem somewhat unimpressed by what you have told us.'

'It is of no consequence to me,' the soldier replies. 'It does not make Diego Velazquez a better or worse man whether he's descended from – what should we call them? Pure Christians? – or not.'

Don Fernando raises his arms and places his palms over his ears in a mock gesture.

'Captain, we thank you for your time, but I think our interview should end there before you go on to say something you might regret. You have been a most . .' Don Diego hesitates, choosing his next words carefully, ' . .enlightening witness. Neither my colleague nor I would like our interview to end on a cautionary note.'

'Cautionary?'

'Let's just say that your candour has been helpful, but being too outspoken can be misinterpreted.'

After the briefest of deferential nods in the direction of each investigator the captain strides towards the open door. His thin upright frame silhouetted in the doorway, he pauses and turns to face Don Diego and Don Fernando once more.

'In all of Don Quixote', the captain says, 'there is only one scene where chess is mentioned that I can remember. As you know, the knight, in his quest for the 'fair Dulcinea' of *El Toboso* cannot distinguish between what is real and what he has imagined, his head being so full of books and chivalric nonsense. He and his dim-witted companion Sancho Panza have just encountered a cart full of actors, still in costume on their way to a performance of The Parliament Of Death, I believe, on the last day of Corpus Christi celebrations. Can you guess at Don Quixote's reaction when he hears the explanation that within the cart are a Queen, an Angel, a Soldier, an Emperor, the Devil no less, and even Death itself' No, sir', the captain says pointing to Don Fernando. 'There is no need to cross yourself. They are actors.'

'Once Don Quixote is reassured they are actors,' he continues, 'he is disappointed. He had hoped that in front of him was another great adventure as a knight errant.

Such was the way his mind worked. After a clown from the troop jumps on Sancho's donkey and brings it to the ground, it is only with difficulty that Sancho dissuades his master from charging the cart of actors on his steed, Rocinante. Later that night Don Quixote asks Sancho if he has seen a play with a cast of characters, good and bad, kings and knights and beautiful ladies. Then at the end of the play all of the characters remove their costumes. In an instant they all become equal before the audience. Sancho says he has. Well then, says Don Quixote, the same thing happens in the comedy of life in this world. That's the word he uses. Comedy. At the end of the comedy of this life, says Don Quixote, death takes away all of the garments and costumes of each of us and we are all equal in the grave. This, sirs, from a man who is deemed to have lost his grasp of what is real and what is imagined.'

Don Fernando opens his mouth to speak but is silenced by the raised arm of the departing witness. 'Let me finish if I may. Sancho, in his response, compares Don Quixote's own comparison to a game of chess. In the game each piece has its own role, he says, but at the end all are jumbled together in the bag. It doesn't matter whether you are a king or a queen, a bishop or a knight, death makes us all equal. Our shared humanity, sirs, regardless of who you are or where you come from. Let me tell you what Don Quixote said at the end of this conversation with Sancho,

'With every day that passes by, dear Sancho,
you lose some foolishness and gain some sense.'
Captain Diego de Vegas Hoyos turns and is gone.

Chapter 3

THE EPIPHANY

The success of Francisco and Leonor's new life in Madrid depends, in no small measure, on their new home. As in all matters of the greatest practicality and family business, it falls to Leonor to make the selection. The unspoken agreement, naturally evolved after fifteen years of marriage, that she would make the decision. Left to her husband, they both knew, the decision would be meditated over to death. In his mind, each day would bring another reason to delay, another all-important dimension to be taken into account, one more worry to be added.

Leonor managed the complexity of choice efficiently. Having determined core parameters of affordability, area and accommodation, she created her own tests of purchase. These tests, or clarifications as she chose to call them in meetings with intermediaries and vendors, eliminated the majority of options presented to her. One principal clarification was sound: how far and how fast it travelled. Sound was a prime concern to a woman who could foresee one possible future as financial ruin and destitution for her children. Sound mattered in a home where she would juggle her responsibilities of mother, family book-keeper, and woman of business trading in jewellery. Too little in the beating heart of the home and they would not be a family. A place where children could not play and argue and spend time with parents was not a home at all, at least not to her. Too much sound, however, too close to her and Francisco's working areas, and their survival in Madrid would be short-lived.

Francisco assumed, correctly, that another of his wife's 'clarifications' would be a working studio for him. She knew his requirement: natural light, minimal street distractions, room to stand several large easels, an alcove for the *prie-dieu*, and a reclining sofa for resting, dreaming or mental painting. Francisco thought less about the bedrooms for the children or the bed they would share as husband and wife. It was not that he didn't care about them, but these features in themselves were not good enough reasons to reject a Madrilenian residence.

Her search concluded, and the patronising condescensions of agents and vendors endured, Leonor had led Francisco to the top of the stairs and along the narrow hallway whose sloping roof created the effect of a tunnel. At its end stood a wooden door, black metal strips at top and bottom betraying its thickness and weight. Nor did the door concede anything to age or use, its strength as foreboding as its makers no doubt originally intended. To Leonor's mind at least, surely they had been commissioned to construct this door for a castle, or as the barrier to a room in which a princess or brigand would be help captive. Yet here it stood - one her father would have prized as a jeweller's door, a solid protector of gold and silver – as a gateway to a new creative life and a sentry to guard the occupant within.

On this December night of 1658 its willing captive reclines on the sofa amid the encircling gloom. The single candle he had lit flickers around the room as directed by the winter draughts, briefly illuminating several unfinished canvases propped against the white painted walls. Some hours ago, as the sun warmed the kitchen with its setting glow, Francisco had collected a lump of bread and cheese for himself, clasped a cup of wine and muttered to Leonor something about working through some new ideas. No need to wait up, kiss the children goodnight for him. Closing the solid wooden door to his studio behind him brought the dual guarantee of solitude and silence. Soon he would have to make his decision about Velazquez. His testimony would be required. The men sent by the Order's Council would want to know for certain whether it was true or not.

Lying back on the cushions of his working sofa, he closes his eyes and smiles at the thought that these representatives, or investigators more precisely, would refer to his old friend as 'the court painter' or 'painter to the king', or worse, 'the Gentleman of the Bedchamber' or whatever Velazquez was supposed to be now. Francisco pictures the great Velazquez as a tradesman reporting to the Escorial each morning to receive his instructions. Maybe that was how it started; but that was not what they would ask him. Confidences are what they would seek, bragging moments of youth when Diego expanded on his noble upbringing.

'Can you, Francisco, describe a time when any members of Diego Velazquez's distinguished family visited him in Seville? Did he speak to you at any other time about his nobility?'

'Not that I can remember.'

'It's hard to believe, Francisco, that you and Velazquez and Alonso Cano spent no time together as apprentices, as friends, as artists in the last thirty-five years and didn't talk about family. In fact, it's hard to believe, Francisco, that you haven't spent any time together at all. You cannot be saying that.'

Francisco, Francisco, why are they calling me, Francisco, he thinks. There it is again. Francisco. Are the investigators calling? No, wait, it's one voice calling. Were there not to be two investigators, but whether it's one or two they would not call me Francisco. The voice is not Leonor's. It is definitely a man's voice. His Spanish is different somehow, a foreigner's accent. He cannot place it. The door is closed and bolted.

'Francisco.'

Keeping his eyes tightly shut, Zurbaran assumes a more dignified position on the cushions, lifting his head to rest on the back of the sofa.

'Speak, Lord, your servant is listening,' he says out loud, he thinks, Samuel's response being what seems to him the most natural utterance to make. 'Yes, Lord, I am here,' he says again.

'You old fool. Do you really think your pathetic incantations are heard? Open your eyes.'

Francisco Zurbaran obeys. In the far corner of his studio a crouched figure encased in black is peering at assorted canvases, twisting his head to left and right. Francisco watches, beyond comprehension. The figure presses up against the latest work almost kissing the easel with his nose. Straightening up, humming and tutting, the thick-set and, Francisco discerns, as he comes slowly to his senses, shabbily dressed shape topped by dark and greasy hair, takes several steps back. Two steps to the left, back to his starting point, two back, two to the right, all the while staring intently, and to Francisco's waking mind, critically, disapprovingly even, at the progress of his hours of painstaking labour.

Distracted by the thought of this unfinished painting and other as yet unfulfilled commissions had filled Francisco with the fear of failing in Madrid even before he had begun. He looks at it again now under scrutiny. Any shock of who this intruder might be or his purpose is surpassed by the sudden memory of this greater catastrophe, the total collapse of his reputation.

'Surprised, Francisco? A little embarrassed maybe? Mmm? Just a little. I mean to say. Speak, Lord, your servant is listening. What were you thinking? First time around, not even Samuel believed it was the Lord come to visit.'

Though still too dumbfounded to respond to the mocking taunt of the uninvited guest, Francisco's artist's eye nevertheless starts to function properly, absorbing more of the detail of what it was speaking to him, whose careful study of the incomplete work on the easel had ended as quickly as it had begun. The two look at each other for the first time. Only now does Zurbaran comprehend the sight. There. In his presence. Real, before his very eyes. Real. Moving, speaking, sounding like a man, he beholds a phantasm. His mind processes the absurd first. How can a phantasm, - no, a ghost, for that is what it must surely be - how can it, this being, have greasy hair, a threadbare black cloak, an attitude? Yet, his eye confirms the spectral nature of the subject. It is both substantial and not, black and grey. Francisco sees through it and he cannot.

Years later, as his mortality approached, Francisco described what he beheld that night in his studio. It was as if, he said, that he was on his hands and knees gazing at a moonlit pool, unable to move, unable to look away. For there, on its surface not his image, but the reflection of another mature man, the lunar white of face and hands clear against the black of his hair and garment; his wide outline distinct but shimmering as the night breeze gently reminded the pool that peaceful sleep was not in its gift. Arched, thick, crescent eyebrows introduced tired, sunken eyes above a long nose spread on the pale face, flattened not by God's design but others who had left their mark. The skin sagged. Nothing. Not the inverted anvil-shaped beard of twisled grey and black strands. Not the mass of black hair, not the flouncy dirty white collar and cuffs, not the mocking tone, nothing suggested harm or threat. Any painting of this ghost Zurbaran determined, without conscious thought, would have to capture alternating themes of confrontation and indulgence, of anger and charm, of darkness and light, a subject to be pitied not feared.

'Painting me, are you, Francisco? You've had a good look, I see. Less convinced of a miraculous vision, I suspect. Not exactly like the visitation of the Blessed Virgin to the cathedral of Toledo only a few months ago. Did you hear about that? Caused quite a stir. She brought a choir of angels with her. Very considerate, I thought. You don't want to disappoint the faithful. I wonder whether they sang their own celestial composition or went with a crowd pleaser. Something by Tomas Luis de Victoria, one of your favourites, I would guess. Am I right? A jovial fellow, I'm told, an Avila man who just wanted to mirror Teresa's writings and visions in music. Sublime sounds, and that requiem of his. To die for, if you'll pardon the phrase. Never met him, though. We move in different circles, you understand. Have you read Dante? Whatever the choir was singing for the Virgin in Toledo, the Greek would have loved it, don't you think?'

'The Greek? Why do you speak of him? Who are you? What do you want from me?' Whether Francisco poses these questions aloud or not, the spectre holds his stare, ignores them and continues on its random monologue.

'Something dark and moody about him. I've only got to know more about him since I have been like this,' he says, gesturing with one hand pointing from head to toe. 'Don't be shocked, Francisco, but the Greek and I are alike. Both rather intense, though I say so myself. Both outsiders, both trying at one time to satisfy our holy patrons in the holiest of places: him Toledo, me – well, we'll come to that. Both rejected. The Blessed Virgin did not see the Greek's painting of the stripping of her son before his crucifixion on her visit to Toledo Cathedral. Did not see it in its rightful home where it was intended to be, because it wasn't there. They rejected it, those zealots, supposedly humble guardians of the same cathedral where, I might add, Ferdinand and Isabella once appointed none other than Tomas de Torquemada as the first Inquisitor General. Need I say more? I digress. Why? Why did the bishops of Toledo reject the Greek's painting?'

'I only want to know who you are, what you are and why you are here.'

'Patience, Francisco, patience. Not one of my virtues, I admit, and maybe if I once had more of it, well . . . let's not go into that for the moment.' The phantasm shrugs its shoulders, simultaneously laughing at its own aside. 'I will tell you, Francisco, by way of my story about the Greek which you have interrupted, for, right now, you have eyes but you do not see, ears but you do not hear.'

The accompanying laugh this time, Francisco thinks, gaining more control of his own senses, is more forced, more hollow. Ha! How can a ghost have a hollow laugh? How absurd.

'Anyway, the reason for the holy fathers of Toledo in their wisdom rejecting this radiant work of art is – '

'El Espolio. Yes. Yes. I know all about it. The Sevillian painter rises to his feet causing the uninvited guest to take two steps back. 'They did not want to see the three Marys in the painting.'

'Or the heads of the executioners higher than Christ's on the canvas. Don't forget that, Francisco.'

'And they only paid a third of what he was due, it is said.'

'You are right again, Francisco – 350 ducats to be precise.'

Zurbaran dares not take a step closer. He stands still, slowly extending his arms in supplication, shaking his head in disbelief at each word he utters, to wake himself up, to rid himself of this spectre. 'Toledo. The Church. The vision of Our Blessed Mother. The Greek. His painting of Her Son. Why are we speaking of this? Why are you here? Who are you?'

'Father, I have sinned against heaven and against you.'

'What?'

'That's what you sound like, Francisco. The prodigal son, grovelling and pathetic, on the verge of tears, 'Please give me a second chance. Please. Please tell me that I have not wasted my whole life in Seville bowing and genuflecting before every bishop, every holy order, so that I am worthy of remaining this town's most favoured artist. Please tell me why. Tell me why, after my decades of service to churches and monasteries and the city elders I am cast aside in favour of Bartolomé Esteban Murillo.'

'Wait. How do you know about Murillo?'

'In my circle of existence, Francisco, I get to see and hear many things, some of which would make you blush.' The ghost laughs at his witty parry of the interruption. 'His work for the Franciscans impressed. It's as simple as that. You are no longer talked about as the greatest painter alive in Seville. No, you know don't you, Francisco, that Murillo is first choice now and Velazquez is the master of

Madrid. He is the master of the king's trust: his confidence, his closest adviser, even the second most powerful man in all of Spain, you might say. But then you know that or you wouldn't be here. It is why you are in Madrid, isn't it, Francisco? To restore your reputation? To swallow your pride and enlist the help of the man you think of as your friend, but who hasn't given you a moment's thought since . . .'

'Since my ten paintings of the Labours of Hercules at the Buen Retiro Palace, it is true', says Francisco, shaking his head in agreement.

'You returned to Seville from Madrid, and then what from Velazquez over the last twenty and more years?'

'Nothing.'

Francisco's interrogator lifts an opaque hand to his beard and turns his head from side to side in mock consideration. 'What does Diego Velazquez care about? Mmm, let me think. Velazquez possibly? No, that is too harsh. There must be someone else, at least one person. Who could that be, I wonder. Maybe it's the one who made him a wealthy man. Have you seen his house here in Madrid, its silverware, tapestries, such exquisite furniture, paintings – he has good taste, let me tell you – and as good a library as I have seen outside of Rome. Of course you haven't. Never been invited, Francisco, have you? Let me assure you in case you are in any doubt. Diego Velazquez cares about Diego Velazquez. Oh, and the king, the provider of his gilded life.'

Listening with rapt attention to this lengthening monologue, the ridiculous thought still creeps into Zurbaran's head that this all too knowledgeable spirit does not pause for breath. He shakes his head again at the absurdity.

'You disagree with me, Francisco?'

'No, I was merely thinking – '

'It is galling. I agree. Here you are, a kept man. Your earnings from scattered paintings in Lima and heaven knows where else, not nearly enough to sustain your family. You have been copied and replaced in the affections and the commissions of Seville. What was it the archdeacon of the cathedral said only a few years ago? I am sure you heard. Dom Juan Federigui paid for Murillo's St Isidore and St Leander and stated publicly that the painting came from, what was it, 'the hand of the best painter in Seville'. It's official. Murillo is the best in Seville. The man who imitated your style of painting – and something of Herrera, I grant you – is here too in Madrid at the invitation of *El Sevillano*. That's Velazquez in case you had forgotten. The great Francisco Zurbaran – copied, broke, surpassed, forgotten and dependent on his wife's jewellery. You are *el sevillano* desperate to find favour with *El Sevillano*.' Once more the spectre emits as hearty a guffaw as a being without substance can utter.

Thus confronted with the truth of his miserable decline, Francisco's legs give way and he falls back on to the cushions. Chin lowered to his chest, eyes closed, he makes a silent prayer, beseeching, begging his crucified Lord Jesus to free him from this devilish intrusion into his consciousness. Hot tears fall onto his tunic. That he should be brought so low as to have to endure this nightmare. At least Juan did not live to see him like this. Nearly twenty years now since the plague claimed him and half of Seville. June 8th 1649. He repeats the date over and over, sees the still life of his son's face, witnesses the funeral procession to and from the Sagrario. The wailing of women he hears is not only for Juan. They are aged by grief for lost fathers and mothers, brothers and sisters, sons and daughters, weeping in black, whispering breathless Hail Marys as if the faster they recite the rosary the more likely plague-ridden corpses would inhale again.

'Jesus, Risen Lord, take this vision of pain from me', Francisco prays, his relief in Juan's absence converted into a deeper sadness. Was that the moment when all he had worked for in Seville, when he, the city's most revered artist, died with his son? The time when the stark choice of living in God's light or living in darkness, as he and his patrons had believed, was no longer one the people of Seville or Spain wanted to see. They had to face harsher truths more fearful even than God's judgement.

'Lord, first Maria, then Beatriz, then Juan. I have lived in darkness and never once thought to express doubt. My work, my commissions, always for your greater glory, that is what I have believed. Never did I let the doubt, the weakness, the fragile nature of who I am or what we as your people endure, the struggles we face; never did I let these shake my faith. I feel so rejected, so broken. Why do you torment me with this nightmarish vision? My neglect, my not praying to be put to the test? So here it is when I am at my weakest. Lord Jesus, Holy Lord, I am thinking now that the devil himself has presented this ridicule. It is he who is trying to lead me to despair. It is he who is laughing at my failures, my fall. I am rejected by my city that put me on a pedestal. I am an embarrassment reduced to begging for scraps from the table of the king, scraps that Velazquez has the power to keep for others or throw at my feet. At his table is Murillo. I am jealous. I am beaten. I am lost. I am foolish to think even for a moment that I can rely on Velazquez to restore my reputation. I am – '

'Am I boring you, Francisco? It hardly seems the time to take a nap.'

'I wasn't napping. I was just – '

'Overwhelmed? Still not sure, are you? Maybe you would like to go through your 'Speak, Lord, your servant is listening routine' again and see what happens.'

'Just tell me who you are and why you are here. You said you had been rejected like the Greek. What did you mean by that?'

'Really, Francisco. I am offended. Are you so dim-witted as not to see who I am, or is it the fading light that obscures my best side?'

'So you are an artist, then.'

'Yes, I am an artist. I came into this world to be an artist. Or at least I was until rejected.'

'Other artists imitated your work?'

'Many. Before and after my death. De Boulogne. De La Tour. Even a woman, would you believe, Artemisia Gentileschi. Let me see. There is my old tutor, Manfredi. Ribera. Rembrandt. Rubens. You.'

Zurbaran is staring at the apparition, eyes widened, pointing with an outstretched arm, as if he has heard a confession from a murderer's own lips. 'You. You are . . .', he croaks.

'I am rejected, copied and replaced as you have been, Francisco. Not always in painting either. Your countryman, Ribera, even insisted that his Roman landlady cut a hole in his room so he could have more light as I had once done a little more forcefully, shall we say, with a less compliant landlord.' The phantasm pauses, amused by the recollection and, as Zurbaran is still too dumbfounded to utter its name and understand how a ghost can gather its thoughts, continues.

'There is an emotion, isn't there, Francisco, when you are given a commission to create a work that will be seen by more people, believers and faithless alike, than you could ever imagine. It is more than a feeling, even more than relief at the hopefully handsome reward which will follow its completion. Who but an artist can understand the ecstasy of possibilities, I ask you. The painting that emerges on the canvas is only the final choice, the winner if you like, over tens, hundreds of other paintings judged and rejected.'

Zurbaran nods.

'You know who I am, Francisco. I am the person nobody wants to be. A murderer. A streetfighter. A drunk. A whoring lecher who would give his love,' the spectre pauses to make an obscene gesture, 'to whoever would have me. Men. Women. I didn't care, whoever took my fancy.' The laugh echoing in the room sounds to the shocked recipient of these revelations more hollow, more melancholic than before.

'Anyone who objected to me I would fight or abuse. It was of no matter to me. At first I had my mother's inheritance to spend as I pleased.' The figure sighs, black head and shoulders pointing to the floor in the pose of a criminal trapped by the truth of his crimes before a jury. 'Then I realised the power of the gift I had. My talent was wasted on pretty flowers and fruit, and musicians, card sharps and gamblers. I could paint *dal naturale,* creating the perfectly lit image in my mind, the detail as clear inside my head as you see it on the canvas. I did not need to make sketches, no drawings, no outlines. Simply an intensity, a clarity, a drama if you like, that I could transfer directly from my brain,' says the ghost pointing to its temples, 'on to the canvas.'

The painting, that marked the change in me, Francisco – and this is what will interest you most – was of Francis of Assisi. *In Ecstasy* I called it. I was as captivated as you have been by the sheer intensity of his belief, the conviction, the certainty, the sure knowledge that he was held upright by a divine shaft of light. Step out of the light and he was nothing, a sad, misguided fool depriving himself of the pleasures of life for no reason. It was a drama, Francisco. I had the gift to re-imagine and re-create in the clearest light moments of divine presence. Anything outside of that light, His light, wasn't important.'

'I understand,' is all Francisco can whisper, his heart beating somewhere outside of his chest, his breathing all but stopped.

'You would think, wouldn't you, that this dawning of the light would have clothed me in humility, made me cast aside my wicked ways, rejoice in my one-man evangelisation for the illiterate masses. The Holy Roman Church should have raised *me* aloft in a sedan chair or at least made me a cardinal for all that I was doing to restore its authority. After all, I was still more holy than some I could mention.'

Spontaneously the two artists laugh together recognising the truth of the last observation. Why Francisco did so he did not understand other than, as he later reflected, an unexpected opportunity to acknowledge what he knew to be true but never had dared to admit.

'But it didn't. Make me more Franciscan, I mean. I became even more arrogant, more difficult.'

'One painting is not going to change the person you are, what's in your heart,' Francisco intervenes, his confidence growing.

'True. I had already experimented with the light of faith in *The Penitent Magdalen* and *The Rest On The Flight To Egypt,* but Francis should have been the answer for me. He was the saint revered more than any other in my lifetime. Don't you see? In my mind as I painted, I allowed myself to be him, thinking I could be re-born as he was, made new by communion with Christ.'

'I have not seen the painting you speak of with my

own eyes but I have heard talk of it. From your new vantage point,' Francisco stutters, 'if I can call it that – from which you appear to have a view of past and present, you will know that I too have turned to Saint Francis. That doesn't matter. It is who you are. I know who you are. I want to say your name so that I know it is you. You are – '

'I am rejected as you have been, Francisco. I told you. The Greek and you were also alike: you by the patrons and prelates of Seville, the Greek by the zealots of Toledo.'

'And you?'

'You wonder why I dress in threadbare black, Francisco? No? I cannot blame the darkness in me on any one moment or rejection. I sought redemption, I really did.' The spectre looks thoughtful for a moment as if deciding where next to take its monologue.

'Then again, I could point a finger from beyond the grave at the *palafrenieri*. Papal grooms, they commissioned me. A *Madonna of the Palafrenieri* for the altar of Saint Anne in the basilica of Saint Peter.'

'In Rome?'

'No, Granada. Of course, Rome. Wake up, Francisco. You seem more dead than I am. It was as high as the ceiling in this room and more than half as wide. The naked Christ child places his left foot on top of his mother's, together squeezing life out of the serpent, Satan. Saint Anne looks on approvingly, hands clasped in front of her, making no movement to intervene. Her daughter is in control, bending over in modern dress, of my time at least, to help the child keep his balance.'

'I understand.'

'Do you? My crowning commission, put on display at the altar of Saint Anne on April 14th 1606, taken down on April 16th 1606, covered up and loaded on to a cart like a victim of the plague. They were ashamed of it, wanted rid of it, and do you know who bought it, Francisco? Do you know who was not as sanctimonious, who recognised its true value?'

'I am sure you're going to tell me.'

'A cardinal. A prince of the Church. A man closer to the Bishop of Rome than anyone else, his nephew in fact, Scipione Borghese. He recognised what I was.'

'A master of light and darkness. An artist like no other who confronts us with the harsh physical truth of the Old and New Testament and the lives of the saints. You take every subject and give it divine clarity. The sharpness of light you create out of the darkness on each of your religious paintings makes them all meditations on the Word Made Flesh, on God's presence in this world. Yes, I know who you are, Michelangelo Merisi da Caravaggio. You are, or were, the possessor of one of the greatest gifts bestowed by God on any artist.'

'Quite a speech, Francisco. Most kind. If only I had heard it in my lifetime I might not have ended up like this. What I was actually going to say,' says the artist's ghost, breaking into hollow laughter once more, 'was that Borghese knew me to be a collector of prostitutes and whores. All for my art, you understand. I wasn't an ordinary street pimp interested only in the money or the free perks of the job.'

Zurbaran starts at the wink from the spectre.

'I am astonished that you look so shocked, Francisco, you, the husband of so many wives, the father of so many children. Sit down before you faint again. I needed models and I didn't want to share them with anyone else, especially *not* junior notaries like Pasqualone. He had to be taught a lesson.'

'What did you do to him?'

'Oh, nothing much, a blow to the head, enough to knock him unconscious to the ground in a pool of blood – I could have drawn my sword if I had wanted to kill him.'

'When was this?'

'So you are curious about me now. You have heard rumours about me over the years, but you have not travelled as Velazquez has done, not seen the work of my artist's hands as he has done, and now you have an opportunity to question a pimp and a murderer about what actually happened at his hands. Is that it, Francisco? You don't see a great artist in front of you now. Perhaps the kindness of my visitation was a mistake.' The spirit folds its faded black arms and tilts its head back in an unspoken challenge: answer that. Justify yourself. Give me a reason to remain and explain why I am here.

Zurbaran stands up shaking as he extends his left arm in a gesture of apology. 'I wasn't clear', he mumbles, barely audible even in the stillness of the room 'how this unfortunate incident with the notary had anything to do with Cardinal Borghese and how you could still work as an artist, I mean, not as a – '

'As a pimp and whore collector, I know, I know. Just get on with it.'

'How could you still be a free man? Was this before the commission of the Madonna with a serpent for the *Palafrenieri* in St Peter's?'

'Pasqualone was a nobody,' the ghost of Caravaggio shouts, stepping forward. 'He deserved what he got from me. Borghese knew what I was, a pimp and troublemaker who would test his skills with a sword on another Pasqualone the next week and the week after that. You are so slow, Francisco that you miss the point. The good cardinal did not care about my soul. As good as my eye was for finding and bedding the most divine prostitutes to sanctify in my paintings, his was as good in recognising art that would live long after his death.'

In this moment of the spectre's rising anger, Francisco finds himself reflecting on what a coward he is, a coward to be afraid of a ghost, a coward to have lived his life without ever questioning the truthfulness of his patrons in Seville. His thought is interrupted by the rant intensifying in front of him.

'You don't think I haven't dwelled upon his motivations in helping me. I was as close to being a leper as it was possible for a modern man to be. Borghese paid 100 scudi for the Madonna of the ungrateful *Palafrenieri*, rescuing it from oblivion. That was nothing. Preventing the Pasqualone incident from becoming a disaster for me was easy for him. He wanted more of my work, could turn a blind eye to my lust and violence. The cardinal could accept that I wasn't like Velazquez's friend Reubens, who would dedicate his work of every day to the Lord at morning Mass. Or Guercino, who still prays for the whole morning before he picks up a brush, though he was not averse to spreading his affections with married women as his assistant found out, but that's another matter. Or Bernini, whose activities behind closed doors were nothing like mine at all. He was more interested in another kind of exercise to mine, he and Saint Ignatius had different ideas on that.'

Francisco notes that the spectre's mood has changed again, not laughing at its contrived contrast between Bernini's following of Saint Ignatius' Spiritual Exercises and its own sordid exertions.

'Without Borghese, Bernini's brilliance would probably have been missed. Rome was not in short supply of artists and sculptors seeking commissions from the Church.'

'Perhaps the cardinal collected art for the greater glory of God. He saw an opportunity in your and Bernini's talent to draw people far and wide back to the one true faith.'

'You are so trusting, Francisco. So straight, it's what I like about you. You could even say it's why I am here. Your blind faith. That quality. What is it – acceptance, a simple belief that all the Church has told you is true – you are not even bitter towards the prelates of Seville, are you? More resigned, convinced that your rejection was in some way your fault.'

'I am not perfect,' Zurbaran snaps back. 'I have my jealousies and weaknesses.'

'Yes, I know you do. These are mere trifles, my friend.'

'I am not your friend and I will not be patronised by a ghost or whatever you are – telling me it knows all of my thoughts and character. I am going to wake up in a minute and this intrusion will be over. I can't even believe I am talking out loud like this, to a vision of Caravaggio. Vision, ha! You're not even that. I am not afraid of you or what you say about me.'

'Righteous anger, too, laced with insult: now I am impressed. No matter. You still possess nothing of the hidden darkness of most mortals and certainly nothing like the depths occupied by men like Scipione Borghese or me.'

Still riled, Francisco takes his turn to shout. 'You cannot possibly know what is in another man's soul, even you.'

'On that we can agree, Francisco. We cannot judge a man by his actions.'

'I didn't say that.'

'So you would be a judge ready to condemn if the evidence presented gave you sufficient reason? Imagine for a moment that my powers on this side allow me to take your hand and lead you back in time to observe Cardinal

Borghese at work and at play, in public and in private.'

'What would you show me?' Zurbaran asks, curious in spite of himself.

'A good man,' the spectre shimmers. 'A man who argued for my pardon when my crimes demanded punishment. A compassionate cleric who exercised his considerable power to make a living for artists struggling from one commission to the next. Scipione Borghese's actions can be seen as very Christian indeed: helping artists; buying collections and individual work of the living and the dead; building his modest villa on the Pincio so that these divine works might be displayed for the illiterate masses to grasp the glory of God, as you said. You can hear, can you not, the glowing tributes, and see the clouds of incense rising on his death twenty-five years ago.'

The phantasm pauses in its narrative as if making its own mark of respect.

'Or I could show you a more temporal man, one who used the power and privacy of his office, controlling the Church's vast funds to promote his interests. You and I, Francisco. We observe. We think about the detail. We make choices. Then we create a new reality. We deliver the painting we want people to see. That is what we want both the educated and the illiterate to believe in, the final work that we choose to show them, not the mistakes, not the other choices that we have rejected, for better or worse.'

'This is beginning to sound like some philosophical treatise in *The School Of Athens*.'

'Precisely my point, Francisco. Miraculously, Raphael has Pythagoras in the same scene as Saint Thomas Aquinas. Beneath the three arches Zoroaster could have just ended a philosophical argument with Socrates. Boethius would have had a thing or two to say to Epicurus or Diogenes the Cynic, don't you think? We don't know why Raphael selected these philosophers and theologians for his painting any more than we know who he decided to leave out, or whether he really knew what he was doing by painting Aristotle and Plato as philosophers of equal standing dominating the frame. Raphael alone has decided who will be in his School of Athens. Averroes but not Confucius. Aquinas but not Augustine. Where are Saint Paul, Origen or even our beloved Saint Jerome? Why did Raphael omit them from the greatest painting of philosophers and thinkers ever seen?'

'Why don't you ask him?'

Ignoring Zurbaran's sarcasm, the insubstantial being appears to its host to have become absurdly breathless by its extended monologue on Raphael. Allowing charity to get the better of him, as it so often does, Zurbaran gives the ghost of Caravaggio a moment to regain its eerie composure and fills the silence with his own perspective on Raphael's omissions.

'Or Saint Gregory of Nazianzus who preserved the theology of Origen, stood up to the Arian heretics and inspired Jerome when he was still a young inexperienced biblical scholar.'

'Ah, Jerome, yes,' the spectre sighs. 'Raphael left him out too. We shouldn't be surprised. True, his translation of the bible into Latin a thousand years ago brought Christianity to millions, but he was an interpreter, not a creator of ideas, nor of philosophies to change men's thoughts. Neither was Gregory of Nazianzus: both were concerned with preserving one absolute truth. They were not thoughtful men. Raphael was never going to put either of them in a toga looking pensive or converting other philosophers with great oratory. Why are you smiling?'

'Twenty years ago, when the Jeronomites commissioned eight paintings from me to keep the spirit of Saint Jerome alive, as they put it, different monks repeated the same story in their conversations with me.'

'And what was that?' the ghost asks.

'In the three hundred and seventy fourth year of Our Lord – '

'Very precise, Francisco. Are you sure?'

'Why do you mock me for no reason? I have barely begun speaking and again you interrupt to laugh at my expense. If this is what you were like as a real person I am not surprised you were disliked so much. You give men reason to pick a fight.'

'Harsh words, my friend, but you are right. This form I now possess has not cleansed me. I still cannot declare confidently with the psalmist 'Lord, open my lips and my mouth shall declare your praise'. I open my lips and words, often the darkest or most thoughtless of words, declare my character. It seems I can control them as little in this existence as I could in the previous one. I am contrite. Please continue. I want to hear.'

'So tell me, then, why you are here. Tell me. Is it because I am going to be like you and will say or do something I will regret? Something that will hurt Leonor or the children? You are here to warn me, I assume.'

'Calm yourself, Francisco. You have nothing to fear from me. Let us talk first about Saint Jerome. He matters to us both.'

'Very well,' Zurbaran concedes, 'but not for long. I am at my wits' end. I cannot endure this conversation much longer, not knowing whether my mind is wandering so badly I cannot control it, or whether you are indeed a vision from beyond this life, from purgatory, for you are clearly not an angel come to convert or change me. I do not know which. All the same, I will continue as you wish. When I cannot take any more I will, I will . . .' he says, pointing with an unsteady finger at the thick bolted door, 'walk out.'

'Only for me to return again at another time,' the ghost replies.

'Let us finish what you have started. Jerome, then explain yourself.'

'You should be flattered, Francisco. I have already stayed this long because I am enjoying our exchange. We will get to my purpose, but please. You were saying about Jerome.'

'I will have my answer?'

The spectre nods.

'As a young man Jerome lived in Rome and dedicated himself to studies of Greek and Roman literature becoming a scholar of some renown.'

'Yes, I know that bit.'

'The Jeronomites told me their saintly inspiration was a man obsessed with detail, at times intolerant of less able interpreters or anyone who distracted him from his purpose.'

'He was difficult and miserable. Yes, I know that too, but continue, Francisco. I want to see where you are leading me.'

'Jerome believed that Rome itself, its excesses, its corruption, its temptations, were in danger of separating him from his connection with God. At the age of twenty-five he left Rome to become a monk, returning to the area where he grew up near Aquilea. Less than a decade later, in the year of Our Lord three hundred and seventy-four, he was travelling to Antioch when he contracted a fever. He became delirious, later claiming that he had heard the voice of Christ Himself judging him. 'Who are you?' the Son of God asked him. 'I am a Christian', Jerome replied. 'No, you are a liar', the Christ told him. 'You are Cicero's disciple, not mine'.'

'Another man who wasn't good enough apparently for *The School Of Athens*', the phantom observes. 'So what did our beloved Jerome do then?'

'He prayed. He fasted. He abandoned the sparse comforts of his monk's cell for the Syrian desert. He wrote. He wrote and wrote. He translated more and more of the Old and New Testaments into Latin. It is said that to overcome any carnal fantasies he would concentrate on repeating Hebrew words and grammar.'

'He never became any less miserable, then.'

Whether or not the sound of the ghost's empty guffaws can be heard, Zurbaran is certain that his uncontrolled laughter would bring Leonor or at least one of the children running to the other side of his door. When the two finally stop, only silence fills the gathering gloom.

To Francisco's eye the outline of the ghostly presence has become less distinct after the laughing outburst, as though vital energy sustaining the apparition has been spent. Accustomed now to the surreal encounter, he realises the lengthening shadows slanting across the white and painted canvases alike could well have been casting their own illusions. Still, he believes that the spectre of Caravaggio before him is fading. The belief prompts fear, a sudden panic that he would lose the opportunity to ever learn the reason for this visitation from beyond the grave. He presses for an answer once more. As he liked to credit himself on later reflection, Zurbaran did so this time in a less challenging, more conciliatory manner. Whenever he thought back to his encounter, he smiled at the thought of how conversational he had been with a man who had died forty-eight years before they met.

'I don't think the Jeronomites I painted were unaware of the joyless nature of their founder', he smiles. 'They admired his single-mindedness.' Seeing the ghost keen to interrupt him, Francisco presses on, discovering a preacher's fluency he had not realised was within him.

'Who can separate us from the love of Christ?', he hears himself say, quoting Saint Paul. 'For Jerome it was not power or women. It certainly wasn't humour or kindness. As he saw it, he was, well, leading a life worthy of his vocation. Sorry. Saint Paul again.' Is he trying too hard? Is it too obvious that he desperately wants to elicit a response? Neither lying nor concealing his intent had ever come easily to him. After what seems to Zurbaran an eternal silence, the ill-defined grey, white and black figure is oddly conversational.

'Jerome took his second chance then?'

'What do you mean, Michelangelo?' says Zurbaran, addressing the spirit for the first time by name. If makes no answer this time and Zurbaran continues with his explanation.

'Whether Christ actually spoke to Jerome in a vision does not matter. The point is that Jerome believed he did. Jerome thought he was another Paul on his own road to Damascus, blinded by the light and told he would need to change his ways. 'Stop following Cicero' is not half as bad as 'Stop persecuting Christians', I grant you, but Jerome wanted eternal life with is God, so he changed. He spent the rest of his days proving that he was not a disciple of Cicero, because he believed God had spoken and given him a second chance.' Zurbaran tries again. 'Was it Scipione Borghese who did the same for you?'

'Was Borghese my voice from heaven, is that what you mean, Francisco? No, he was not sent from God to save me from myself. Borghese recognised me as an asset, nothing more, nothing less. He concerned himself with the darkness of my soul as much as I did with the injuries I inflicted on Pasqualone. It satisfied His Eminence's princely calling and his conscience to rescue me from the law. He detested scum like Pasqualone as much as I did. The painting of Saint Jerome after this series of disasters felt to me more like payment than gratitude. Borghese collected art and sculpture for treasure in this world for him and his family. He believed that by enabling the most talented artists he could find to produce more, and share their divinely inspired gifts, he was serving the illiterate faithful and storing up treasure for himself in the next world. Scipione Borghese was fully expecting his eternal reward.'

'That seem a harsh and cynical judgement to me. The cardinal was helping you after all when your reputation and earnings as an artist were about to collapse. Why are you so bitter about him?'

'And why not? He could have done more for me. If I was that good, why did he not give his full protection or the patronage of his uncle. Then I might never had had the misfortune to mix with Ranuccio Tomassoni.'

As quickly as its anger had arisen like a storm at sea, the spectre is overwhelmed by grief, sobbing, causing an unfamiliar feeling of compassion to well up in Francisco.

'I killed him. With these hands. The same hands that only weeks before had brought Jerome to life . . well, you know the story.'

'Is it not true that Tomassoni could have killed you?'

'I brought it upon myself. I painted Jerome as if he were my penance so that my confessor Borghese could see how grateful I was for his aid, how much I needed forgiveness. I did not deserve his favour, whatever his self-interest or lack of interest in my redemption had been.'

To Francisco Zurbaran, the phantasm appears as empty, broken, abandoned by the world, dead as the Caravaggio is claimed to be. How he can feel such sorrow for a being, such desire to give what consolation he can, so soon after being mocked?

'I killed him on a Sunday. Did you know that?' the spectre of Caravaggio asks.

'No, I didn't.'

'His brother nearly killed me after I delivered the fatal thrust with my sword. Had it not been for Petronio Toppa stepping in after I had been struck on the head, I would have died on that twenty eighth day of May of 1606 in Rome and not four years later. It would have been a just reward.'

'But you got away.'

'I escaped to Naples and painted in hiding there, earning what I could, in fear of my life every day. Me! An artist. A murderer. A wanted man. And let us not forget who desired to end my miserable life.'

'The Tomassonis?'

'If they could find me, certainly. Mariano Pasqualone too, and any number of artists, or brothers or fathers of models and whores who learned of my rough hands.'

'They didn't find you? You escaped and you had another chance to restore your name.'

'Look at me, Francisco. You can see right through me. See how disfigured I am. I don't exactly cut the dashing figure of an arrogant artist who could seduce women at will or triumph in duels. They didn't find me. Not then, but later, after I had been given my second chance.' Seeing that Zurbaran is poised with another question, the phantasm raises its faded black arm for silence.

'I wasn't looking for the crowning of my career the way Velazquez is,' it continues. 'The certainty of resurrection was not what mattered to me. Maybe it should have been and I wouldn't have ended up like this. I needed a way out. I know you want to ask, Francisco: was I sorry for what I had done? You may wonder whether I was repentant, seeking forgiveness, deliberately deluding myself into thinking it, so that I could do what was necessary to restore my reputation.'

'Your freedom too,' the Spaniard inserts.

'Freedom? Since the day my father died of plague and I watched him thrown on to a cart of corpses I have never been free.' The spectre pauses. Zurbaran dares not interrupt again. This may be the moment of revelation.

'Never been free,' it repeats. 'You do wonder, don't you, why Raphael never placed Thomas Aquinas in his *School Of Athens*. We have the greatest freedom, Thomas would say, when we do what is good. We are made in God's image. We are intelligent and free. He has willed us to be. We are the authors of our own actions. Aquinas would say that being virtuous, doing the right thing if you want to think of it that way, Francisco, is being true to ourselves, because we are made in God's image. Do you see?'

'I am trying. I'm not sure how this relates to Scipione Borghese, or the death of Ranuccio Tomassoni, or why you are here, but if you would continue, I will listen.'

'When I finally left Naples for Malta a year after I had killed Tomassoni I believed my freedom could be obtained by becoming a Knight of the Order of Saint John. I would change. I would be granted sanctuary, immunity, forgiveness, a papal pardon, all in one step. I would have my freedom again, Francisco. All I had to do was show contrition and make reparation. Be good. Act from the very core of my being to choose good, to finally exercise my deepest freedom, if you think of how Thomas Aquinas might put it.'

'What did you do?'

'Do? I beheaded John The Baptist of course,' the phantasm booms, shimmering in delight at its spontaneous humour, relieved, as it seems to its audience, to find an escape from reflection.

'It is true, Francisco. I gave Grand Master Wignacourt and the Order the head of John the Baptist on a plate. You look shocked again. You shouldn't be. You want to know who gave me the opportunity I craved for redemption? Not Borghese. Not Jerome, though I did commit his learned figure a second time to canvas for a close adviser of the Grand Master's, Ippolito Malaspina. Funny that after my Jerome became my payment to Borghese he would be my first trade on Malta. Malaspina was one of the Council of the Order who voted for the Frenchman, Alof de Wignacourt, to become Grand Master. Before you ask, not Malaspina either. Not any of these, but Wignacourt himself.

You ask me what did I do. I demanded an audience with the Grand Master. Here was a man who had proved his courage and skill at Lepanto and in countless other sea campaigns. When he first became Grand Master, or master of Soldiers, as they called him then – '

'When was this?'

'At least five years before I arrived on Malta. He made Malta secure by launching sea attacks on the towns of Mahomeeta in Africa, on Passava, on Patras, and even Lepanto in Greece – all successful. He once told me that while one of these raids was underway and the fate of the knights on Malta still unknown, an eagle of a size no-one had ever seen before flew over the belfry of the Church of Saint John, and then landed on the top of its mast. The people believed it was a sign from God.'

'I am curious to know more about Wignacourt and you seem ready to speak more about him, but how much longer will it take? If I can say this to you, Michelangelo, you seem to me to be fading and I am more worried now that our meeting, wherever this is, will be at an end before you tell me your purpose.'

'Wignacourt is at the heart of my purpose, I assure you, and you will know it.'

'Very well. It was Wignacourt who gave you a second chance then.'

'Not immediately,' the phantasm responds, warming to its theme. 'Some obscure law of the Order prevented any man from becoming a Knight until he had been living on Malta for one year. Would you believe that they actually called this law 'the Convent'? No matter. I bided my time and enjoyed the protection of Grandmaster Wignacourt.'

'You were safer on Malta than in Naples?'

'Not a single man on that island would dare interfere with a guest of the Grandmaster. Mark my words, Francisco. Wignacourt was the King of Malta. Not a tyrant, not a monk, a king, subject only to the laws of God and his representative on earth, the wearer of the Fisherman's Ring. A king, whose left hand was occupied with war, or should I say the *Corso* as the Maltese called it: one long sea campaign against the Turks, corsairs and any other usurpers of the faith. And whose right hand was building churches like the Oratory of the Church of Saint John. The same Knights whose job it was to cut down any Turks, petitioned Wignacourt to build it. They needed an Oratory to be part of the grand Church of Saint John, they told him, but separate, a secret room where Knights could petition the Lord their God privately, a sanctuary where novices of the Order could be instructed and moulded in the spiritual. Most of them I can tell you, Francisco, already knew enough about matters temporal.'

'When did this happen?', Zurbaran asks, sensing the spectre is losing the thread of its story and readying for another rant.

'Wignacourt granted their wish only five years before I arrived on Malta. It took two years to build. On the façade of the Choir in the Oratory they placed an image of Our Lady of the Seven Sorrows and that was why it was known first as the Oratory of the Pietà.'

Caravaggio's ghost falters, his thin voice drying up at the recollection. Zurabaran, believing now that the time for the revelation of its purpose has come, does not intercede.

'But not for long,' the phantasm continues, even more melancholy. 'Within a few years a shabby and disgraced, yet accomplished artist had landed on Malta to seek entry into the Order in reparation for his sins. And what does an artist of repute do when his life is held in the hands of the Grand Master?'

'He paints him,' Zurbaran volunteers.

'Yes. He bestows on him all the military and spiritual might that is due a divine intercessor. Without Wignacourt's direct appeal to Pope Paul V for a dispensation, no man could enter the order as a murderer. The Statutes forbade it. Only a papal dispensation could allow it. Only a man whose heart and soul were so flooded with light would ask for it. From the moment I first met him I knew. He received me so warmly and we bonded in an instant. He would be the source of my redemption. Wignacourt and the Order were all I could think about. Every conversation in the street and in the taverns, 'Tell me more about Wignacourt', I said. 'The Knights in the Infirmary, tell me what they do'. The Grand Master even entered my subconscious thought. He found his way on to the face of Saint Jerome, my first painting on Malta, for Malaspina.'

'Yes, you told me that already. You started talking about the Oratory.' Zurbaran tries not to sound impatient.

'And I told you that I beheaded John the Baptist,' Caravaggio smiles through the flickering gloom. 'This painting,' it says, pausing at absorbing the enormity of the divulgence. 'This painting mattered more to me than you can possibly imagine. Papal forgiveness or not, Wignacourt and the Council could still have rejected me, judged me an undesirable, made me an outcast, sent me back to a doubtful fate.'

'Please continue. Don't stop now.'

'When I revealed the Beheading of John the Baptist to Wignacourt and the Council; when I explained the purpose of this gift of the largest and most symbolic painting I had ever done, it was though the gates of heaven itself had opened in front of me. Every time the priest raises his eyes to heaven, holds the sacred Body of Christ in his hands or lifts up the blessed cup of His Precious Blood, as he commemorates the Last Supper in the Oratory, he will be reminded of his Saviour's words, 'No other child born of woman is greater than John.' Each Knight, each member of the Order and every novice could be truly present at the moment of their patron's sacrifice. As long as the Order of St John existed and held the Oratory to be the inner sanctuary of their faith and hope for eternal life, they would behold the altarpiece of the Beheading of John The Baptist by Michelangelo Merisi da Caravaggio. That is why, Francisco, it is no longer the Oratory of the Pietà but the Oratory of the Beheading.'

'You became a Knight of the Order through Wignacourt's intervention with Pope Paul and the Council's acceptance of the Beheading as atonement for your crime?'

Don't you see, Francisco. Don't you understand yet why I am here?'

Zurbaran stares at the apparition unable to speak. He had felt like this before: moments when his legs could no longer support him; when the beating of his heart pounded his ears; when he seemed to be floating, conscious, but no longer awake; days when he understood his son had been claimed by the plague; when he stood alone, broken, a widower once more; when speech failed him.

'You look as if you have seen a ghost, Francisco.' Caravaggio was not laughing now. 'I made a terrible mistake. Killing Ranuccio Tomassoni, you might say, but that is not what I mean. Whilst the Tomassonis and the Pasqualones and the fathers of whores were all seeking their just revenge, I believed that I could be redeemed. Arrogantly, vainly, naively, I was worth saving. I was a murderer who made a choice to buy his freedom and redemption. At least that is what I tried to do.

I could make up some story for you now, Francisco, if you like, seeing as you appear to be struck dumb as I tell you why I am here. I'm hardly Nicodemus, am I, and you are not without sin, are you? Still, here I am. Caravaggio visits Zurbaran by night. I could tell you in my made-up story that after I murdered Tomassoni I was filled with the deepest remorse. I realised that I had to finally reconcile my two personalities, make sense of the darkness in my head. It was time to test resurrection.

Perhaps you would still have believed me, Francisco, if I had asked aloud whether I might still recognise Christ himself in the breaking of the bread. No, this is better. I could say to you that I had reflected on the story of the adulterous woman whom Christ saved from stoning. Was his command, his life-saving intervention, so strong, that she really could 'go and sin no more'? I could say anything to you, to myself, tell any story of divine recognition and redemption, and you would believe me, wouldn't you; that I turned to painting and to the island seclusion of the Order of St John to reveal who I truly was, or rather who I could truly be.'

Zurbaran nods in silence, but thinks the spectre of Caravaggio must hear the pounding of his heart.

'I have to tell you, Francisco, that is not what happened. I thought I could buy my freedom. Not so completely lost as a soul that I didn't feel some regret for the life I had taken, for the abuses I had delivered. Only what mattered so much more than repentance was resurrection. That was my terrible mistake. I thought I would be free, redeemed, because of the choice I had made. I deluded myself into thinking that all I had to do was tell the Grand Master what he wanted to hear and give the Order what they wanted to see. I gave them the most learned of saints in whose face they could see their own Grand Master, builder of churches, hospitaller, defender of the faith at sea, in war and in peace. I gave them the very reason for their existence. Ironic, isn't it, that I, Caravaggio, the murderer, should point to an execution to gain entry to the Order of Saint John as my own path to eternal life?'

Throughout Caravaggio's explanation Zurbaran remains still, his legs like pillars of stone, eyes wide, barely comprehending how he beholds the artist of his dreams, how he hears this confession.

'I succeeded,' the penitent continues. 'I thought I was free. Grand Master Wignacourt, Malaspina, members of the Council and Knights of the Order, embraced me in the Oratory. They beheld my Beheading of John the Baptist and rejoiced.

Listen to me, Francisco. I was deluded. I had no loyalty to Wignacourt or anyone else. I could not become virtuous by submitting to the Order's vows, fighting the Turks, or treating lepers in the Infirmary. I may have been accepted into the Order of St John but I was not free.

This is why I am here. Your friend, the man of whom you are so jealous in spite of yourself, is not free. Velazquez sees acceptance into the Order of Santiago as the crowning of his career. He thinks he is choosing eternal life, that the habit of the Order on his cold body in death will be the reason for the warm embrace of the saints in God's heavenly kingdom.'

'I still do not see', the only words Zurbaran's lips can form.

'Have we really been talking this long, Francisco, and yet I must still spell it out for you. I told you I was deluded. Velazquez is deluded. You are deluded. What do you say to those who are certain that their last breath on this earth is the end of their entire existence? Answer me that.'

'Please calm down. The children or Leonor might hear you.'

'Maybe they should hear me. You don't with your self-pitying whimpering.'

'Calm down. What was it you were saying about Velazquez being deluded – surely you do not mean him as one of those who think their death is the end?'

Zurbaran later recalled how he now peered through the dim light to note the apparition shimmering, and his fear that it might vanish altogether before he fully understood its purpose. At that moment, he remembered, the apparition of Caravaggio gazed at him with a look of compassion and entreaty, its light all but extinguished, and spoke to him for the last time as a father might have spoken to his prodigal son.

'There are many, too afraid to speak now, whose heart and mind tell them that believers in resurrection of the body have been indoctrinated, deceived or deluded. That they are the ones who do not know their own mind. They would say that John the Baptist was beheaded for nothing. Jerome's self-denial was his loss. Francis was just talking to the birds. Christians and Muslims alike in the Holy

Land, at the Siege of Malta, Lepanto, wherever they killed each other over their version of divine revelation, died in vain. David was not saved from Goliath by his God but by quick thinking and his own skill. The Supper at Emmaus is a painting of what we want to believe. Even the arrival of the saints to claim the Count of Orgaz for his heavenly reward is only the work of El Greco's vivid imagination. Whatever his true motivation, Scipione Borghese did not denounce me for what I was. It would have been easier to look away. Grand Master Wignacourt knew that I was not a Knight of the Order, but he argued for my acceptance regardless. As actually happened, he knew that sooner or later the darkness at the very core of who I was would overwhelm me. I would be de-frocked beneath the Beheading by the same Knights who had so warmly embraced me as one of their own.

Gaining acceptance as a Knight of the Order of Santiago will no more guarantee Diego Velazquez the freedom of eternal life than becoming a Knight of St John made the kingdom of heaven a certainty for me.'

Its waning energy almost spent, the spectre pauses for the weight of its words to fall on the witness.

'It is you who have the greater opportunity here, Francisco, by granting Velazquez his wish. You do not need to paint the Beheading of St John or a portrait of the king's family, ladies-in-waiting, dwarves, dogs and all, to justify your place in heaven.

There is nothing and no-one of whom you need to be jealous and certainly not *El Sevillano*. You are only deluded and deceive yourself if you think that having the right ancestry or painting for your masters what they want to see, or putting your own eternal salvation before love and loyalty, before Leonor, before the lives of your children, before your lost son, Juan, matters more. Velazquez' two daughters, Ignacia and Francisca, died as well, remember.

Show your friend, Velazquez, what it is to be free, Francisco. See the price I have paid for seeking to control my destiny. I could have acted from the very core of my being, from the good in me, to reward Alof de Wignacourt for my second chance. I failed and look at me now, trapped in this state.'

The ghost raises its arm to prevent Zurbaran taking another step forward.

'See how compassion moves you now, Francisco, weeping for a ghost. There is no reason for you to do anything, nothing you can do. It is too late for me. Ah, of course. Ringing in your ears are the Lord's words that it is a faithless generation that asks for a sign. Call it proof, evidence, whatever you wish. It cannot be tested, but you will know when your friend acknowledges his debt to you. I promise you. He will show you when he understands it is you who has given him his freedom.'

'But how can I possibly – ' Zurbaran starts to remonstrate, when the last of his flickering candles dies. As quickly as his shaking legs would carry him he pulls the door open, recovers a torch from the top of the stairs, rushes back into his studio and looks to where the spectre of Caravaggio had stood. It is not there. He strides to every corner waving the torch not willing to accept its fiery bright light illuminating the entire space. He is alone.

Chapter 4

THE AWAKENING

Francisco dare not open his eyes. Not yet. The darkness has passed, of that he is sure. He is touched by the light and chill of the early morning. Whenever sleep did overwhelm him, so strong was its embrace that he was powerless to resist, no time to prepare for a comfortable rest with blankets layered over his shirt, shutters closed. It does not matter. He allows his fingers to stretch and feel the uneven bunching of the cushions crumpled under his weight. The cushions are his own. He is certain of it. He lifts one from behind his head, places it over his face and breathes in its scent. Yes, his own! It is real.

Francisco smiles in blindness, a grin so broad his eyes are pressed tighter shut. Resolving not to open them in case he loses this moment of inexplicable happiness, he lies still, his thoughts turning even more inexplicably to St Benedict's phrase. Run, run, Francisco, run while you have the light of life. It is not too late. Live and love and paint in the present. That elusive peace can be found, he whispers to himself.

'Your peace comes from painting. It is your calling, what you are meant to be doing. Whether Murillo and others have taken your place in Seville or not is of no consequence to you now. You should not be trying to lead a life worthy of their vocation. It is your life to lose, to waste in bitterness and regret if you choose. You do not honour Juan's memory by denying anyone else from becoming what they want to be.

Is that it, the reason why you resent Diego so much, why you reacted the way you did to Alonso Cano? Because Juan rejected your expectation, because Juan died knowing you thought of him as a failure who had chosen the wrong path, because you never could accept that he was the kind of man and painter he wanted to be? Different from you. Not just different, though, was it? You worried about your reputation, what your patrons would say, what whispers there would be in the monasteries.

'You've heard about Zurbaran's son. Doesn't believe in God, some have said. Doesn't ever attempt to glorify God, or His Blessed Mother, or the saints, in any of his paintings.'

You let those thoughts torment you. True, but there was worse. You told yourself over and over that Juan could not be allowed to become like the so-called *Sevillano,* Diego Velazquez, who became so preoccupied with painting anything but divine revelation. You resented Diego for his influence over him. The man your son had never met. What was your worst fear? That Velazquez would call this talented painter of still life into the royal court and not you? Not you, in spite of the friendship of your youth. Not you, the man who gave his life to painting God's divine intervention. Not you, who would not show any gratitude for Diego's invitation to paint for the Buen Retiro Palace. No surprise then that Diego was less inclined to offer again.

But your son was a different proposition. Given time – ah, there's a phrase for me to think about. Given time.

Given time, Diego Velazquez may have presented Juan Zurbaran with an opportunity that he hardly afforded his father. Given time, Juan Zurbaran could have become court painter, one to eclipse his predecessor, one of whom Church and King and Country and Empire could be proud. And then, a reconciliation of Francisco with Diego, Diego with Francisco. Had Juan lived. All that might have been had Juan lived. You cannot go back in time. You cannot say now what you should have said to Juan then or to Diego.

Maria. To think of the life we might have had together with our three children and, who knows, maybe more. The two of us growing old together. Looking back on a life well lived. Had Juan lived. Had Maria lived. Maria, how you would have embraced our baby daughter, Paula Isabel. Loved her as you did five-year-old Maria and Juan, what was he, must have been about three then. Instead, God called you back to Him, asked for an exchange. One life for another, gave me Paula Isabel and took you to heaven with Him, your salvation guaranteed. Who could be angry with Him for sparing you from the trials and poverty of this later life? Not Paula-Isabel, that much is certain. But why she nurtured such a resentment, no, reserved such an anger for me, is a mystery. The life we might have had together as father and daughter.

If only Paula-Isabel could have accepted Beatriz as her step-mother even if she couldn't bring herself to love her. And why Paula-Isabel would not show any outpouring of loving consolation, or prayer, or compassion for Beatriz, never mind her father, when our beautiful baby girl, Jeronima, died. That too will never be known.

Though Paula-Isabel had always wanted to hear stories about her mother as a little girl. She was so proud of the fact that she came from a humble family rooted in Spanish soil, her grandfather a lowly pig-gelder. Poor Beatriz. Poor, sad Francisco to marry into the Morales, one of the wealthiest families in Llerena and to settle into one of the *Casas de Morales* in the main square. She probably shook her head in disbelief and disgust three years after Beatriz died when her father married for a third time, and this time a woman whose life and heritage glinted with gold and silver.

No sound, it must still be early. That's assuming these cushions are not another one of Caravaggio's tricks. That it is morning and now two days before Christmas. You thought it, or you knew it was there deep in your mind, all of your pain over Maria, Beatriz and Paula-Isabel, but you never mentioned any of this to him, none of it. He knew. Of course he knew. It didn't need to be said. Caravaggio knew about Diego's suffering when both of his two daughters died. Still didn't stop him from saying what he had always assumed to be true: that Velazquez only ever cared about Velazquez. Why does it seem so harsh to say that now, when yesterday I would have agreed wholeheartedly? Why can I think now of Maria and Beatriz and my children and not feel the anger, the grief, the bitterness I felt yesterday?

Think. Think. Remember what Caravaggio said and why he has made you feel so elated. Where is your jealousy of Velazquez now? The guilt you have felt about Juan for nearly ten years of waking thoughts – where is it now? That pain about Maria, Beatriz, Jeronima, you could never discuss with Leonor – it is as though it has been lifted from your shoulders, your heart and soul. You were so afraid of appearing weak, dwelling in the past, not dealing with the present necessities of providing for your family. You could not face the fact that you were out of touch.

Surpassed in Seville. Outwitted, outperformed by the man you once thought of as your equal. Caravaggio thought he was free. That was it. Indoctrinated into the ways of the Order of Saint John, or was he deceived? Wait. Deluded. He said he was deluded. Deluded into thinking that passage into the Order would make him free, would bring him peace, would guarantee a restoration of the life he had led before. Just as Velazquez is deluded if he thinks that proof of his nobility and admittance into the Order of Santiago will bring the certainty of resurrection.

You are released, Francisco. Released from your jealousy, guilt, anger and bitterness, if only you will stop deceiving yourself. You cannot hope to restore your reputation, to be the loving husband and father and artist you are meant to be, as long as you are a slave to the past, chained to your fear and persecuted by it. You will know, Caravaggio said. Know when you are free. Know when Velazquez acknowledges what you have done for him. He might as well have said 'Know, too, that when you open your eyes in the morning you will feel as though an angel had visited in the night, your chains had fallen off and that you had walked past the sleeping guards of your prison'.

'Yes! More precious than gold,' Francisco repeats, sitting up suddenly, rearranging the cushions and absorbing the awakening. 'That is what I will tell Leonor. Our love, our children, our time together in this life are what matter to me. I will let others worry about whether my past work is remembered or not. Let my Lord and the Immaculate Conception and the prophets and the saints be the judge of how I have painted them when we meet in the life to come, but not now. 'Look at these hands,' he cries, laughing and holding them up to the light of the open window for any passers-by to hear. 'They are the hands of a man who can still paint,' he shouts leaning out of the open window. 'I am happy to be in Madrid, not somewhere else. I am Francisco Zurbaran, not someone else. I am not the Spanish Caravaggio. I am the Spanish Zurbaran. That's good enough. I am here and I have time to bring my gifts to the Christ Child born in Bethlehem.'

Not unhappily shocked by his proclamation to the largely sleeping residents of Madrid, Francisco turns his back on the street and looks around his brightening studio. The spread of blank canvases still lie on the floor, leaning expectantly against the wall, waiting their turn. Francisco stares at them. They seem less demanding than before, the colours on the work in progress clasped by the easel above, brighter than he remembered.

'There,' he says, looking past the easel. 'That is where the ghost of Caravaggio stood. I am sure of it.' Francisco steps up to the spot, positions himself facing the sofa where he had lain, and waves his arms in silent conversation with the velvet cushions. By reliving the visitation he imagines, gesture by gesture, that he will hear again the voice of the opaque Lombard. 'So much I could have asked him,' he says, exchanging places in his mind with the master of chiaroscuro who is now reclining open-mouthed and speechless on the sofa before him.

'Tell me, Signor Caravaggio. Now that you are here, tell me please when your ideas to paint with such stark contrasts of light and shade first formed in your mind.'

Holding up his hand in mock objection to halt the secret being told, Zurbaran offers reassurance to the subject of this interview.

'Let me say first of all, before you speak, that I am concerned with your art and your gift to the world. For God Himself will be your judge. I cannot possibly know, nor will I ask you now, whether you sought His forgiveness and found peace in your last breath. For I cannot say, who can, what you were capable of until your last moment. But I ask you again. Was there a painting, a sculpture, an artist, an experience, that inspired you to turn away from the conventions of art that had gone before?'

Francisco pauses, adopts a mock quizzical look, and resumes when it is clear no response is forthcoming from his dumb witness.

'Very well, then. What came first in your head, the light or the darkness? How was your work conceived, that's what I want to know. I am also minded to ask which paintings you conceived but never committed to canvas because patrons never commissioned them or because, let me put it delicately, other distractions got in the way. The return of the prodigal son, I wonder, or the Risen Christ appearing to Mary of Magdala?'

Zurbaran shrugs, arches his eyebrows and makes an exaggerated forward tilt of his head like an actor on stage in the town square making sure that the person standing at the back of the crowd can see his intention.

'You have no answer for me,' he declares, laughing, as delighted with himself and his charade as he possibly can be.

'Then let me try one more time to hear the truth from your own lips, Signor Caravaggio,' he says, pointing at the empty sofa. 'Tell me how you made your escape from Malta. I find it hard to believe that you simply set yourself free and were lucky enough to find a boat. Was it Grand Master Wignacourt himself who arranged it because he took pity on you; or because your very presence on Malta shamed him after proving you could not control yourself? He believed in you, didn't he? Of course he wanted your divinely inspired hands to glorify the Order of Saint John, to make the city named after Jean de la Vallette one of the most envied in Europe, so magnificent would its art be. That is of no consequence. I think that he understood your character better than you realised at the time. Wignacourt knew all about your weaknesses before you sought refuge in the Order.

But I know it now, my dear Caravaggio. I can see more clearly than I have ever done before,' chokes Zurbaran, laughing and crying at the same time, dancing around the sofa.

'I know it. I know it. I do not need your answers. Wignacourt set you free. The Beheading of Saint John The Baptist set you free. Not the boat, a mere detail. You could not see it then, but he redeemed you. Yes he did.'

In his excitement Francisco dances to the corner of the room and splashes the previous day's water from the basin on to his face.

'See, Signor Caravaggio. I am not dreaming. I am awake. Christmas is coming. Wait. Is it here already? No matter. It can't be, not yet. You took the light that Wignacourt gave you like a flaming torch, and you used it on The Beheading of Saint John. It has taken you some time, I admit. Not in your sad lifetime. Coming to me, I mean. You have passed on the light, setting me free too. O Caravaggio! It is wonderful to be so redeemed, so restored, so – '

A sudden thought stops Francisco in the middle of his outburst. Running back to the open window he yells at a passing market trader pushing his barrow of fruit.

'Sir, can you tell me what day it is today. Is it Christmas Eve or Christmas Day?'

'You would make fun of me at this early hour asking such a stupid question,' the man shouts back.

'No, not at all. Not a bit of it. I have slept for far too long, that is all.'

Picking up his barrow the plan plods on, uttering in first steps clearly enough for Zurbaran to hear. 'It is December 23rd.'

'Thank you. Thank you indeed. Today is the day then. There is still time!'

Facing the empty room once more, Francisco grips the window ledge at his back. He cannot move. The courses of action form faster in his mind than the command to his legs. There is still time, he repeats to himself, but what must he do first. Wake Leonor? Paint? Wash properly and change his clothes, for his appearance today will matter. He must be a credible witness, dispel any perception of dress betraying a careless mind, a bitter mind, or heaven forbid, an old mind. There is still time. Rouse the children. Sit Marcos down, and Jose Antonio and Micaela if they will listen. Hug Eusebio and Agustina, one with each arm. Tell them he will be a better father. They can grind pigment, help with his work anytime they want. He would be very happy for them to do so. And if any one of them wanted to learn more about painting he would be happy, thrilled, to show them. He would not tell them what to paint of course. That would be their choice.

There is still time. To make amends, to account for himself, to take responsibility, to show Leonor that her sacrifices have not been in vain, to restore –

The knock on the door startles him.

'Francisco. Are you alright? You didn't come to bed and I heard voices.'

Leonor's voice instantaneously releases Francisco. In three bounds he crosses the workshop of his room, unbolts and swings open the door to face her, beaming.

'Francisco, what has happened? You seem so happy. Look. You have not changed your clothes from yesterday. Have you been painting all night, finally worked out what you want to do with that canvas you have been staring at for so long? Is that it? Since that visit from Alonso Cano I have been so worried about you.'

'Hush,' he says, gently placing a finger on her lips. 'There is nothing to worry about. I am going to visit Alonso Cano this very morning to make my peace with him.'

'What? Now? The investigators from the Order of Santiago are expected to interview you about Velazquez, or have you forgotten that? You haven't slept much, have you? You haven't changed. We need to buy food for breakfast for the children, not to mention our guests. You haven't answered my question either.'

'I know. You are right. I will not be long and I will buy whatever food we need on the way, he says, pulling her close to him, wrapping and rocking her in a warm, tight embrace. 'You have worked so hard to establish a new jewellery trade in Madrid so that we can live and eat and give the children any Christmas at all. I have been so difficult – '

'I do think you should wash first with the fragment of scented soap we have left before Micaela finds it' she says smiling, pushing him away. 'And find a fresh doublet.'

'Of course. Of course. I will do it all. There is still time.'

* * *

The two investigators, Don Diego and Don Fernando, thread their way along the Calle Mayor, the irregular clip-clops of horses lost in the competing cries of market stall-holders, alarm calls of caged birds and the chorus of challenges issued by itinerant water-sellers marking their territory. It is still too early for Mary and Joseph to be seen with attendant shepherds, sheep and oxen. Their awaited presence and the ceaseless notes of *villacancicos* between the Puerta del Sol and the Plaza Mayor, will be confirmation that the star has reached its divine destination of Madrid. The Spanish empire's capital city was chosen by King Philip IV's grandfather nearly a century before for its broad thoroughfares lined with shade-giving trees between churches and palaces, so regally defined. There had been a time within living memory of only a few remaining survivors of the 1500s when Philip II could have chosen Lisbon as his capital. He had, after all, been proclaimed king of Portugal in 1581, and had watched a combined Spanish and Portuguese fleet set sail for the New World only a year later. Persuaded more by the drift back to Castile by the Spanish nobility than by the beauty of Madrid, Philip eventually abandoned any notion of Lisbon as the seat of the Spanish empire and returned to his designated new capital city. Though not with triumphant processions of a conquering Roman emperor, he reportedly entered El Escorial with an Indian elephant and a rhinoceros, the ancient spoils of conquest.

Mindful of these facts, Don Fernando does not permit any speculation into his thinking, the 'what ifs' of the past translated into a new interpretation of the present. Madrid is the capital. That is the fact of the matter. Why wonder whether war with Portugal would have been avoided or whether Diego Velazquez would ever have become the king's favoured court painter-curator-adviser. There is no merit whatsoever in wishing these interminable travels and interviews never had to take place, nor making a judgement on the worthiness and nobility of Velazquez for the Order of Santiago. That would be pointless. The facts counted, nothing else. At least today marked the end of the process. That was a fact too.

Don Diego is too preoccupied with his own reflection

of the investigation to notice the heralds and glad tidings of Christians in every street. He does not see the Advent wreaths or the large purple and red candles attached to columns and archways ready to guide the night-time procession of shepherds and sheep to the stable. It is a still morning, too early yet for the winter wind to rise. The expectant throng of flags and tapestries will wave and flutter in praise of the new-born king. They hang idly for now, waiting. The time is near, their presence declares. Christmas is coming.

Oblivious, the lawyer is re-examining the evidence presented on his and Don Fernando's return to Madrid by the artist and sculptor, Alonso Cano. He had stated even before being asked the question that he had known Diego Velazquez and his family for more than 40 years. Though he had settled in Granada, it was of Seville that Cano had the fondest memories, of a youth spent there with Diego Velazquez. And his family? Cano barely mentioned his mentor, Pacheco, and at no point did he talk about the coming together of these two supposedly great families when Velazquez fell in love with, and finally married, Pacheco's daughter, Juana.

Cano could not relate the detail of a single specific occasion of meeting Velazquez's parents when they spoke of their proud heritage. Odd that they wouldn't. Odd that their son would not make more of his nobility in youthful boasts to his friends or future father-in-law. If Alonso Cano had known Diego Velazquez and his family for over 40 years, why could he not speak of parental visits, of ancestral trips to Portugal for his father's family?

Don Diego considers another reason for Cano's lack of explanation. Interviews in court and with other artist witnesses, those who knew Pacheco, and his own reading of Pacheco's *Arte de la Pintura* , published five years after his death, all confirmed that Velazquez and Pacheco had become close friends. Pacheco was quick to recognise the teenage talent of his student and just as sharp in cultivating the most profitable relationships in Seville. Whatever the great and the good might have thought of Pacheco's own rather old-fashioned style of painting, they admired his nurturing of new talent, of whom Velazquez was the shining star. In those days, let's suppose, that the young Velazquez was as quiet and reserved as they say; but inwardly bursting with confidence, arrogant even, as young men can be when they know they are superior to their peers.

Let me think, then, that his only true confidant is Pacheco, not his friends Alonso or Zurbaran. Velazquez understands that it is not in Pacheco's interests or good for his own prospects to do any more than adopt his mother's name. He is a private man, reserved and considerate of her more humble Sevillian origins. Open discussion about maternal humility and paternal nobility – Portuguese at that – would not suit his purpose, not as a young man being pushed towards opportunities at court at any rate by Pacheco, a man acutely aware of his daughter's reputation and comfort, and not forgetting his own. The forty years of knowing the family of Diego Velazquez as Alonso Cano had testified, therefore only refers to Velazquez's marriage to Pacheco's daughter in 1618 and the birth of two girls in 1619 and 1621. What was Pacheco thinking? What was he saying to Velazquez?

'Honour your parents in your own way, but do not forget in this time of war with Portugal, this moment of golden opportunity in your life, this new life of responsibility to my daughter, that there is no benefit in ever publicly drawing attention to your heritage.'

Is that the counsel Pacheco gave to him? Don Diego

considers this point and looks across at Don Fernando riding alongside him. He is satisfied that he too is lost in his own thoughts. His companion of these past months would surely dismiss his theories. 'You have no evidence of facts to support them', he would say. 'You are a lawyer. You should know that. As investigators and representatives of the Council we are bound by duty and the king's command to deliver our verdict based on testimony given to us. We cannot ignore the fact that Señor Cano confirmed both how long he had known the family of Velazquez and believed he was descended from noble stock.'

Don Diego says nothing. They will soon reach the house of the final witness, Francisco Zurbaran, and their long journey together will be over. Don Fernando had not been keen to discuss with him, after the last interview, why Cano had been so dismissive of Zurbaran. No, Velazquez and Zurbaran were friends no more. It wasn't so much that they had fallen out. They had gone their separate ways and their paths were unlikely to cross because Zurbaran was not a *magistral:* he did not take the prescribed master-painter's examination at the end of his apprenticeship. When Velazquez moved to Madrid and was appointed court painter to the king, that truth made any association with Zurbaran all the more awkward. It was in fact an act of great kindness on the part of Velazquez that he should have asked Francisco to paint the Labours of Hercules for the Buen Retiro Palace twenty years ago. Velazquez and Zurbaran are such different people that it's no surprise they weren't close. Velazquez never took any interest in Zurbaran's son, Juan, for example, before he died. Zurbaran would have been too proud to ask for any court favours from Velazquez, and it would surely have annoyed him that his teenage-friend-turned-painter-to-the-king took no interest, especially as Juan seemed as keen as him to capture on canvas much more of this life than the next.

Cano did not need two investigators to tell him, Don Diego reflects, that they would also be interviewing his apprenticeship friend of whom he has little positive to say. Apparently it did not occur to Cano that putting down Zurbaran would hurt the case for his friend Velazquez's admission to the Order of Santiago. Saying that, they had no love for each other and, in as many words, that arrogance, pride, jealousy and selfishness all made it far less likely that the two artists would ever in the past 40 or more years have talked about one's nobility when the other had none. Suddenly, his thoughts are interrupted.

'Don Diego! Are you listening? I've been calling your name. Are you praying?' asks Don Fernando with a hint of mockery.

'No.'

'What were you thinking then? About the torchlight processions and praise of the shepherds to come when Our Saviour is born? Or something more specific, like whether Diego Velazquez will be granted his wish of a place in eternal life? About whether Zurbaran will be the one to help us make up our minds?'

'You are right about the shepherds at least,' the lawyer replies. 'I was thinking about Don Quixote's encounter with goatherds and shepherds. They think he is mad of course. One of the shepherds, Vivaldo, wants to know what it means to be a knight errant. Don Quixote tells him that it's his calling to roam lonely and deserted places fully armed, so that he is ready to help the weak and the needy in harm's way. He will do whatever it takes at whatever cost to himself to save them.

Don Quixote then explains to Vivaldo and this group of shepherds that it's impossible for a knight errant to be without a lady who is his love and purpose. It is as natural and right for them to be lovers as it is for the heavens to have stars, he tells them. Even you can imagine, can't you, Don Fernando, the look that Don Quixote would have given these simple men, the one that said 'Do you think I would dress up like this and put up with being a knight errant if it wasn't for a lady? That really would be mad, wouldn't it?' '

Don Diego laughs, leaning so far back in his saddle that Don Fernando fears his partner will fall on to the unforgiving cobblestones.

'I still don't understand why you are telling me this,' he says, 'though I confess the workings of your lawyer's mind have been beyond me for some time. What possible relevance can your story have for this day?'

'Obviously Vivaldo is curious and keen to discover who Don Quixote's lady is. As you would expect – or, as most would, Fernando – our errant knight tells Vivaldo that her name is Dulcinea. She is more radiant and beautiful than any other woman. In Dulcinea all of those ideal qualities poets ascribe to women become real. She is from Toboso, a village in La Mancha, Don Quixote tells Vivaldo, and she must at the very least be a princess. Tell me more, then, says Vivaldo, about her heritage, her family and lineage.'

'What does the mad knight say to that?'

'That's the interesting part. At first Don Quixote gives a long list of families that she is not descended from, as if what follows must be absolutely true. Dulcinea is not descended from the Moncadas of Catalonia or the Villanovas of Valencia or the Gurreas of Aragon, or a host of other families he lists that I cannot remember.'

'So who is she then?' asks Don Fernando, more in hope of moving on to another less fictional topic than any desire to know.

'Dulcinea is of the lineage of El Toboso de La Mancha, he says. As simple as that, and Don Quixote adds that no person should contest this. Nor should anyone doubt that, though this is a recent family line, it could well be the beginnings of one of the most illustrious family names for centuries to come.'

'Are you telling me this story because you have reached the conclusion that proof of the noble line of Velazquez does not matter? Please tell me that is not the case, Don Diego. This is not a great deceit created by the Order to satisfy its own ends. We are not deluded fools. You would have been better served preparing for our investigation by reading the Gospel of Luke rather than Cervantes. Look around you, my friend. We are celebrating the birth of Christ, the Son of God, and will do to the end of time. Luke went out of his way to explain the Messiah's ancestry, his time and place in history. Resurrection awaits – '

'Calm down, Don Fernando. I am not questioning the importance of an investigation or what it will mean for Velazquez's salvation if he is admitted to the noble Order of Santiago. I was merely struck by the idea that Don Quixote loved his Dulcinea so much that it mattered less where she sprang from and more the lineage that would spring from her. His love is unconditional and does not depend on her family name. Her name will be known and she merits Don Quixote's love because of the person she is and not because any of her forbears amassed great wealth or achieved some distinction that gave them titles or land.'

Very profound, I'm sure, but he was mad this knight of yours. That's the whole point Tof the story, isn't it. Dulcinea is a fiction within the fiction. However fair and virtuous she might appear; however much she might not care or seem to need to come from a noble family, she does not exist. She is nowhere to be found in the real world.'

Don Diego pulls on the reins and turns his chestnut mare around so that he is stirrup to stirrup with his companion's horse where he can look Don Fernando in the eye. 'We are nearly at the house of Zurbaran now,' he says. 'We have been on this journey too long together to reach this final interview arguing with each other.'

'In the final days of this Holy Season of Advent, too,' Don Fernando smiles and simultaneously extends his hand. Don Diego shakes it warmly.

'Let us focus on the task at hand and the facts of the evidence put before us,' continues Don Fernando. 'Let us hope that after so much opinion and hearsay these past months we finally hear testimony that is definitive. Then we can look at the whole board and decide our next move.'

'Spoken like a true chess player who always thinks he is in control of the game,' laughs his partner, swinging his horse around in the direction of the house of Francisco Zurbaran.

* * *

'Look who I have found!' declares Zurbaran stepping to one side of the threshold for Leonor to see who is standing behind her husband. Francisco's guest bows respectfully before telling Leonor with his eyes, 'I know that I am the last person you wanted to see. I would rather be anywhere else but here, but what could I do? Your husband virtually dragged me to you front door.' Leonor acknowledges the look of embarrassment mingled with apology, giving a nod that is gracious, not warm.

'Come, Leonor,' says Zurbaran as a prelude to putting one arm over her shoulder and another around his discovery. 'It took some persuading, I admit, to bring my old friend to our home after all that has been said.' Releasing his companion, Zurbaran stands back. 'See. Here he stands, Alonso Cano, my old friend, in a spirit of good faith and forgiveness. In the spirit of Christmas, too, I should add.'

Francisco crouches, elbows on thighs, hands open, balancing on the balls of his feet, and whispers to Marcos, Eusebio and Agustina who have all gathered in the refuge of their mother's skirts. 'Nor has Señor Cano come empty-handed. He has helped your papa carry fresh fruit, ripe melons and oranges and figs too, and all kinds of sweetmeats and cheeses and breads from the market for our feast on Christmas Eve tomorrow. Do you like the sound of that? Well, how about this. There is cake as well.' Curiosity and expectations satisfied, Marcos takes his brother and sister by the hand, knowing that the prospect of any cake before Christmas would depend on silence and invisibility when a guest was in the house.

'I have asked Alonso to be here for when the investigators arrive. They have already interviewed Alonso about our friend Diego's . . .'

'Eligibility,' prompts Cano.

'That's it. Thank you, Alonso. His eligibility to be a Knight of the Order of Santiago and the certainty of his eternal reward that this will bring. I have nothing to hide in the testimony I will give and I want both you and Alonso to be alongside me during my interview.'

'Will the investigators allow it?'

'They cannot object, *mi amor*. They are Christian men and will not wish me to bear witness under duress. I will tell them, if I need to, that your presence is essential for my willing co-operation. They are also guests in our house and must comply with our rules.'

'You are very welcome, Señor Cano,' Leonor adds finally, making way for the two men to enter, and allowing them to pass into the kitchen further down the hallway, pausing before following. It is time enough to feel her heart beating from surprise to concern to panic. On this second arrival of an unexpected guest her mind does not present the comfort of scripture or the familiar repetition of a *Pater Noster* still less an *Ave Maria*. Leonor's worries, in the slow steps from her front door to the kitchen, are not separated for solution as is her way in money matters. They collide with one another, the realisation that a defining moment has arrived clashing again and again with the reality of concerns which she cannot control or comprehend, the critical compromised by the comical. What is Francisco thinking of, promising cake like that to the children before Christmas Eve? He will not have given a second thought either to the money she had carefully worked out as to what they could afford for food and gifts over the twelve days of Christmas.

He has painted so little since they had arrived in Madrid, and never once slept in his workshop without so much as a word. It wasn't as though he was bursting with energy and enthusiasm before he went up there last night. Too worried about the investigators over his past; the best thing was to leave him to his own thoughts. Keep the children out of his way. Let him paint if he can. For him to emerge this morning as if he had just returned from the stable in Bethlehem does not make sense. That is not Francisco at all. It is not Francisco either to almost come to blows with a man in his own kitchen and then days later bring him back to the house the best of friends. It's as though Francisco actually went looking for Cano, thinking he would find him at the Plaza Mayor – a reasonable assumption that Cano like anyone else wanting to buy the freshest food on offer at the market, would be there early before the stampede of last-minute *Madrileños*.

Francisco hates confrontation. Normally, whenever he raises his voice or loses his temper it can take him days to recover. He has had this decision about Velazquez hanging over him, all the while thinking about the blank canvases in his studio, the absence of money-making commissions, his dependence on his wife to feed the children, to see the family through Christmas, and the very idea that jewellery not art is what enables the Zurbarans to live. Why he would want the very person with whom he argued so bitterly over Caravaggio and Velazquez to be present when he is at his most vulnerable with these investigators from the Order of Santiago. It makes no sense.

If only Sor Maria could be here. Seat her on one side of the kitchen table between Francisco and Cano. Place myself directly opposite, flanked by the two investigators. Meeting her eyes would keep my nerve steady. The abbess can see into my soul. That calm certainty she had. We do not know until the very end what is in a man or a woman's heart. We are in no position to judge whether Caravaggio finally found peace whatever he might have said or done. We cannot be sure that Velazquez is as selfish or self-serving or as obsessed with his resurrection in the life to come as he appears. That was what she said, more or less. None of this, none of it fits with the reality we face, Francisco and I. Not with his declining reputation, not with the little money in my purse to pay for what the children need; not with the other untrustworthy and possibly violent man in my kitchen; and definitely not with all I know about Velazquez.

I wouldn't have gone to Sor Maria had it not been absolutely necessary. Francisco was losing his mind. Day by day in Madrid his confidence, his belief in himself was draining away. What does it matter whether he blamed Velazquez or himself or the elders of Seville, the result was the same. To think of where he was in his mind and then to seek out Alonso Cano like that. There is no rational explanation for it. For Francisco to act as though he, and not Sor Maria, had seen a vision, or at least received private correspondence from the king himself. 'You have nothing to fear, Francisco Zurbaran. Your art is recognised, your reputation is secure, your best is yet to come, for the glory of the Spanish empire, for eternal life through Christ Our Lord.'

Leonor jumps at the loud knock on the door behind her. Instinctively she raises a hand to touch her gold ear-rings, turns and opens it.

'Señora Zurbaran?'

'Yes.'

'I am Don Fernando de Salcedo and this is my colleague, Don Diego Lozando Villasandino. We are representatives of the Venerable Order of Santiago and are here by appointment of the Council as investigators in a case of the greatest importance to members of the Order, and to His Majesty, King Philip. Your husband is a key witness and we are here to interview him.'

* * *

Leonor cannot help smiling at Francisco. He might as well have suggested to the two investigators that Mass on Christmas Day be said in Spanish not Latin given the shock registering on their faces. Their key witness is so welcoming, so tactile, greeting them like returning prodigal sons, stopping short of a full embrace, but clasping hands, enclosing them in his own and not letting them go. The look of bewilderment when he tells them how much he has looked forward to this day is only matched by the sight of Alonso Cano falling into his chair, his legs buckled. As quickly, Francisco releases his grip on the two interrogators of the Order and shepherds each to an allocated chair at the kitchen table simultaneously signalling to his wife that she sit between the two, and insisting that he will serve all of them with food and drink.

It occurs to Leonor in this moment that Francisco might start serving from the store of morning market purchases. Inexplicably, she is not worried. Equally incomprehensible is her position at table, seated, arms folded, contented, ear-rings untouched, happy to be waited upon in her own kitchen. Francisco's joyful fearlessness discovered somehow in the night has affected her too. That must be it. At first she didn't understand, sceptical about any good that could possibly come from inviting Alonso Cano back to their home on this of all days.

Most surprising of all to Leonor, she is regarding and smiling in turn at Alonso Cano, then first at the bald, rounder investigator and lastly at the thinner man who, though younger, has the bearing of a man closer to old age, a man incapable of feeding and looking after himself, a man without the physical strength to fight off any disease. These men, whatever their intentions or motivations, she thinks, cannot hurt her or Francisco now. She does not need to understand how or why Francisco has resolved his doubts and fears about Velazquez or his own reputation. She knows. The evidence is clear to see in Francisco's every movement and word. He is possessed by a peace and joy that not one of his guests has ever known. Of this she is sure. There is nothing to fear in the outcome of this interview.

'Are you sure, Señor Zurbaran,' begins Don Diego when Francisco the waiter finally sits down and Advent greetings exchanged, 'that you wish your testimony to be given in this case of personal interest to His Divine Majesty, King Philip, in the presence of your wife and your fellow artist?'

'I do not believe we should allow Señor Cano to attend,' interrupts Don Fernando. 'He is also a witness in this investigation and should not hear what his close friend of forty years has to say. We cannot have a situation where Señor Cano, however well-intentioned, might lead the witness by, say, completing a sentence or helping with the memory of a past event.'

'Or winking at me,' says Francisco. 'We can't have that.'

'This is a serious matter, Señor Zurbaran, and I am surprised you make light of it.'

'We are not close friends,' mutters Cano.

'Ah, but we used to be, my dear Alonso, and there is still time for us to be so again.'

Astonished, Leonor watches her husband stand up suddenly, go over to the hunched figure of Cano resting on folded arms, and throw his arm around him as a brother would comfort a grieving relative. Cano does not react and Francisco, seemingly satisfied with his action re-takes his seat.

'That settles it,' says Don Fernando. 'We must ask Señor Cano to leave. He clearly does not wish to be here and we have already obtained all of the pertinent facts from his perspective.'

'We are not close friends. Never have been, never will be. He doesn't care for Velazquez either. Thinks Caravaggio is the greatest artist of this or any other century.'

'Precisely my point. We cannot have these – '

'Opinions,' sighs Don Diego.

'I will decide the matter for you.' Francisco takes Leonor's hand as he speaks. Something he has never done publicly in front of strangers, she notes. 'You are guests in our home. You may represent the most noble and holy Order of Santiago and even the king himself, but here Leonor and I have authority. If you wish to question me and record my testimony, you must do so with Leonor and my old friend, Alonso Cano at this table. I want him to hear what I have to say. If you will not, then I must ask you to leave in the peace and joy and spirit of Christmas.'

'We are not close friends.'

Ignoring the voice at the end of the table, Leonor marvels at her husband's assertiveness. More than that, his readiness to court confrontation with two men, oddly contrasting though they may be, who can dismiss him. Has he forgotten what he says will go straight back to Philip? If it became known that the king and the Order were displeased with him, Francisco, dear Francisco, the fight to restore his reputation in Madrid would be over before it had begun. He could not live with himself, his children surviving on their mother's jewellery business. 'If it became known', how ridiculous to think that. Every wealthy patron, every religious order, every competing artist, would know. Of course they would.

'Very well. If you insist, and if that is what will hopefully be the last word from you for the time being, Señor Cano, then we can begin with Don Diego's first questions.'

'That didn't take too long.'

'The last word, I believe I said.'

What Leonor cannot believe is that her husband is smiling throughout, as composed and content as she had ever seen him.

'You are Francisco Zurbaran,' Don Diego begins, 'the legitimate son of Luis de Zurbaran, a haberdasher in the village of Fuente de Cantos, and Isabel Marquez.'

'All true, all true. My father's shop was on the Calle

de los Martires in the main square, so everyone in the village knew the Zurbarans. My father, God rest his soul, had a good business.'

'That may be so,' says Don Fernando, 'but Fuente de Cantos, even today, is a village of fewer than one thousand. Your father was by no means a wealthy man. He must have struggled at times.'

Francisco bursts out laughing, as if Don Fernando had told the funniest of stories. 'No doubt, no doubt,' he replies without a hint of mockery. 'Whose father has not at some time or another, or every day indeed, struggled to survive, labouring for his family? And from this great struggle to survive in Fuente de Cantos emerged the son desperate to break free from the grinding poverty of country village life to find his fortune in the great towns and cities of Spain where wealthy merchants and nobility lived. The son of the poor haberdasher from nowhere would say and do anything to escape, to be noticed, to be someone that his father was not.'

'Well? Was that the case? Did you grow up dreaming of the day you could be someone else?'

'Fuente de Cantos may have been small, but you forget I told you that our house was on the main square. A haberdashery shop like my father's was so much more than it suggests. I remember the women of the village buying scents and spices, even lace collars, and colours. Yes, my father sold colours.'

'So you started painting with the colours from your father's shop?' Don Diego sees the opportunity in the good humour and awakening nostalgia of Zurbaran to draw more from him than the direct questioning and insinuations of Don Fernando could do.

'We used to say the rosary together, my parents and I, reciting all of the mysteries. It wasn't enough for them to link each decade to a mystery. Our *Pater Noster* and *Ave Marias* were always preceded by what they could see with their mind's eye of whatever it was, the reaction of Simeon when he realises that the child before him at the presentation in the temple, is the Christ-child; or the crushing weight of the cross on the way up to Calvary. As a boy I marvelled at the way they could be taken so far out of themselves as they described each mystery. When they could barely read and had seen so little art, only witnessed the most basic market-place feast day processions and staging of the Nativity or of the Lord's Passion – '

Pausing, Francisco looks across, first at Leonor, then to each of the investigators in turn. 'And then, somehow, to paint a picture for me of the astonishing scene, the dazzling light of Our Lord's Ascension, or the colour and majesty of the crowning in heaven of Mary, the Mother of God. From what they knew of them, the lives of the saints were described just as vividly. What my father and mother didn't know, they imagined. How strong the light in which God must have held the saints, they used to say, to overcome temptations, torment, even fear of death. You ask me about the colours in my father's shop. I don't think any boy, presented with such visions in his youth would not try to re-create them.'

'Can we get to Velazquez?'

'In a moment, Alonso. Before I joined the studio of Pacheco and met my new friends, Alonso here and Diego Velazquez, my father found a painter who would take me on for a three-year apprenticeship. His name was Diaz de Villaneuva.'

'We are not close friends.'

'I left home. You can imagine how excited I was. Even more so when my apprenticeship began. It was then that I was so captivated by the work of a great Carthusian painter called Fray Juan Sanchez Cotan. I was not so naturally gifted, but had enough talent to be noticed by Pacheco.'

'Not enough, though, to be mentioned in his book *Arte de la Pintura*, published five years after his death,' interrupts Don Fernando, drawing a reproving stare from his partner which he ignores. 'I am simply stating a fact, Señor Zurbaran.'

Leonor notes her husband nodding in acknowledgement, seemingly unperturbed by a comment that would normally have hurt him. Before she can dwell any further on where Francisco's recollections will lead, or what pressure the two investigators and the surly Cano might put on him, the pale investigator fills the silence.

'Pacheco invited you to become a pupil at his school of painting in Seville?'

'Not exactly. I had been apprenticed to Pedro Diaz de Villanueva. Let's say that I was a frequent visitor to Pacheco's school and spent much time in the company of his pupils. It was there that I met Alonso and Diego. We became good friends.'

'What was Velazquez like then?'

'Do you mean his art or the kind of person he was?'

'Both, if you like.'

'I remember catching Alonso's eye on many occasions when Diego would show us his latest work.'

Cano immediately lifts his head off folded arms, opening his mouth to intervene, and would have done but for the pointing finger of Don Fernando.

'At first,' Zurbaran continues, 'we couldn't believe how different it was from anything Pacheco, or Villanueva for that matter, had been teaching. It was nothing like the style of Pacheco himself or the Dutch schools of painting. In Diego's paintings nature seemed so real. The subjects of his religious paintings had this divine light on them. I thought then it was the intense light my parents believed in. It was the light that shone on the day of the Ascension.'

'Were you jealous?'

'Of course. How couldn't we be? We had never heard about this *chiaroscuro* style of Caravaggio. Not then. Pacheco was not trying to teach it, so where this gift, this intuitive understanding of what Caravaggio's style could be like in art, only God knows. Alonso and I hoped and prayed some of Diego's gift would rub off on us. Pacheco saw it too. You should be in no doubt that Diego Velazquez was the first person in Seville, or all of Spain for that matter, to create such a natural style in art, comparable only with Caravaggio. Diego's talent eclipsed everything Alonso and I were working on. We wanted to be like him, to copy him, but never reached the same level.'

'Speak for yourself. I – ' shouts Cano, rising to his feet.

'I wasn't expecting you to be so generous in your assessment of your rival,' says Don Diego, cutting off Cano.

'Nor was I. Nor was I', repeats Francisco. The chuckle with which he says this, and the speed in the single step to the side of Cano, and the hearty shake he gives the miserable sculptor, and the delight dancing in his eyes, are surprise enough for the two investigators. Leonor is the most taken aback of the three when her husband takes the hands of Alonso Cano in his own.

'Then let us be close friends,' he laughs, spinning them both around to face his wife and the two inquisitors. 'Gentlemen, I assure you that Alonso and I were so envious of Diego Velazquez. Did I say that already? Yes, yes, of course I did,' he says chuckling again. 'The way the beautiful Juana looked at him, the way Pacheco was ever fawning over him, and the way his painting seemed so, so, what's the word my dear Alonso?'

'Effortless.'

'Yes, yes, that's it. It seemed to us that he didn't even seem to be trying.'

Throughout this exchange Leonor glances from the beaming face of her husband to that of the gaunt and undoubtedly more measured of the two investigators, the one with half of the life sucked out of him. He is aware, she thinks, of life's energy draining slowly away from him, knows he cannot reverse the process. He accepts the change taking place. It makes this task all the more important for him. If he is indeed a lawyer he will not be distracted by the display of this witness. He will overcome his surprise of the unfolding scene, return to the core purpose of the interview. Make the wrong decision; present a weak recommendation to his elders of the Order; let the king think even for a moment that he and his overbearing colleague have not been diligent, and *his* reputation, all that he has achieved, will be broken. In his mind at least, and for his family. That's how he and they will see it. This Don Diego – maladies eating away inside will deprive him of old age, and he knows it, my God he knows it. As a member of the Council of Santiago his eternal reward should be guaranteed. Fail the king. Fail his peers, and even that certainty could be taken away from him, his legacy, and family name of no consequence in this life or the next.

'Were you envious of the family of Diego Velazquez also?' asks Don Diego. 'By your own account, Diego Velazquez possessed this extraordinary gift for painting and, it seems, had everything else going for him. Did that extend to his family?'

Leonor immediately sees the trap sprung for Francisco. If he does, he gives no indication.

'Of course. Of course. A splendid woman, Doña Jeronima. So down to earth and kind, I remember she was always telling her son to notice what was going on around him, to see the quiet devotion to God in the way people went about their ordinary lives.'

'Doña Jeronima and her family came from Andalusia, is that right?' Don Fernando again. 'Do you know of their origins?'

'Of that I cannot be certain, except to say they were Andalusian in character and generosity', replies Zurbaran, extending his arms in apology. Leonor observes Don Diego, impressed with the honesty of the response.

'And Velazquez's father, Juan?'

'A proud man, I recall. Distant, a disciplinarian who demanded respect from his children, and expected them to behave in a certain dignified way. Diego could not cry or show emotion as a boy in front of him, I know that.'

Leonor tries hard to read her husband's face. Does he know what he is doing, constructing his responses to lead the investigators in the direction they want to take? Francisco is not a calculating man. He is not a manipulator of truth, of people. And yet, this switch from disarmingly cheerful to candidly frank does not seem like him at all. Hidden in his tone is something else.

'If his father was such a dominant figure, then surely he would have asserted his authority in the family name', Don Diego insists.

'He respected the Andalusian custom to take the mother's family name. It is as simple as that.'

Leonor smiles, noting Francisco employ the same open-armed 'Trust Me' gesture with this response. Don Diego nods in acknowledgement.

'In your encounters with the family, you never heard Juan Velazquez speak of his family heritage?'

'That would be surprising, wouldn't it?', replies Francisco, shrugging shoulders, showing the palms of his hands and nodding in a movement that says 'I am being straight with you and have nothing to hide'. This is planned. Leonor is certain of that now. Wherever, whatever, whoever has given Francisco his change of heart, his confidence – no, his guile – the evidence is before her very eyes. 'Diego's father was not going to start discussing his Portuguese heritage in front of mere boys, the teenage friends of his son'.

'That is a fair point', Don Diego concedes.

'Forty years ago wasn't the time either, Zurbaran continues, 'to be speaking openly in Spain about ties with Portugal when – '

'Tensions between Spain and Portugal were rising', says Don Fernando completing the sentence. 'Nevertheless, you are speaking of Velazquez's father's Portuguese ancestry as if it were a fact. How can you know that?'

Ask Francisco a question, any question, thinks Leonor. He will pause before answering. He will repeat his first response. He will measure the impact of his words. It is his way of showing consideration, not blurting out the first reaction, what he thinks, what he wants. On every occasion he frames his answers in an understanding of what response is being sought. When she desires directness, which is most of the time, Francisco's thoughtfulness is infuriating. It is also why she loves him so much. Now he does not hesitate for a moment.

'We talked about everything, Diego, Alonso and I. Diego took some coaxing, I must admit. He doesn't like to give much away, unlike Alonso here who will tell you what's on his mind almost as soon as the thought enters his head. Won't you, Alonso? Then you are just as likely to say or do what's in your head on the spur of the moment.'

Cano nods. Leonor sees that it has finally dawned on Cano, the role he has to play here. He is the foil. His reluctant compliance makes Francisco's evidence all the more plausible.

'You see. Diego became obsessed', continues Zurbaran, quieter, more serious.

'With his father's heritage?'

'With Juana, Pacheco's daughter. He confided in Alonso and me, always consulted us about the next opportunity for him to impress. Should he ask her to accompany him to some festival or other in Seville? Would she like him to paint a portrait of her? Should he tell her that he is born of a noble family, that his father's De Silva family are descendants from Silvius, from whom sprung the Portuguese nobility.'

'Are you certain of this?'

Zurbaran gives another immediate response.

'Yes. Diego Velazquez has the blood of nobility. We told him not to talk about it because Alonso and I thought it would create more problems than it would solve at the time. Apart from the politics, you have to remember two things: first, that we were in Andalusia, Diego's family held the Velazquez name and he did not want to alienate or embarrass his mother in any way; and second, that Juan Rodriguez de Silva was a church notary, hardly a sign of nobility.'

'Why did you not tell us about this, Señor Cano?' asks Don Fernando.

'We agreed, that is why', answers Zurbaran, giving Leonor confirmation if any were needed. Her husband is a false witness. He is not the man that he was, even yesterday.

'Gentlemen, we agreed. To protect our friend. You understand. Sharing the facts of our friend's Portuguese nobility could so easily have ruined his prospects. He might have been subject to ridicule, or worse. Pacheco could have forbidden him to take the hand of his daughter, and Juana might not have wanted any more to do with him anyway.' Francisco throws his hands into the air, issuing his own challenge to the silent investigators, 'What could be more conclusive than that? What further evidence could you possibly need?'

* * *

The star above Madrid sheds a new light on its people. The Messiah is born in a manger in the Plaza Mayor. Shepherds abandon their flocks outside the city. Torches are held high to guide them. Laughter from candlelit roasted feasts spills out onto the streets, mingling with bells pealing, children singing carols, families celebrating. Peace and goodwill are in the eyes of Mary and Joseph who only the week before were seen squabbling over the price of bread in the market. Now they are smiling at the gathered children who are kneeling, pointing, praying for their faults and failings of the year to be forgiven and forgotten. One day, Mary and Joseph look out across the Plaza Mayor. The children have parted to make way for the arrival of three mysterious wise men from the East, led by the star to Madrid, so that they too may worship the king that is born there. For the children, for *Madrileños*, for all of Spain, the day of redemption is at hand.

The Zurbarans do not see or hear from the investigators or receive any communication from the Council of Santiago on Christmas Eve, Christmas Day or any of these twelve holy days of Christmas. Of the nativity in her husband's head, Leonor can only ponder. Not once has he spoken of the visitation. Even in the stillness of the night or in the dawn of birdsong, in their waking and sleeping moments in bed together, has he said 'I don't know what came over me to act and speak as I did.' She has not challenged him, the celebration of Christmas being more than enough reason to put the children and family first. Time, and no doubt the Council of Santiago's decision on Diego Velazquez will tell whether this brightness in Francisco will last.

For now, the Zurbaran she does not know is finding pleasure in everything. One minute he is kissing her on the cheek telling her what a fine year, the year of Our Lord, One Thousand Six Hundred and Fifty-Nine, is going to be. The next he is patting the children on the head, joining their games and insisting that they make one more family visit to the manger in the Plaza Mayor. Two days after the Epiphany, Leonor can hear so much laughter coming from Francisco's upper room that she has to investigate. Through the open door she sees Marcos teaching Eusebio to grind pigments, whilst Francisco and Micaela are finding the greatest amusement in capturing the essence of the caravan of the three kings with camels on canvas.

Returning to the kitchen, she passes the spot where she had stood reciting Ecclesiasticus to herself on that first visit of Cano. What has come over Francisco? To think she had been so fearful for him and their future in Madrid, so desperate as to deceive him, making the secret trip to the convent at Agreda. What would the abbess think of all that has happened since their meeting? Surely she would not ask Leonor to believe that the Lord had spoken to him as he had called Samuel; had asked him to lie, if that's what he did. Francisco was no more sure of Velazquez's nobility than he was of his own.

Lost in these thoughts, Leonor sits at the kitchen table. She should be pleased, she tells herself. Francisco did not denounce Velazquez after all. He did not betray years of bitterness for being passed over, ignored, forgotten.

Velazquez, the friend who never was. That Velazquez might now be the man to save Francisco's reputation, but why should he open the doors of the royal palaces to him? Cano, other witnesses, will have given the investigators what they expected to hear.

The knock on the front door is soft. Expecting to find that Cano or the investigators have returned, Leonor straightens what she can in the kitchen in the seconds available. Walking to the door, she fingers her ear-rings, retrieves straggling hairs, tucking them behind her ears. Like a fisherman bracing himself for a torrent of water to engulf his boat, she grips the door post with one hand, pulls the door open with the other.

'Señora Zurbaran?'

'Yes.'

'I have a letter for you.'

'For me? Not my husband?'

'For you, Señora, I am certain.'

The messenger, a young lad dressed head to toe in black, lightened by eyes of sky blue and a sheepish grin, bows, turns, and is gone. Leonor hears jovial exchanges continuing above and knows she will not be disturbed. Seated again in the kitchen, she prises open the wax seal.

My dear Leonor,

I have held you in my heart and prayers since our meeting and throughout the Holy Season of Christmas whilst celebrating the Word made flesh in Our Lord and Saviour, Jesus Christ. As your sister in His name, I am filled with joy and thanks for your Advent visit. You opened my eyes. You laid bare your pain. You exposed the depth of your love for your husband, Francisco, and the desire from the very core of your being, to protect him.

I am humbled by your sacrifice and ask for your forgiveness too. I said too much of my past trial and tribulations. It is not for me to unburden myself to you and yet, with good grace, you listened with the generosity of a confessor. Keep what you learned of me in the silence of your own prayers, I beg of you. There are many, both living and yet to be born, who will see my life as one of delusion and deception. They will wonder what has been real and what are the workings of an imagination. They will doubt whether I have ever truly known my own mind and assume I have allowed my thoughts to be controlled, my experiences a desire for attention.

Remember me as one who tries not to pass judgement on any man or woman. I do not know the good or evil any child of God is capable of until their last breath in this life. Think of me who struggles every day with the certainty of doubt. It is my greatest temptation. I am as misguided to say that I know for certain who is deserving of redemption or condemnation, as any non-believer to say that God does not exist.

You have shown this nun the meaning of redemption. Your husband, as I now believe, has placed the needs of the king's painter above a burning desire to restore his own reputation. I have it from the highest authority, whose confidence or name I cannot divulge, you understand, that Francisco Zurbaran's testimony was the convincing evidence needed by the two representatives to recommend the knighthood of Señor Velazquez to the Council of Santiago. Word will reach you in the coming days, I know, but I wanted you to hear from me first. You took me into your confidence and I hope that in some small way I can now repay your faith in me.

Whoever believes in me will have eternal life, said the Lord. Think now about what Francisco has done for the path to eternal life for another man for whom he had no love. We do not need the certainty of knowing what brought about this conversion of heart. Our certainty of doubt about what is in a man or woman's heart so often deceives us. It is we who are deluded by thinking love has boundaries.

Let me remind you, Leonor, of our conversation about the 'Portrait of the Family', the painting completed two years ago by Velazquez of their majesties King Philip and Queen Mariana and their family. You have seen it and I have not, but allow me to describe its detail from letters I have received. The painting is of a room in the royal palace where Velazquez has his studio. In the foreground stand Princess Margarita Maria with her *meninas,* a dwarf, servants and a dog. We see the scene through the eyes of the king and queen whose image is painted as a reflection in a mirror. Earlier paintings hang in the shadows. It is not clear what they are. Standing in the open doorway at the back of the studio is the queen's palace marshal. Whether he is entering or leaving, no-one can say. He may be taking an instruction from the king and queen. He may be looking at the centre of attention, the Infanta herself. She is, after all, the heir to the throne, the only living hope of the king and queen to extend the Spanish branch of the Habsburgs. Velazquez will not say.

If I tell you that word has reached even the inner sanctum of the royal court of the debate far beyond its walls, about this work, you will understand. Some say it is political, pointing to a fleeting moment in time when the king and queen's line and legacy depends on the Infanta. Others say Velazquez wanted to create the past, present and future of the Spanish empire in one painting. Some have whispered that the Portrait Of The Family was a vanity project for Velazquez. He has painted himself standing behind and to the right of the Infanta. He is dressed, I believe, as a courtier in a plain black doublet, paintbrush in hand, the key of his office as Palace Chamberlain dangling at his waist. It is, some have said, such a blatant act of self-promotion, even if he is in the painting by virtue of the possibility that he is painting a full-length portrait of the king and queen together.

The several letters I have received from an observer of this painting – yes, several – have described the observer standing far back from the painting so that the illusion on the canvas could be seen clearly. The observer would edge nearer, then nearer still, until what was a dress, a hand, a mirror image, dissolved into a mass of brushstrokes. There is not a single point standing back from the painting when it is possible to see where the work of the artist ends and the illusion of reality begins.

In recent days this same observer, my correspondent, made his latest visit to the painting. Another attempt, you might say, to understand what is actually happening and what is not real at all. On entering, he found Velazquez himself standing back from the painting, a paintbrush in his right hand, a palette of red colours in his left. When the court painter stepped to the side, the observer could see his purpose.

'I have made a sign of the cross for him', he said.

'For whom?' my correspondent asked.

'Francisco Zurbaran. I am thanking him in a way he will understand. We have not spoken for many years. I have allowed our friendship to die and yet he still testified to my nobility. He knows what the Order of Santiago means to me.'

Velazquez made only this request of my correspondent, Leonor; that he should make it known to his old friend that the red cross added to his doublet on this Portrait Of The Family is a mark of thanks to him, a gift of eternal life from Diego Velazquez to Francisco Zurbaran.

Now you know, Leonor, go and tell your husband. Pray for Diego Velazquez. Pray for your beloved Francisco. Pray for your children. Pray for me, and pray for us all to act in love until our very last breath.

Your servant,

Maria, Abbess of Agreda +

Leonor allows the letter to fall from her hands and runs towards the sound of laughter from Francisco's studio above.

HISTORICAL NOTE

On 24 October 1609, Caravaggio was attacked on leaving the Osteria Cerriglio in Naples. He was so badly beaten that he was left for dead. Whether agents of the Tomassoni family or the notary, Mariano Pasqualone, or aggrieved artists from Rome, or even Maltese Knights, had finally caught up with him, cannot be said. There is no conclusive evidence. The vicious assault did, however, herald the beginning of the end of his turbulent life. Still not recovered and fearing for his life, in the second week of July 1610 Caravaggio set off for Rome from Naples, hoping that his pardon from Pope Paul V had finally been arranged. It had not, and was still in progress.

The felucca transporting him and his paintings docked at Palo, outside of Rome. It is not clear exactly why, but he is imprisoned there, and detained long enough for the felucca to set sail with his paintings, without him. Knowing it was destined for Porto Ercole on the Tuscan coast, some 50 miles north, he sets off in pursuit by land. The final achievement in reaching Porto Ercole costs him his life, most likely on 18 July 1610. He may have died of a heart attack or heat exhaustion but whatever the cause, he died alone, without comfort, without any final testimony, and without anyone knowing whether the storm of light and darkness that had raged in his head for so long, had finally abated.

In telling Caravaggio's story on Malta, the name of Francesco dell'Antella has been changed to Vincenzo, simply to avoid any possible confusion between Franciscos and Francescos. The real Francesco Dell'Antella, however, did indeed serve Grand Master Wignacourt of the Order of St John on Malta for many years. He was a friend of the brothers, Giovanni Ottone and Giacomo Bosio. In 1581 Giacomo had murdered the brother of the Viceroy of Calabria at the Vatican Palace but, says Helen Langdon, one of Caravaggio's biographers, 'so great was their diplomatic power that they had been pardoned by the pope.' So, for this reason I have described him as tolerant of Caravaggio.

Giacomo was commissioned by Wignacourt to write a history of the Order of St John. His *Historia della Sacra religione di S Giovanni Gerosolimitano* appeared in 1594. The book is illustrated by a drawing of Valletta by Francesco. Giacomo describes it as 'done by the hand of the most virtuous, valorous and courteous Cavalier Fra Franceso dell'Antella, now Secretary of the most illustrious Grand Master.'

The relationship of Wignacourt with his Secretary, Francesco dell'Antella was tested only the year after Caravaggio's death in 1610. After he had been provoked, Francesco dell'Antella killed Wignacourt's nephew, Cavalier Henrico de Lancry de Bains. He offered to withdraw from Wignacourt's service, but Wignacourt insisted that he stay and continue as secretary. Wignacourt said he was satisfied with the 'modesty of dell'Antella'.

The works of Caravaggio were known in Seville through copies or prints. It is not known exactly how Caravaggio's influence reached Spain after his death in 1610, but

Zurbaran, Velazquez and a host of other Spanish artists, most notably Jusepe de Ribera and Esteban Murillo, were strongly influenced by his work and use of *chiaroscuro.*

Of the fact that Francisco Zurbaran testified favourably for the admission of Diego Velazquez to the Order of Santiago in December 1658, there is no doubt. Equally clear is that Alonso Cano did so too. Both men asserted that they had known Diego Velazquez and his family for more than 40 years since they had been apprentices together in the studio of Pacheco in Seville.

Francisco Zurbaran and Alonso Cano were two of no fewer than 148 witnesses who were interviewed by the two investigators, Don Fernando de Salcedo and Don Diego Lozano Villasandino. They began their weeks of interviews on 1 November 1658, based principally in the Spanish town of Tuy in Galicia and Madrid. Even after the investigation ruled in favour of Velazquez, a special dispensation was required from Pope Alexander VII, the successor of Pope Innocent X, whose portrait Velazquez had painted in Rome in 1650.

On 27 November 1659 the title of Knight of the Order of Santiago was conferred on Diego Velazquez by King Philip IV of Spain. Due to his extended royal service, he was given a special exemption from the normal obligations of a Knight, namely service in the galleys and profession in a convent. Less than a year later, on 6 August 1660, Velazquez died and was buried dressed in the habit of the Order. His wife, Juana, followed him only a few days later and his son-in-law, Juan Bautista Martinez del Mazo, who had continued to live in the household of Velazquez even after the death of his wife, Francisca, succeeded him as court painter.

Though Velazquez was as wealthy as he was enigmatic, debts were still unpaid on his death, possibly due to expenses incurred in striving to prove his nobility. He left behind no letters or other writings, but an expensive collection of furniture, tapestries, paintings, silverware and books. He had produced a small number of paintings in his lifetime, relative to his decades as an artist and the output of many of his contemporaries, only 120.

Maria de Agreda has often been called The Lady In Blue or The Blue Nun, a mystic known for reports of miraculous bi-location, appearing to the Jumano Indians of New Mexico and Texas. As a girl she had visions and, when still a teenager, she joined her mother and sister in establishing a Franciscan convent through the Order of the Immaculate Conception in the family house at Agreda. Such was Maria and the family's reputation, demand grew and a new convent was built in Agreda in 1633. Maria was elected Abbess at the age of 25 by her fellow nuns and she remained there until her death.

In July 1643 King Philip IV of Spain, stopped in Agreda on his way to the war with Portugal at the Aragon frontier beyond Zaragoza. He was determined to meet the Abbess of Agreda. From that meeting to her death in 1665, shortly before the death of Philip, they exchanged more than 600 confidential letters. The king's difficulty in reconciling his desire to reform the Spanish empire with his love of pleasure and fear of punishment for his own sins, is laid bare in these letters where he seeks the mystic nun's prayers and counsel. He thought that the Abbess could intercede on his behalf. He, in turn, is believed by scholars to have interceded for her, protecting Maria de Agreda from the worst outcome of the Inquisition's investigation of her in 1650.

The plague of 1649 claimed the lives of over 50,000 people in Seville alone, including Francisco Zurbaran's son, Juan. By that time Zurbaran and his third wife, Leonor, had three children of their own: Micaela-Francisca, born in 1645; Jose Antonio, born in 1646; and Juana -Micaela, born in 1648. Three more children, Marcos, Eusebio and Agustina-Florencia would follow in 1650, 1653 and 1655 respectively.

In these years with so many young children, Zurbaran had the least income. He and Leonor moved from house to house in Seville, where his star was falling. He tried to keep the family out of poverty by earning money from commissions in Latin America. Leonor brought a generous dowry into her marriage with Francisco, thanks to her father's success as a goldsmith.

Zurbaran outlived Velazquez by almost four years. More work did follow his testimony in favour of the friend of his youth. In 1661 he worked at San Jose, a church of the Barefooted Carmelites in Madrid, producing two paintings. His last known painting was *Virgin and Child with St John,* painted in 1662. It is a work notably softer in tone, the contrast between light and dark less stark.

At the time of his death on 27 August 1664 Zurbaran was not in debt. Leonor owned notable items of jewellery and in her husband's workshop were, as the inventory states, 'nine primed canvases, a stone for grinding pigments, two easels and about sixty engravings.' Alonso Cano, arguably the most versatile of artists of Spain's Golden Age, survived Zurbaran by another three years before dying in Granada in 1667.

Las Meninas, literally The Ladies-In-Waiting, but originally called a Portrait Of The Family, is one of the world's most celebrated paintings and widely regarded as Velazquez's masterpiece. The appearance of Velazquez in the painting is one of the very few likenesses of him and the only surviving self-portrait. Some scholars have argued that the painting itself, completed in 1656, was a part of the artist's campaign to be accepted as a Knight into the Order of Santiago. Certainly, his desire to be a Knight of the Order was well known for years before the final judgement was made in 1658.

No incontrovertible proof of the nobility of Diego Velazquez was ever found. Nor have any documents or correspondence been discovered to prove the intention of Velazquez in *Las Meninas*. Nor can anyone say for certain precisely why or when the red cross on the doublet of Velazquez was added to *Las Meninas* several years after its completion. Some have said that Velazquez added it in celebration on his acceptance into the Order. Others have surmised that the king himself added the red cross. To this day, why the red cross was added, or who the artist was thinking of when doing so, and whether in celebration or thanks, are all open to interpretation.